FERRUM CORDE

Terran Armor Corps Book 6

by

Richard Fox

Copyright © 2019 Richard Fox

All rights reserved.

ISBN-13: 9781794370821

Chapter 1

The silence felt wrong. A strike carrier's flight deck was the beating heart of the ship, always moving as fighter craft came and went while crew prepped other craft. The stillness—the emptiness—of the space struck Roland as an affront to the ship's purpose.

Especially a ship as storied as the *Breitenfeld*.

He turned slowly, taking in the details of the unmoving lifts, the spars of the superstructure across the ceiling, the faint smell of incense…though he wasn't sure if that last sensation was a trick of his imagination.

His gaze lingered on a line of bullet holes in a bulkhead. Bloodstains on the deck.

"I can't believe we're here," Morrigan said. "You know what happened here, don't you, Roland?"

"This ship won the Ember War," Roland said.

"Took the battle to the Xaros Masters in their world ship beyond the galactic rim. Of course I know."

"Ach, don't you remember anything?" She strode across the flight deck, her eyes low and searching, the long red tail of her hair draped over one shoulder, the metal rings from her skull plugs glinting in the light. She froze for a moment, then crossed herself.

"Here! It's here." Morrigan rushed to one side then went to her knees. She reached to the deck with a trembling hand, then pulled her fingers back to her lips.

Roland made his way to her slowly. Morrigan's chest heaved unevenly as she tried and failed to stifle tears. A few inches in front of her knees was an even cut almost six inches long in the deck.

"What is it?" Roland asked.

Morrigan wiped a sleeve across her eyes.

"You saw our Templar ceremony back on Navarre," she said. "Put it together."

Roland's eyes narrowed.

"The ceremony…the initiates knelt in prayer and a hologram appeared of Colonel Carius from the night before the final assault on the Xaros." He looked around and felt sick to his stomach. "Carius asked for volunteers and the initiates…they all said, 'Take me.' This-this is where it happened, isn't it?"

Morrigan nodded quickly.

"Saint Kallen was here," she said. "Right here. She was with them all at the end, just as she promised her Iron Hearts. And this was where Elias stood. This is where he drove his sword into the deck and prayed that Kallen would find him worthy…to stand beside her in the world to come."

Roland's skull plugs tingled ever so slightly. The vision of Saint Kallen on Ouranos, a vision he'd shared with Morrigan and the other Templar Armor, still haunted his mind. The power of Kallen's presence had left him uneasy in the days that followed. The rest of the armor had acknowledged the event to each other, but none had been willing to speak of it openly.

Morrigan put her hands to the deck and leaned forward. She kissed the deck where Elias's sword had pierced the metal, then got back to her feet.

"It's right that this ship belongs to the Ibarra Nation," she said. "The Union doesn't deserve it. Saint Kallen's mantle has passed to us."

"You sound like the Lady," Roland said.

"Is she wrong?"

"No," Roland said quickly. "But Stacey Ibarra didn't send Admiral Makarov to capture this ship for religious reasons. She was after the Keystone jump gate the

Breitenfeld carried." He gestured to the bloodstains a few yards away. "And this ship didn't go easy. The Lady…she snatched this ship *and* Admiral Valdar, hero of the Ember War, right out from under the Terran Union. Things were bad enough between us and Earth."

"Earth has real problems." Morrigan shrugged. "The Vishrakath bombing colony worlds. Kesaht invasions on multiple fronts. They used this ship as a glorified museum piece. It wasn't ready for the war, but Valdar threw it into the fire anyway…you saw all the work being done to her when we shuttled in."

"We may stand apart from Earth, but we're still human," Roland said. "This ship isn't the same as when you and the rest of a fleet defected…left the Terran Union with the Ibarras. She means a lot to people. Earth can't slap 'Breitenfeld' on a new carrier and call it a day. They will want this back. They'll want Valdar back. There won't be peace until that happens."

"The Union can sod off and—no," Morrigan said, shaking her head quickly. "I owe the Rosary for that sin. You're right. They are all human and our oaths as Templar don't stop at politics. Still, the Union's not our ally. You were there on Mars—you saw our brothers and sisters cut down as we tried to escape their prison."

"Tongea deserved a death in his armor," Roland

said.

"We didn't leave Earth behind because we cared about what Phoenix, or President Garret, or the aliens on Bastion wanted. We followed Saint Kallen here. We fight for humanity. And Lady Ibarra needed this ship and the Keystone gate to win this war once and for all, to make the galaxy safe for us," she said.

"I barely understand what Lady Ibarra wants with this ship…or what she needed from Trinia on Ouranos," he said. "The Keystone is a mobile Crucible gate. The Nation already has that technology."

"Our mobile gates are limited in range to a few dozen light-years. The Keystone is next generation, far better design. As for Trinia…faith, Roland." Morrigan gave his shoulder a gentle squeeze. "How can you lack any after what you've seen?"

"How indeed," Roland said with conviction, though doubt gnawed at his heart.

"Soon we'll do our pre-battle rights here." She raised her arms to her sides. "Where Carius and the first Templars made their oaths and blessed their weapons. Iron Hearts. Hussars. Warriors of legend were here."

"May we be as worthy," Roland said and went to one knee next to the tear in the deck. He ran his fingertips along the edge and looked up, imagining the armor named

Elias beside him.

He thought back to the mausoleum on Mars where Saint Kallen was buried in her armor, *momento mori* of those that died on the Xaros world ship around her. The only thing Elias had left was a face mask, a face mask he ripped off one of the Xaros leadership caste.

Of all the feelings swirling through his heart, worthiness—when compared to Elias—was not one of them.

The screen on Roland's forearm buzzed with a message.

"Back to the *Warsaw*." Morrigan frowned at her own screen. "In armor drills."

"I'm not sure who's the harder taskmaster, Nicodemus or Martel," Roland said.

"Fire makes steel, boy-o," Morrigan said.

****

Amniosis sloshed around Roland as it filled his womb, the armored pod within his suit. Filling his lungs and stomach with the fluid was never a pleasant experience, but after so long, he'd become accustomed to the sensation and the slightly sweet taste of the amniosis.

The umbilical attached to his plugs vibrated and his armor's HUD appeared on his vision. Video feed from his helm fed to his brain and he took in the cemetery, his lance's maintenance bay on the *Warsaw*.

Master Chief Eneko stood on the catwalk running parallel to the armor's waist, his attention on a data slate held in the crook of an arm.

Roland's mind still clung to the events on Ouranos as he and his armor integrated. The process was almost second nature to him by now, but something the Aeon Trinia had said to him in her laboratory itched at the back of his thoughts.

He ran a quick diagnostic, then pulled up a schematic of his suit. His hands wavered slightly with sympathetic motion as he searched through status reports on components attached to his womb. He accessed a small device built into the umbilical system and got an error notice.

"There a problem?" Chief Eneko looked up from his slate to Roland's helm.

"What is…regulator CD-999B?" Roland asked.

The maintenance tech's face scrunched up with confusion. "You getting a function alert off that component?" he asked.

"No. But I'm locked out from monitoring the

internal controls. There a reason for that?"

The chief sighed and began swiping across his slate. "Your suit's designed so you don't have to worry about the inner workings. You plug in and you *are* the armor. Screw around with the fine-tuning, you run the risk of redlining or screwing up your sync rating. Why you doing this to me, sir? Think me and my guys aren't busy enough patching up your battle damage?"

"Do you know what it does or not, Chief?"

"I'm inclined to answer, as you might crush my skull as part of your customer service feedback," Eneko said. He doubled-tapped his screen and lifted an eyebrow, then whacked the side of the slate against the handrail, tapping the screen repeatedly. "Well…that's funny."

"What?"

"System locked me out. Unauthorized access. Though I did get that regulator CD-999B is coded for specialty techs to service…thing is, me and my wrench monkeys are the only ones on your maintenance records. That part comes installed from the foundry that makes the wombs. I've never had to work on them. Weird."

"Can you tell what it…regulates?" Roland asked.

"It's housed with the neural buffers. Works with the input/output through your umbilical is my guess. I worry about what's broken, not what's working just fine," the maintenance chief said.

"Roland, we're on holo range seven for gunnery," Colonel Martel, his lance commander, sent to him.

"Roger. Moving." Roland activated his armor's servos and Eneko stepped aside as the catwalk lifted up and away from the maintenance bay.

"You want me to keep digging?" Eneko asked.

"No, Chief, forget we ever mentioned this." Roland gave him a thumbs-up as he walked out of his bay.

"Mentioned what?" Eneko whacked his slate hard against the railing and the screen came back to life.

Chapter 2

Candles flickered in front of Roland as he lit another votive. He said a silent prayer for his parents and watched as the smoke rose from the fire. He was alone in the chapel, and the relative quiet served to heighten the religious nature of the space, at odds with the emptiness of the *Breitenfeld*'s hangar.

"Up to heaven," he said quietly. The traditions aboard Ibarra Nation ships were slightly different from what he'd experienced aboard Union vessels. There, open flames were forbidden, so shrines to Saint Kallen were tucked into corners of work areas and chapels were plainer. Aboard the *Warsaw*, Saint Kallen was front and center, embodied in a stained glass window backlit above the pulpit.

Roland looked up at the Saint. The art held her in a wheelchair outside the gates of the Armor Center at Fort Knox, where she waited for days before being accepted to training.

"Things would be easier if you were still here," Roland said. "We'd know what you'd want. We would only follow you. Fight beside you. Never for something…abstract."

His breath fogged and a chill nipped at his ears. Roland swallowed hard, knowing who'd just arrived.

Stacey Ibarra stood behind the rear pew, her silver hands resting on the wooden back. She wore a black robe run through with a tight pattern of wires. Her face was still, the candlelight reflecting off her metal face.

Roland beat a fist against his heart in salute.

"My Lady."

"Ro-land." She pronounced the syllables separately without moving her lips, but her shell wavered as she spoke. "You spent some quality time with the last Aeon…with Trinia. She tell you anything…interesting?"

"I left nothing out of my report, my Lady. And Marc Ibarra was with me the entire time I spoke to Trinia," Roland said, suddenly realizing what a fool he was to try and delve into the inner workings of his armor. Of course the Ibarras would keep an eye on something that could be incriminating.

But if she—of all people—were here…

"Grandfather says you're truthful," Stacey says. "Honest. Honorable. He doesn't like you. And when you were with Trinia, she…mentioned something while examining your armor."

"She claimed she designed the armor and that there were components she wasn't familiar with," Roland said evenly.

Behind Stacey, blocking the doorway, was one of her honor guards who were heavily armed and wore ornate power armor. They were formidable warriors and Roland knew he had no chance in a fight against them outside his armor.

His mouth went dry. The Ibarras were known to kill to accomplish their goals.

"And you got curious." Stacey put her hands behind her back and walked down one side of the pews to Roland. "That's not a trait we encounter with our armor. Curiosity. How curious."

Roland remained silent.

She stopped near the votive candles and the chill from her presence bit through Roland's clothes. Flames flickered, fighting against the cold.

"Do you know what you went looking for?" she

asked.

"Trinia said there were components she didn't recognize. Given her expertise as a scientist working for millennia—according to her—and her involvement in creating the armor …it sparked questions."

"Questions you haven't shared?" Stacey looked up at him, her doll-like face almost unnerving.

"My crew chief looked into regulator CD-999B for me," Roland said, turning his face to one side. Had he doomed Eneko too?

"And you found something," Stacey said, walking to the pulpit and looking up at the stained glass depiction of Kallen, "but you don't know what."

"That is correct, my Lady."

"And should I tell you? Remove all doubt? What would happen then?"

"The decision is yours," Roland said and felt his uniform stiffen as Stacey's metal body leeched heat away.

"I should be honest, Ken. You deserve honesty. I never had the chance to tell you the whole truth before you left," Stacey said.

"Ken, my Lady?"

Stacey's head cocked to one side for a half second.

"How to tell you the truth without ruining everything? All my armor is so honorable. They don't take to being tricked. Oh no, no, no." She wagged a finger next to her face. "But Grandfather said it had to happen. We needed you in Navarre. We couldn't wait decades to grow our own true born to recruit into armor. What choice was there? He…he's not to blame. I know what I did."

Roland rubbed his thumbs against his forefingers. What was she getting at?

"She was real," Stacey said, raising a hand to Kallen. "I remember seeing her. I know how you can venerate her. A cripple, a quadriplegic, but she had the strength to be armor. Impressive for anyone. Back then, I was just a junior navigator on the *Breitenfeld*, then the Ember War began and everything went sideways. I didn't see much of her after the war started.

"After it was all over, armor began to pray in her name. Then it spread to the Navy. Then to the Rangers. Then everywhere. Not that I cared. My own faith was in danger." Stacey touched where her heart would be if she was still flesh and blood.

"One day a Pathfinder team brought back an artifact from a dead world and it gave us quantum communication technology and I was able to modify it—not perfect it, just get it to work well enough as a monitoring device. One I could even send data through. Grandfather had them installed in every armor's womb as a 'system improvement.'" Stacey was still for a moment, then whirled around and thrust a finger at Roland.

"And I don't regret what I did, Ken! You were on New Bastion negotiating away our future and what was I supposed to do? I needed them!"

Roland backed up until his legs touched the votive stand.

"My Lady, I don't understand why you—"

"You think I wanted to be Saint Kallen?" Stacey balled her fists at her waist. "Think I wanted to masquerade as someone noble and pure while I was trapped in this thing? Yeah? Do you know how hard it is to project onto the armors' minds? What it does to me?"

Roland felt ice in his heart, a feeling that had nothing to do with Stacey's presence.

"No…no. I saw the Saint," Roland said.

"You 'see' what the armor feeds to your brain," Stacey said, "not with your own eyes. Your suits are all tapped. Have been for years. I can dip into the feed of any suit in the galaxy when I want and blast my own reality to you." She rapped the side of her head. "Remember back on Barada? When the Vishrakath nearly disabled your armor? I needed the Union to get the archaeotech, so I stepped into your data and sent Kallen to you. Got you back on your feet and fighting."

"It can't be…" Roland shook his head.

"'Roland, you have to get up. Fight.' You remember that? 'Let her go.' I said that to you all on Ouranos so you wouldn't get Trinia killed for your damn honor." Stacey kicked a pew, breaking a corner into splinters and knocking it into the row behind it.

"Why? Why lie to us?" Roland asked.

"Ibarra tradition," she said, picking up the remains of an armrest. "Lie and just keep at it. Ends are all that matter, Ken. You know us. So why don't I just go to Nicodemus or Martel and tell them the truth? That Saint Kallen is a fraud!"

She whipped around and drew an arm back to hurl the splinter at the stained glass window.

Roland grabbed her by the wrist before she could let fly, ice biting into his flesh as he tried to hold her back. The strength he felt in her arm felt like he was struggling against armor.

Stacey stared at Roland, her dead eyes locked with his.

She dropped the splinter and pulled free of Roland's grip.

"You're not Ken Hale," she said. "Where am I?" Her head snapped from side to side.

Roland tried to squeeze his freezing hands shut,

but they creaked like there was rust in his joints.

"I...I'm sorry, Roland," Stacey said. "I need to show you something." She reached into her robe and pulled out a small triangle. She tapped the pad of her thumb against the apex and the chapel vanished.

A playground appeared around them. Skyscrapers of Navarre's capital city soared into the sky, disappearing into the ever-present cloud cover. Excited shouts of children playing filled the air, but there was no one there.

A moment later, figures materialized around them—kids and their parents. Roland recognized Nicodemus and his wife, carrying a newborn. Their eldest son, Jonathan, sat on a swing as his father pushed him, a toddler on his hip.

Roland stepped to one side and bumped into a pew that flickered in and out of view.

"Hologram," Stacey said. "Live feed from the hab blocks."

"Why are you showing me this?" Roland asked.

"They are why," she said sadly. "They are why I've lied to the armor. I couldn't win without them. Without you. Do you think armor would have come to Navarre with us if we hadn't had Saint Kallen urge them to do it?"

"We are loyal unto death," Roland said. "Ideals first. Politics second."

Nicodemus's son, Jonathan, kicked his legs forward, jumped off the swing, and arced up, giggling. He hit the ground hard with a yelp. The boy grabbed his ankle and began crying. Stacey lunged forward and her arms passed through him.

Nicodemus arrived a heartbeat later to comfort the boy.

"This is why." Stacey stood and ran her hands down the front of her robe. "The future. Children, Roland. The Ibarra Nation is my child. It must grow. I was there in Phoenix when we first returned to Earth. Saw my childhood home being dismantled by the Xaros. My life came apart in that moment and I've never really been able to piece it back together. But this…this I can control. Our Nation free and safe. Free to live as we choose. Safe from those that would harm us. Armor is the key to that. There is no victory without you, Roland. I'm so close to finding it…so close."

Roland looked at Nicodemus as he hefted Jonathan onto his other hip. The boy flung his arms around his father's neck, tears streaming down his face.

"The lies are worth it," Stacey said. "To me, at least."

"You think the armor will turn on you if they know the truth about Kallen," Roland said.

"Will they?"

"I think so," Roland said, nodding slowly. He looked across the playground to where he remembered the door to the chapel to be, waiting to see if her honor guard would come through and finish him.

"Then it is in your interest to lie to me now. Buy time to get this back to the Templar. Yet you're being honest…" Stacey asked.

"I betrayed the Terran Union when I escaped that prison on Mars. It was the right thing to do, but it still wears on me. I don't want a second burden. Do what you will." Roland straightened up.

The holo fell away, leaving him and Stacey in the chapel.

"What should I do with you, Roland? A traitor once. Would my armor believe you?" she asked.

"Almost every armor you have came from the Terran Union, all traitors one way or another. What do you want from me, my Lady? Do you want me to tell them or keep this secret?"

"Roland, you are armor. Your soul is strong. I know your type. You can't carry a lie with you. It will eat away at your soul, a black cancer that will bring you down." Stacey sat on the step leading up to the pulpit and rested her forearms on her knees.

"That's how I live," she said. "My dark path goes back for decades. Marc Ibarra set me on it before I was even born. I carry the guilt *and* I carry a burden to protect the Ibarra Nation…and by extension, the future of the human race. Let me eat that sin for you, Roland."

"You want me to tell them that you're Kallen?" he asked.

"I'm not going to tell you what to do," she said, shaking her head. "I'm not going to hurt you. I'm not my grandfather. I just want you to know that we're close…close to a final victory. The *Breitenfeld* and the Keystone gate it carried were the last pieces of the puzzle. Malal's Ark is just out of reach."

"My Lady…I am sworn to your service and my oaths as a Templar haven't changed," Roland said, "even if Saint Kallen is not—if what I've experienced is not true. But now I'm in the middle of something that could throw the entire Nation into chaos. If the armor turn on you, then the—"

Stacey raised her face to him.

"I'm wrong," Roland said. "The Ibarra Nation will never turn against you. You brought almost all of them forth from the procedural tubes. They will never believe me. Neither would Makarov."

He and the youthful admiral had grown close

since Ouranos; her favor was still in his breast pocket. They'd done their best to keep things quiet, but there was no point in keeping things hidden from Stacey.

"She's different," she said. "Couldn't make one of her caliber without loosening the controls."

"But the rest of the Nation?"

"My children. I love them, and they me. The Legions are mine, all mine, Ken…No. Roland."

"Why do you keep calling me Ken Hale?" Roland asked.

"I…am slipping." Stacey turned her palms up. "When my soul rushed into this ice cube, my body was dying. The matrix holding me wasn't designed for that degree of trauma. Sometimes things get a little muddled. You've…seen that in me more than once. Trinia could have fixed me, stopped the slide, I hoped. There might even be a transfer point on the Ark, get back to my old self, but I'm not what matters. That's not why I need the Ark.

"And Ken Hale…was a good man. A better person than I would have ever amounted to. You remind me of him. I do miss him. Miss the chance I lost to be with him. I don't blame him for leaving. He deserves to be happy. I want that for you. For everyone."

"Thank you, my Lady," Roland said as he sighed

and looked up at Kallen before the gates of Ft. Knox. "I am Armor. I've fought battles and foes I never imagined when I joined the service, yet I still feel like a damn kid."

"I was a damn kid when the Ember War started," she said. "I sure as hell didn't sign up for the Xaros. But one thing I've learned about life—it isn't fair. Ever. But we must fight for the future, no matter the blows we take or how hard we fall along the way."

"I will…I will do what's right," Roland said.

Stacey stood and walked up to him. As she raised a hand, frost fell from her fingers.

"Ken, I wish we could have…it's not our fault." Stacey wrapped her other hand into Roland's and he stifled a cry of pain.

She brought his hand up to her still mouth and pressed it against her lips. The flesh between his thumb and forefinger burned with pain then went numb. She let him go and walked out of the room.

Roland kept his bearings until the honor guard shut the door, then he gripped his wrist and fell against the shattered pew, his hand throbbing with pain.

Scar tissue matching the imprint of her lips began to burn as the cold wore off. He hadn't felt pain like this since a Ranger's bullet had taken a chunk off of his arm back on Mars.

He looked up to Kallen.

"What now? Pray? Who's going to hear me, Saint, you or Ibarra?"

He kept himself propped up against the broken pew until the pain in his hand ebbed away. The agony seemed to focus his mind on his situation. Tell the truth of Ibarra and Kallen and risk fracturing the Ibarran Armor? Keep what he knew secret and hope Stacey could win the war before her mind finally unraveled? Play along with Saint Kallen and abandon his morals?

Roland thought back to Mars, when Tongea had taken him and Aignar to see Saint Kallen's final resting place. He remembered feeling something, a presence that he couldn't explain. But he wasn't plugged into his suit then, so was that just a figment of his imagination or did Stacey's deception go deeper than what she claimed?

He clutched his hand to his chest and looked up at the stained glass window.

"Who says...who says I have to decide now? There's still a war to fight. My lance needs me. Doesn't matter what Ibarra is, the Kesaht still want to kill us."

He got up and winced as he moved his thumb against the new scar tissue.

"Duty calls." He beat his damaged hand against his heart in a salute to Kallen and left the chapel.

Chapter 3

Stacey Ibarra walked down a narrow, windowless corridor. A pair of honor guard followed just behind her, unaffected by the cold aura her silver body generated. At the end, a single legionnaire armed with a snub-nosed gauss carbine stood guard next to a vault door. Another silver being—Marc Ibarra, wearing a lightly padded jumpsuit with wires running through it in small square patterns—stood on the other side of the vault frame.

"Stacey!" Marc held his arms wide. "I knew you'd take this call, so important. So diplomatic. I knew you had it in you."

"Shut up." Stacey held up two fingers pressed tightly together and swiped them to one side. There was a rumble within the walls as unseen gears began turning. The vault door rotated slowly.

"Talk is always good," Marc said. "Much better than shooting. Better hurt feelings than blood all over the place, yes? Yes?"

Frost grew on the walls and over the legionnaires' armor as the two immortals spoke.

"Talk is useful only when the truth is told," Stacey said, turning her metal face to Marc, "not lies."

"Well," Marc said as he wrung his hands together, sending bits of ice falling to the floor, "it depends *which* lies are told. And to who. And when. They have their uses, certainly."

One edge of the door opened as the vault continued to rotate.

"Legionnaire," Stacey said, pointing to the guard. "Medvedev, yes?"

"Yes, my Lady." He bowed his head quickly, his hands still on his weapon.

Stacey's finger swayed to Marc. "If he speaks in there, shoot him."

Medvedev flipped the power setting on his carbine to high and a low whine filled the air. He hefted the carbine's stock to his shoulder.

"Now that's a bit much," Marc said.

The legionnaire raised his muzzle.

"Whoa, meathead! We're not in the chamber yet. Heel, boy. Heel." Marc raised his palms up defensively.

Medvedev grumbled and turned the muzzle away from Marc.

Stacey sidestepped through the opening and into a small, cylindrical room bare of any decoration. Floating over a small plinth was a box, glowing from within. Stacey went to the box and began tapping in a code on a panel as Marc and his guard followed her inside.

A lens on one side of the box lit up and a middle-aged man with a slight paunch and thinning hair appeared on the other side of the plinth.

"—of goddamn time, Keeper. She won't…oh, Marc." Garret, president of the Terran Union, put his hands on his hips and nodded to Marc. The silver man, his back to the curved wall, gave Garret a quick wave.

A woman stepped into the holo projection from the quantum box. She was tall, her blonde hair run through with gray, her face lined with wrinkles. Her fit body was in stark contrast to the age in her face.

"Speak," Stacey said, her elbows slightly bent, fists held at her waist.

"Thank you, Stacey." Torni took a step closer to the box, half reaching toward the leader of the Ibarra Nation. "I know there's been some strain between our—"

"*Strain?*" Stacey leaned toward Keeper. "You call this *strain*? You murdered an Ibarran in cold blood. You know you did this. His name was Tyrel, and the Terran Union put a bullet in his head simply because he existed without your permission."

"The Hale Treaty tied our hands," Garret said. "There were observers from Bastion there. If we hadn't complied with the Omega Provision, we'd be in a war with every race in the galaxy, not just the Kesaht, the Vishrakath, and their allies."

"You murdered him," Stacey said. "Murdered."

"We've suspended the Omega Provision," Keeper said. "It was wrong to ever put it into effect, we know that. And nothing we can do will bring that man back, but there are more lives at stake now than before. Hear us out."

"I don't care," Stacey said. "It doesn't matter what happens to you. To Earth. To anyone but my Nation. You want my children dead. All of them."

"No, that's not true." Garret motioned to one side and a pair of Strike Marines in power armor materialized at the edge of the holo field, a hooded woman grasped by the arms between them.

A Marine pulled the hood off, revealing a mess of blonde hair. She flung her head back to clear her vision, and deep-blue eyes looked from Stacey to the legionnaire behind her.

"Masha!" Medvedev took a step forward then snapped back and brought his carbine level with the elder Ibarra's chest.

"I failed you, my Lady," Masha said, "but the target is still alive on Eridu. She—" The hood went back on and the Marines carried the spy away as she screamed Basque obscenities.

"One of yours, obviously, given how much trouble she's caused through the Union," Garret said. "And she won't be killed by us. The Omega Provision is over."

"Only because no one on Bastion knows you have her," Stacey said.

Garret and Keeper shared a look.

"You have our people too," Keeper said. "What did you do to the crew of the *Breitenfeld*? To Admiral Valdar?"

"They're safe and sound," Stacey said. "I'm not you. I don't kill prisoners."

"Moral superiority aside," Garret said, "we have a chance to end the war with the Kesaht. Right now. You interested?"

"They want peace?" Stacey crossed her arms.

"No. Bastards are still attacking our colonies and

killing every human they can get their hands on. There's only the sword with them," Garret said.

Stacey nodded slowly.

"We found their home world." Keeper held out a palm and a map of the galaxy projected from her palm. Keeper wasn't human, at least she wasn't anymore. She was the mind of a slain Strike Marine within a Xaros drone, one capable of reforming into the shape of a woman, but so damaged that Keeper had to mask the cracks as old age.

"Epsilon Iridani by our star charts," Keeper said. "Outside the original Crucible network. Bale must have jumped to the system before the Qa'resh destroyed all the jump drives. He built a Crucible gate and whipped the Kesaht up to fight this damn jihad of theirs. But we've got that Toth bastard now."

"Good for you," Stacey said.

"The Kesaht won't stop with Earth," Garret said. "You know they won't rest until they come for your worlds too."

"Won't be my problem," Stacey said.

Marc raised a hand to speak, but Medvedev put his finger on the trigger and Marc's hand snapped back down.

"We're launching a mission to defeat the Kesaht

in their home system," Garret said. "From what we know about them, if we kill Bale, the rest of the Risen commanders and their deployed fleets should fall back. Then we can turn our forces to the Vishrakath."

"I don't care," Stacey said.

"The Vish have killed millions with their mass drivers," Keeper said. "Innocent civilians. They've sent dozens of city killers through Crucibles at Earth. We've knocked them all out of space, but the attacks are only getting more frequent. We are running out of time and ships, Stacey."

"I told you," Stacey said, shaking her head. "I told you this would happen. You were so eager to get New Bastion up and running that you agreed to the Hale Treaty and gave up the only thing that gave us an edge over the aliens: procedural technology. Now you're desperate because you don't have the manpower to fight and win and you have only yourselves to blame."

"And you were right!" Garret shouted. He dug into a pocket and pulled out a small pill bottle. He twisted the cap off and tossed two small white discs into his mouth as Keeper watched, her disgust evident on her face. "You were right all along. That good enough for you, Stacey? Ibarrans good. Union bad. We turned our galactic expansion into a goat screw when we sent Ken Hale to negotia—"

"Don't you dare!" Stacey swiped at Garret, her fist passing through his projection a split second before he reacted and ducked away. "Don't you dare blame him. He was *your* pawn. The treaty—and everything that happened after—is on you!"

"I get it." Garret bit down on his pills and swallowed hard. "I get it, Stacey. Pin it all on me. Doesn't matter right now. What matters is that we know where the Kesaht's base is. We're set to go there and smash it to pieces, knock those bastards out of the war and back to their Stone Age for all I care…but we need you."

"You what?" Stacey cocked her head to one side.

"We need your help," Keeper said. "We're throwing every available ship into this mission. Pulled out of three different systems to build an armada that can win this fight."

"But it might not be enough," Garret said. "Intelligence is spotty. And after that Toth dreadnought smashed the Cyrgal in Ouranos, we'd rather bring too many guns than too few."

"You want Ibarran ships to join your assault?" Stacey's voice went an octave higher, almost like she was laughing.

"They'll have opeational control," Keeper said.

"We have—"

"You want us to be your cannon fodder," Stacey said. "First you execute us for the crime of being alive, now you want us to die in your place?"

"The Union doesn't shirk from a fight," Garret said. "Fight beside us as allies. As humanity united in purpose. After this, we'll work out a mutual defense treaty. Full diplomatic recognition. We'll even restart our procedural program. To hell with Bastion."

"Come back to Earth, Stacey," Keeper said. "This division between us was wrong. Help us make it right."

Stacey uncrossed her arms then strode around the quantum box with her hands clasped behind her back. She stopped and looked to Marc, who nodded quickly.

Stacey turned her gaze to Garret. "No."

Garret's head jerked back like he'd been slapped. "But…we're giving you everything you want," he said. "This is your fight too and we can win it together if—"

"Never."

Stacey chopped a hand across her chest and the box shut off.

She went to Marc and poked a finger in his chest. "This war ends on my terms, you understand? *I* will bring this galaxy to its knees with the Ark and then *I* will burn every planet that refuses to obey the Ibarra Nation. No compromises. No ally that can betray us when we need them the most. *Our* strength will keep us safe. *My* Nation over all. To hell with Earth."

Stacey stormed out of the vault, leaving Marc and Medvedev behind.

Marc motioned to the quantum box, but Medvedev shook his head. The metal man shrugged, dejected.

Chapter 4

Aignar's gauss cannons snapped as he put two rounds down the hexagonal cavern running down the keel of the Toth dreadnought. He ducked behind the shield mounted on one arm as energy bolts burst into sparks against it. A threat warning popped up on his HUD and he swung his shoulder-mounted rotary cannon around to spray an open hatch with a torrent of bullets.

A Toth warrior crashed to the ground beside him, body shredded but not bleeding.

Aignar stomped the Toth's head with his heel and blasted a Kesaht armor berserker in the sternum as it ripped through the deck plating a few dozen yards away.

The rest of the Iron Dragoons picked off targets as they appeared down the massive corridor. The snap of gauss cannons and whirl of spinning barrels echoed down the long tunnel.

"This is taking too long!" Aignar kicked a bulkhead next to an open hatch too small for Armor to pass through.

"This is delicate work, thank you very much!" a man shouted over the IR.

"Don't rush him." Cha'ril pulled one arm back and a punch spike popped out of the housing to replace her fist. She rushed forward and bashed her shield into the chest of a Kesaht berserker, lifting the metal monstrosity off its feet as long claws flayed against her back and shoulders. She slipped the shield to one side and rammed the punch spike through its chest, stopping it cold. She put a foot against the berserker and kicked it off, blasting another of the Rakka-piloted suits as it got tangled in its fallen comrade.

"And time!"

A team of Strike Marines hurried out of the open hatch, their smaller gauss rifles covering the angles as they emerged. Their weapons snapped, picking off Rakka troops that Aignar had ignored. The brutes' weapons were little more than a nuisance to him in Armor, but the Strike Marines weren't as resilient.

A Strike Marine a head taller than the rest barreled

out into the open and stomped a heel against the deck. Struts shot out from his lower leg and braced him against the deck. The batteries of his heavy gauss cannon, a single-barreled version of what Aignar had bolted to one forearm, hummed to life.

"Kill enemy!" the Strike Marine grunted and opened fire.

SIMULATION PAUSE flared on Aignar's HUD, and the enemy fire ceased.

The Marine heavy gunner shook his gauss cannon. When it refused to function, he shook it even harder.

"Stand down, Opal," the Strike Marine lieutenant said. "Inspectors don't like wandering into a live fire exercise."

Aignar cycled fresh rounds into his weapons and checked his battery reserves. After running this simulation for the last six hours straight, he'd need to swap out his capacitors soon.

"I did it right this time." A Marine tapped an empty satchel bag strapped to his lower back. "Promise."

"That is what you said last time, Corporal Garrison," Cha'ril chided. "And the time before that."

"You want to try mixing a binary denethrite explosive while under fire *and* set up a tamper proof timer?" The Marine pointed at the Dotari Armor. "Those big metal digits of yours aren't designed for delicate work. Gor'al, tell her something rude."

"Her big metal digits could crush your head if she wanted," a Dotari Strike Marine said. "And I've taught you enough of our language."

"You have." Garrison took a deep breath and whistled a call, then clicked his tongue twice.

"You want to mate with my hydraulics?" Cha'ril asked.

"No, I said—" Garrison raised a finger.

"That's what you said." Gor'al nodded furiously.

"You're just taking her side because you're really on Team Dotari," Garrison snapped.

A hidden door behind them opened and two Naval officers in light fatigues stepped into the passageway.

"Key leaders." A commander set down a tablet and pushed it away from him. It floated a few inches off the deck and emitted a holo field. Video of Iron Dragoons and Strike Marines breaching the ship's hull played out.

Gideon, Lieutenant Hoffman, and another Strike Marine went to the projection and spoke with the two Navy officers.

"I did it *right*," Garrison said, almost at a whine.

"If we have to get into the tactical insertion

torpedoes again," Aignar said, "I'm blaming you."

"Oh thank God." Garrison shook his head. "I thought I was the only one that hated the TITs."

"That acronym." Santos shook his helm. "I still don't get why we have to set the denethrite bomb inside the Toth dred. Denethrite ain't gentle. Just slap it on the outside and run like hell."

"It's physics, my big metal friend," Garrison said. "Even if I set a shape charge to blow a lance of graphenium through the hull, too much explosive force is lost to backblast. And the hull plating on that beast is no joke. You see the video from Ouranos? Took a hit from the Cyrgal and kept on ticking. We get the bomb inside and all the boom-boom will be contained within the hull. Difference between having a firecracker go off in the palm of an open hand—singed skin—or inside a closed fist— lost fingers."

"All these years on the same team and you finally say something intelligent," the Marine Sniper, Duke, said.

"Opal's wearing off on him," said Booker, the medic.

Aignar felt a sense of kinship with the Strike Marines. Their banter reminded him of his time in the Rangers, and if he still had a mouth, he would have smiled. He looked at the tall Marine next to the lieutenant. One of his hands had four fingers; the other was mechanical like the prosthetic Aignar used outside of his armor and bore five digits.

"That really Steuben?" Aignar asked. "The Karigole from the Ember War?"

"Yup." Duke lifted his visor and put a pinch of chewing tobacco between his lip and gums. "He ain't all cuddly like you may have seen in that crap *Last Stand at Takeni* movie. Guy's a real hard-ass. Hates Toth. Don't get between him and the high priority target named Bale, if you know what's good for you."

"I love that movie," Cha'ril said. "Dotari networks play it on a loop every *Breitenfeld* day."

"There's a day?" Santos asked.

"On the anniversary of when Admiral Valdar saved us from the Xaros," she said.

"What about us?" Garrison flopped his hands to his side. "We rescued that Golden Fleet of yours. Cured the phage? Not even a Valdar's Hammer commercial break?"

"That was you?" Cha'ril asked.

Garrison pointed a thumb at the patch on his left shoulder.

"Yup. We're banshee slayers. Lieutenant Hoffman dusted the last Xaros drone in the galaxy."

Cha'ril bent down, bringing her helm level with Garrison's face.

"Why couldn't you have been a few days faster?" she asked, a growl to her voice.

"Whoa, whoa." The breacher backed up, hands next to his head in submission. "We didn't exactly go sightseeing in the *Kidran's Gift*."

"Got a good look at the sewers," Duke huffed.

"Bad smell." Opal, the doughboy, nodded.

"Team." Gideon walked over, his foot falls echoing off the wall. "Mission objectives were achieved…marginally. Planting the explosives took five minutes longer than projected."

Garrison was about to protest, but Duke put a heavy hand on his shoulder.

"The sim runners will give us another shot." Lieutenant Hoffman removed his helmet and wiped sweat from his brow. "Then it's back to the *Ardennes* for final load out. It's up to my Hammers and Gideon's Dragoons to take the Toth dreadnought out quick. Soon as we hit the Kesaht system. We screw it up and the fleet's going to take one hell of a beating before they can wear down the dread's shields."

"No pressure," Santos said.

"Fifteen minutes for reset," the team's head NCO,

King, said. "Then back in the T-I-T simulator."

Garrison snickered.

Aignar pointed a big finger at the breacher.

"Yeah yeah." The Marine shrugged. "All my fault."

Chapter 5

Cha'ril ducked under an Eagle fighter and looked around. Crewmen shouted to each other and ran carts of tools and bullets between the void craft.

"Darling." A hand grabbed her by the elbow, and she spun around. Man'fred Vo gave her a brief hug and led her away to a less noisy spot just around a corner from a maintenance lift.

"The next time you say 'meet me on flight deck Bravo,' be a little more specific." She flicked a talon under his beak.

"Sorry, I don't have much time before I leave," he said.

"Leave? You're assigned to the *Ardennes*. You should be at the same briefing I'm about to be late to." She placed her hands on his forearms.

Man'fred Vo shook his head, his quills rustling.

"The Council of Firsts ordered all our Union advisors back to Dotari. My father tried to delay it, but he's not a First. Overruled. I take a transport home in less than an hour," he said, his eyes cast down with shame.

"The Firsts know how important this mission is. It will end the war if—"

"There's a Kesaht fleet within range of home," Man'fred Vo whispered. "The Union pulled the task force they had stationed to protect us to bring more firepower to this mission. The Council panicked. Pulled everything they could back to Dotari."

"There are dozens of Union fleets that can jump to Dotari through the Crucible gates within minutes. There's no reason to panic." Cha'ril snapped her beak as she said the words, realizing just how foolish they were.

"The Solar System's holding up to the Vishrakath bombardment," her joined said, "but just barely. The Council's putting everything they can into more macro cannons. I've already got my work detail to fly ore shipments from the asteroid mines."

"You're a fighter pilot, not an ash and trash hauler. Wait, why haven't I received recall orders?" She scrolled through messages on her forearm screen.

"The Union insisted on keeping the integrated Armor," Man'fred Vo said. "They're shorthanded."

Cha'ril hissed with annoyance.

"But this is what we promised each other," she said. "One of us must be there for our hatchling."

"And I hate this." He turned away and crossed his arms. "I am your warrior. Your protector. Why else did I beat the hell out of Fal'tir but to prove that I am strong enough to care for you and our hatchling?"

"I am Armor, my love. I can take care of myself."

"You don't live in that metal, darling. There is more to life than war…I hope."

"Then this is fate." She wrapped her arms around his waist and hugged him from behind. "For now. I don't fight with the intent to lose. My lance is the best in the Corps. Don't worry about me."

"But I will." He turned around and removed a wooden box from his flight suit. He popped the lid open and showed her a leather bracelet, woven through with small gems and carved bones.

"You can't be serious," she said.

"I should've done this on Mount Chatarall just as dawn broke over the bay and the *vinit* burst into morning song. I know you love that part of the old love stories, but proposing to you in a flight bay is the best I can do on short notice. I'm not happy just to be your joined. Be my wife. Let us raise our many hatchlings together."

She touched the bracelet with a talon and looked into his eyes.

"Your timing is awful," she said.

"That a yes?"

"Of course it is. I don't want anyone else, and if another female batted her eyes at you, I'd crush her in my Armor." She slipped on the bracelet and tugged a cord to tighten it around her wrist. She turned her arm from side to side, examining it in the floodlights.

"Oh…thank the ancestors." Man'fred Vo nuzzled the side of her neck.

A chime sounded on her forearm screen.

"Duty calls," she said, fingers tugging at the bracelet. "Your timing…ugh. I still love you."

"I will see you after the mission to Kesaht'ka," he said firmly. "The humans always say 'be safe' to each other at times like this."

"I am Armor, my love." She tucked the bracelet under a cuff. "Safe isn't what we do."

"I don't want to go." He balled his fists in anger. "I want to fly for you. Keep your skies free of danger."

"Go home, and make our skies safe for our egg," she said. "You will do your part. I will do mine. There's no dishonor in either."

He touched the side of his beak to hers and gave her hand a squeeze before he left.

Cha'ril watched him go, an ache building in her heart.

****

Santos pushed the prosthetic hand and forearm against the bolt attached just below Aignar's elbow and it attached with a snap. Aignar worked the fingers open and shut, then gave Santos a thumbs-up.

The younger Armor stepped back and opened his locker. He was still in his skin suit, hair damp and unkempt from the shower he'd just taken. Santos stepped into a jump suit and glanced over at Aignar as he put the nub of his left leg into a boot already holding his mechanical foot.

"You good?" Santos asked.

"I can take it from here," came from the speaker in Aignar's throat.

"Can't believe Admiral Lettow wants us in person for the final briefing. He knows we lose synch every time we unplug." Santos pushed an arm through a sleeve.

"Admiral's ship. Admiral's mission. Admiral can

tell us to do whatever the hell he wants," Aignar said. "It's only for a couple of hours. We'll be pegged out by go time."

"If you say so." Santos frowned and zipped up his uniform. "You going to the service?"

Aignar stopped. His left ring finger trembled and he put his other metal hand on top of it to silence the noise.

"I'm not Templar," he said.

"Neither am I. No one is anymore." Santos shrugged. "But the squids and jar heads didn't get that memo. Every time they spot my plugs, they ask if Armor's going to be at pre-battle rites. We're getting too close to the ceremony. It's hard for me to stay noncommittal."

"Saint Kallen's an important part of the fleet and the Strike Marine Corps," Aignar said. The Saint had once been key to much of the Armor Corps. The memory of dead and bullet-ridden Templar on Mars still haunted his dreams.

"But I'm not Templar. You're not Templar. Nobody's Templar anymore," Santos said. "But can we still go to the ceremony in Armor? Let the crunchies do their knock for luck." He rapped his knuckles against his locker.

"Who's going to stop you?" Aignar asked.

"The captain." Santos glanced at Gideon's locker. "He...I know he doesn't care for religion."

"Captain Gideon doesn't have a problem with Saint Kallen; it's the Templar he...has history with. Why are you sitting on the fence over this? You want to be used as an icon for the ceremony or don't you?"

"It's not about me." Santos looked down at his boots. "I've never asked the chaplain to bless my gear before a fight and I don't think it'll matter this go-around. But you know how some of the crunchies are about us. We're in the fight with them and it's like the Saint's there. Gives 'em hope. Bit of solace in the middle of a shit storm. You know this assault on the Kesaht home world isn't going to be a walk in the park. This is the big show. Not everyone's going home...even if we do everything right."

"Then you should go to the ceremony." Aignar snapped his other foot on and stood up. "Your head's in the right place. The captain won't bother you about it."

"Oh...good." Santos reached into his locker and removed a small gold crucifix on a chain. He put it on and tucked the cross under his shirt.

"Thought religion wasn't for you," Aignar said.

"Dad sent it to me. Says he wore it during the war and it got him through without a scratch." Santos rubbed his chest, adjusting the necklace. "You...you're good? All set for this mission?"

"Kid, you go on enough drops and it gets to be old hat. Work yourself into knots before every mission and it doesn't make a damn bit of good. Have your Armor locked and loaded. Know the mission. Head on a swivel. And be prepared for the plan to go right down the toilet the minute we step off. Murphy's Law."

"Makes you wonder why we go over the plan so many damn times when it never works out the way the brass thinks it'll go." Santos and Aignar walked to the doors, Aignar's steps slow and stiff.

"So long as you understand the commander's intent and keep working towards it—and stick to the plan when you still can—the chaos is manageable," Aignar said.

"I know the intent: Assault the Kesaht home system. Beat them down and force them to surrender. Then get back to Union space and proceed to beat the hell out of the Vishrakath."

"You got it…we still need to go to the briefing," Aignar said.

"Figured you'd say that."

****

Admiral Lettow waited for the murmurs to die down in the briefing room before he walked onto the stage. Ericson, the captain of the *Normandy*, picked her notes off the lectern and nodded to him as she moved away.

"Captains, ground force commanders, Armor," he began. "Ericson just laid out the operational plan for the assault on the enemy's capital, which we've learned they call Kesaht'ka. Roughly translates as 'Heart of Unity.'" He touched a fingertip to a screen and a blue-green planet with a single large moon appeared in a holo over his shoulder.

"Thanks to fine intelligence work and Armor terminating a Risen commander on Umbra," he said, "we know where the Kesaht home system is. Relic light, several hundred years old by the time it reached one of our telescopes, shows the world to be inhabitable and Earth-like. The system is *not* within the network of Crucible gates created by the Xaros, but beyond their advance before we put an end to them during the Ember War. Best assessment is that a Toth overlord jumped to the planet after the war, before the Qa'resh disabled all the jump engines, and proceeded to build a Crucible gate of his own in the Kesaht system.

"But now we've got them." Lettow heard a

number of enthusiastic remarks from the crowd. "And now the Terran Union will bring this war to an end. The Kesaht have pushed everything they have in their attack on us. They're overextended and vulnerable. The planners down in Camelback Mountain have pulled together every ship—not already on the line—and together we will be the hammer that crushes the Kesaht.

"Mission is simple. Jump in. Seize the Crucible and proceed to destroy everything they have in space. Star bases. Shipyards. Every last damn satellite. Once we hold the orbitals, we will demand surrender."

"And if they refuse?" The question came from General Laran, head of the Armor Corps.

"Intelligence is positive the Toth leading the Kesaht is a coward. He'll accept any terms that don't involve his death. President Garret wants the Kesaht out of our space and their threat over. Then we will take the battle to the Vishrakath. Make them pay for the lives lost on Novis."

He touched the screen again and a list of the ships assembled to fight under his command replaced the Kesaht planet.

"Let me play devil's advocate," he said. "Yes, this is our entire reserve force. Yes, the Vishrakath are attacking Earth with mass drivers sent through off-set gates. But the Solar System's defenses are holding. What happened to Iapetus—while tragic—was a fluke. We will smash the Kesaht before they and their allies know what's hit them. We have the element of surprise; they have taken massive casualties in the past few weeks attempting to take our casualties. This is the turning point of the war, and we can end it with one swift stroke."

Officers banged fists against chair arms and tabletops.

By the Saint, I hope I'm right, Lettow thought. *We botch this and the war will be over…for us.*

"If there are no questions, then return to your stations for final prep. *Adversor et admorsus.*" He ended with the *Ardennes's* motto. Resist and bite.

Chapter 6

Bale stomped down the wide corridor of his star fort, the four legs of his tank moving like insect legs as they carried the gilded tank containing his nervous system. Toth warriors flanked him, each bearing a crystalline halberd in their reptilian hands.

Kesaht Risen, both Ixio and Sanheel, followed close behind, their hands carrying oversized data slates.

"Our offensive on Umbra has suffered a number of setbacks," an Ixio said. "Remaining forces have shifted to hit-and-run attacks to harass the Terran devils still there, but the local weather patterns are causing—"

"The commander returned to us, did he not?" Bale asked.

"Yes," a Sanheel grunted. "His mind is readapting

to a new body. A few more days until he's capable of answering questions. We do not recover from a Risen transfer as fast as our Ixio brothers. Earlier reports from Umbra mentioned a significant Terran Armor presence, though they've largely been absent from the battlefield in the past week."

"Always their metal suits," Bale said. "What of the improvements to our own countermeasures?"

"The installation of Rakka brains into combat armor has been…irksome," an Ixio said. "They lack the coping skills to adapt to their new bodies. They revert to atavism, brutal insanity. Useful as little more than terror troops and a danger to our own forces when encountered after their release."

"And the project to adapt the rest of the Kesaht members?" Bale's neural tendrils poked at a Sanheel and an Ixio.

"Your glorious Risen technology will not integrate with the suits," the Ixio said. "Any who make the transition to…your more glorious state of being…are cut off from immortality."

"Criminals. Cowards. Find volunteers. The Rakka solution is unsatisfactory," Bale said.

"My Lord." A Sanheel worked his thick jowls nervously. "You promised Risen immortality to all of the

Kesaht deemed worthy. Every soldier on the front lines fights for that honor. If we turn away some to the metal-clad, then it—"

"We're still in the earliest iterations!" Bale's tendrils squirmed. "All Sanheel—or Ixio, we should try them too—that have their brains installed into suits are still very much alive. We'll find a solution to the current design flaws. Do you hear me complaining about being in this tank? No. It's quite liberating. Get volunteers or make some. Status report tomorrow."

"Yes, my Lord," the Ixio said.

"The Council of Risen awaits you in the command deck," the Sanheel said. "They have an update from our Vishrakath allies."

"They can wait. I have another matter to attend to. Now go away." Bale went to a lift door and shooed away the Ixio and Sanheel with his back leg. He took the elevator with his Toth warriors, a long trip that went the entire length of the star fort.

The doors opened to a vault, and Bale issued a bird call from his tank. A force field dropped and the vault door opened with a series of clanks as massive gears moved the two-yard-thick metal out of his way.

Bale went into a laboratory. Rows of liquid-filled tanks with frost-encrusted data lines that ran to the ceiling made up most of the lab. Dark figures floated within ruby-colored fluid. A work area with oversized desks and a cot was in the middle. A very tall green-skinned humanoid woman stood next to a gurney holding fully grown a man, almost child like compared to the alien next to him. His skin was alabaster, and thick blue veins stood out against his skin.

"Trinia…you're too slow," Bale said to the Aeon.

Trinia touched a finger to a sensor cupped in her palm and traced circles over the man's bare chest.

"It takes nine days to grow these procedurals," she said without looking at Bale. "You demanded them faster and you saw what happened. Cellular disintegration and subject loss. You wish to keep rushing me?"

"You've made little more than playthings for me and my soldiers." Bale lifted a metal claw and nudged the man. He moaned and tried to sit up. Trinia pushed him back down and hit his neck with a hypo spray.

"I don't want meat puppets. I want something that can be put to useful work. Something made to suffer," Bale said.

Trinia glanced up at the ceiling.

"The bodies need the procedurally generated minds to go with them. You had the raw genetic ingredients from corpses and prisoners. You don't have the memory generations software or databases. It took me decades to prepare all that with Marc Ibarra. I've managed to cobble together a framework that will result in something viable. Something for your…needs."

"No, no." Bale extended the feeder arm from beneath his tank, a bronze spike encrusted with old blood. The spike opened and a tiny tendril reached out to caress the man's skull. "No, I won't feed on these. All it takes is one mistake, yes? You upload a burning mind to the meat and I'll end up like Doctor Mentiq, my brain exploding and lining the inside of my tank like paint. Not that you'd mind that, eh?"

"Then why do you want procedurals at all?" Trinia asked.

"Because soon you will perfect the process. Patience, yes? You will recreate the procedural framework to create functioning humans, all programmed to be my willing servants. Then they will have children, children not of shallow minds and weed bodies, but minds that I can savor."

"Consuming one so young can't be—"

"Patience! Their minds will ripen as they age. I fed from Mentiq's human stock on Nibiru. Exquisite taste! Long-term planning, my dear Aeon. In the meantime, there are more than enough true born humans on Earth and their colonies to tide me over. Once the war against the Terran Union is won…what remains of the humans will exist solely to serve me and my appetite."

"Then don't rush me." Trinia tossed her sensor onto a tray.

"But who says I have to wait so long for a taste?" Bale struck out with a leg and knocked over Trinia's cot. A human girl squealed, her hiding place gone.

Bale grabbed the girl by the wrist and lifted her up. She sobbed, eyes squeezed shut.

"Stop, leave her alone!" Trinia reached for the girl, but a Toth warrior slapped the flat of his halberd against her chest and stopped her in her tracks.

"What do you call this vermin?" Bale poked the girl in the stomach with his feeder arm. "Such a mistake to get attached to meat. But the children look so much like juvenile Aeons, don't they? Shall I sample the bounty you're breeding for me?"

The feeder arm snapped open and the wire-thin tendrils grasped at the girl as she kicked at the air.

"Bale, I'm working as fast as I can," Trinia pleaded. "Stop torturing her. It helps nothing!"

"Reminds you to keep at it, yes?" Bale dropped the girl and she curled into a ball, still sobbing. "Besides, too much stress ruins the taste. Best to eat when they're willing meals."

The Toth warrior snapped his halberd away and Trinia scooped the girl up and held her against her chest.

"Faster…Aeon," Bale said. "Your work will satisfy me, or that thing against your breast will."

Bale's tank twisted around and he went back to the lift.

Trinia clutched the girl for several minutes more. She brushed blonde hair out of her face and smiled down at her teary eyes.

"He's gone?" the girl asked.

"He's gone." Trinia nodded. "I can't keep him away, little one. Remember what I told you? He's only scaring you. He won't ever hurt you."

"He will!" She wiped a tattered sleeve across her eyes. "Once he has the proccies he wants, he won't need you. Then he'll-he'll—"

"No." Trinia smiled at her. "Bale is a monster. Evil. But he is no fool. I am too valuable to him to anger. And if he hurts you, then I will never rest until I can hurt him. He knows that."

"So we just stay in this place?" The girl peeked over Trinia's shoulder to the man on the gurney. "Stay here with the zombies?"

"Bale's not the only person that knows I'm

valuable." Trinia sighed. "Someone will come for me. And when they do, you'll come with me. Okay?"

"Will they come soon?" the girl, Maggie, asked.

"Maybe yes. Maybe no." Trinia smiled slightly. "Back to our lessons, yes?"

"Will you teach me how to make an explody-mind?"

Trinia gave her a pat on the head.

"Not just yet, little one. Not just yet."

Chapter 7

Roland tugged his cuff toward the raw, frost-burned flesh of his left hand as he made his way down the steps of the *Warsaw*'s briefing amphitheater. Staff officers and commanders from across the Ibarran fleet were already present, grouped together by ship. Legionnaires, hard-eyed and well-built men that stood half a head taller than everyone else—even out of their power armor—took up a back corner of the seats. Legion and Navy all kept their military bearing, but Roland could feel the nervous tension in the room.

Roland spied the glint of skull plugs through the crowd and caught a glimpse of white tabards down in the front rows. He hurried down the steps.

A one-star general with a gold cord wrapped

beneath his right shoulder—one of Marshal Davoust's senior staff—stepped to one side to let Roland pass. Roland nodded quickly, still unused to the amount of deference the Ibarrans gave to Armor. That the prevailing faith within the Ibarra Nation had a locus on Saint Kallen—and Armor as her *de facto* avatars—gave Roland his explanation, but what he'd just learned from Stacey had sown doubt in his heart.

Roland slipped into the seat at the end of a row next to Nicodemus. The older man glanced at a clock over an exit and then to Roland.

"Sorry, sir," Roland said, tugging at his Templar tunic. "Got...delayed in the chapel."

Just then, Admiral Makarov walked onto the briefing stage and spoke quickly with one of the officers tending to a holo table. She was young, in her early twenties, at odds with her senior rank.

Nicodemus raised an eyebrow at Roland.

"No, no, that's not—" Roland held up his left hand and swiped it back to his waist when he realized what he'd done.

Nicodemus took Roland by the wrist, but Roland twisted it free and half turned away from his lance mate.

"It's nothing," Roland said.

"You wouldn't hide 'nothing.'" Nicodemus

crossed his arms over his chest. "What's wrong?"

Roland swallowed hard and looked back across the crowd. Nicodemus and the other armor present might—might—believe him. But the legionnaires and Navy present were almost certainly from the procedural tubes and hardwired to obey Stacey Ibarra no matter what her motives were…or her level of self-control.

"Nothing that will affect the mission, sir," Roland said.

"You know where we're going?" Nicodemus tilted his head toward Makarov.

"Why would—why would she tell me anything? I-I…" Roland yammered for a moment before Nicodemus put a heavy hand on his shoulder.

"You're young. Ignorant in things you haven't even considered," Nicodemus said. "Even on an Ibarran ship, which is more regimented than anything I saw back in the Union, there's scuttlebutt."

"Scuttlebutt about what?" Roland looked to the stage and briefly locked eyes with Makarov. His cheeks flushed and he had to look down to examine his shoes.

"Boy-o still trying to play it cool?" Morrigan leaned over from beside Nicodemus, her long braid of red hair falling from her shoulder.

"He is," Nicodemus rumbled.

"You two don't—" Roland cut himself off. Morrigan had been engaged to her lance mate, Bassani, who died in battle. Nicodemus had married not long after the initial defection from the Union. Arguing with those two, each better versed in all things relationship, felt disrespectful.

"Tell you this," Morrigan said, flipping her braid behind her head. "There's always a war. There's always a reason to say 'no.' There's always an excuse to be alone…but you'll never get back the time you could've been together. Take it."

Gripping his right hand over the fresh scar Stacey had given him, Roland said solemnly, "Who knows how much time any of us have."

The lights in the auditorium brightened and then dimmed. The briefing was about to begin. Conversation died down and stragglers hurried to their seats.

"Is it Mars, Roland?" Morrigan asked. "Is it time to bring Saint Kallen's bones home?"

"Your guess is as good as mine." Roland shrugged.

Marshal Davoust walked onto the briefing stage and the room came to attention. Light shone off the man's bald pate as he made his way to the holo table, clenching a baton in his hand and tapping it against his flank.

Davoust set the end of the baton into a port and twisted it to one side. The lights lowered to almost nothing and a holo screen appeared high over the table. The words TOP SECRET, bordered by yellow and black chevrons, flashed several times in the holo.

"Warriors of the Ibarra Nation," Davoust began, "you are all now on commo lockdown. This mission comes direct from Lady Ibarra…who will be joining us."

Roland's hands clenched into fists.

The holo changed to a map of the galaxy. Pinpricks by the thousands peppered the stars—locations of Crucible gates—through a good three-quarters of the Milky Way. Roland knew almost all had been built by the xenocidal Xaros during their long purge through the galaxy. The aliens' drones had massacred any sentient life encountered and built Crucible gates over habitable worlds, or worlds containing relics of already extinct races. Several dozen more appeared through the remainder of the galaxy, new gates built by the races that made up the old Qa'resh-led alliance against the Xaros.

The holo zoomed in toward a section of the Outer Arm, devoid of any Crucible gates for thousands of light-years.

"Our target is a planet designated Nekara." Davoust removed his baton from the port and tapped the end cap against a screen. The holo closed in on a star and the orbits of several planets appeared, a target icon over the fourth ring. "All we have on the system's composition is what we can pull from old light that's reached Ibarran space. Much of the finer data is lost to nebulae between the galactic arm with Nekara and us. But we can deduce where the habitable zone is and, therefore, that is where we should start looking."

Davoust took a step away from the holo table to address the crowd directly.

"Lady Ibarra has spent years searching the galaxy for a Qa'resh artifact." Davoust tapped his baton against his leg and the holo changed to a picture carved in stone: a vessel with a conch-like shape floating over crude drawings of humanoid figures. The marshal kept tapping his baton, and the images snapped to different depictions of the same vessel: one, an elegant glass etching; another of the ship carved into a mountainside; yet another, a picture taken from orbit of the ship scraped into a continent of an alien world.

"We call it the Ark," Davoust continued. "Now-extinct races recorded its appearance across the galaxy. The Qa'resh dominated the galaxy until they vanished several million years ago. But this ship, the Ark, was recorded in the outer edge of the Perseus arm several times since their disappearance…the last sighting was a few thousand years ago.

"Lady Ibarra, through study and decryption of Qa'resh artifacts obtained on many missions some of you were part of," Davoust said, "has tracked the Ark to Nekara."

Roland looked at Nicodemus. The other armor had ambushed Roland and Aignar in the depths of a Qa'resh artifact hidden in the upper layers of a gas giant. Nicodemus and Stacey had taken him prisoner, setting him on the path that eventually led to his defection to the Ibarra Nation.

Nicodemus shrugged.

"Lady Ibarra has asked me to add," Davoust said, his demeanor changing slightly, a hint of apprehension in his posture, "that this world was known to the Qa'resh that led the old Alliance on Bastion. During the Xaros's long advance across the galaxy, the Qa'resh sent probes to star systems where they might have recruited allies against the Xaros. One such probe made it to Nekara and a single message was sent back to Bastion. Upon receipt of that message, the Qa'resh cut off all further exploration of the Outer Arm. They destroyed all other probes en route to the area. Lady Ibarra has no knowledge as to why this happened."

Trinia might know, Roland thought. The Aeon scientist was millennia old and had worked with Marc and Stacey Ibarra to create the procedural and armor technology. That Roland had failed in his mission to recruit Trinia to the Ibarran cause—and had even lost her to the vicious Toth—filled him with shame.

"Until only a few weeks ago," Davoust continued, shaking the end of his baton toward Makarov, "we lacked the ability to reach Nekara. A one-way jump from the nearest Crucible would only get us halfway across the gulf between Crucible space and the unknown regions. But then we…liberated the *Breitenfeld* from the Terran Union. We brought the ship—and the Keystone jump-gate technology it carried—into our fold. Well done, *Warsaw*."

Makarov gave him a nod.

"Instead of taking years to build a chain of Crucible gates to Nekara, gravity tides currently allow for a jump from the Gethsemane III gate to the target system. Once there, we will assemble the Keystone gate over Nekara and use it to return to the Crucible network and back home. We have our own portable Crucible technology, but what the Terran Union dogs had with the Keystone was a generation ahead of us. 3rd and 18th Fleets will hold the Gethsemane gate until our return. If we lose the gate on Gethsemane, the *Warsaw* and the rest of the forces we send to Nekara will be stranded for years."

Roland wondered which part of the mission was more critical for his lance, finding the Ark or making sure it could return to Ibarran space.

"The Fleet under Admiral Makarov's command will escort Lady Ibarra to the Ark and protect her while she takes control of it," Davoust said. "Armor will protect the Lady. We don't know what else we'll find on Nekara, but if the Templar can't handle it, then the mission is a failure."

Roland had his answer.

"What can the Ark do?" Makarov asked.

"It is Qa'resh technology." Davoust went to the table and tapped on a screen. "This video was recorded on Sletari, during the final days of the Ember War."

The holo changed to a starship gunnery camera feed, overlooking a blue and white planet from orbit. In the distance, a murmuration of millions of Xaros drones poured out of a Crucible gate. Two bands of yellow light sprang around the planet's equator and struck each other. An energy beam miles wide sprang out from the convergence and burned through the drones.

Gasps came from the crowd.

"The Ark holds the secret to this technology," Davoust said. "The power of a race that once controlled the entire galaxy. The Lady believes the Ark will shift the balance of power in the Ibarra Nation's favor. Forever. We accomplish this mission, the wars will end. The Nation will be safe. Our enemies finished."

Nicodemus smiled and rapped a knuckle against the back of the chair in front of him.

Roland's mind went to Stacey Ibarra, to the near-lunatic display she'd just put on in front of him. If she really was going mad and she gained that much power…

"I will personally command the ground forces for this mission," Davoust said. "The 13th Legion will provide security around the Ark while Lady Ibarra and the armor take control of the ship. Admiral Makarov will oversee the construction of the Keystone carried within the *Breitenfeld* and maintain void supremacy.

"I have no information on potential hostile forces on Nekara," the marshal said. "Gethsemane III is in Haesh space, but they haven't settled the system. If they don't show up looking for a fight, we won't give them one. The single message Bastion received was the last trace of data on Nekara…and we don't know what was in that message. But it was faith that led us to Navarre. Faith that founded this great nation. Faith in Saint Kallen and Lady Ibarra that has brought us to this point…Faith is not how I prefer to plan operations, but it is all we have now. One final stroke to end the war and preserve the Ibarra Nation—and a future for humanity—once and for all."

Davoust rapped his baton against the holo table and the screen vanished. "Are there any objections?" he asked.

Roland started to raise his hand, but he sent it back to his lap. Nicodemus didn't seem to notice.

"Then to your stations." Davoust raised his baton and the room snapped to their feet. "For the Lady!"

"For the Lady!" roared the auditorium—everyone but Roland.

****

Navarre's cloud cover drifted across the planet. Alone on a wide catwalk, Roland peered through the observation window at his adopted world. Rain was a near constant on the planet, lashing against the arcology towers and domes that made up the Ibarra Nation's capital. From orbit, one wouldn't know there was a thriving colony, one growing by leaps and bounds every nine days as new procedural humans came out of the tubes.

Small void craft flit between the *Warsaw* and the planet, running last-minute supplies and personnel up to the assembling fleets.

Roland, an armor soldier who fought battles within a fifteen-foot-tall killing machine, felt small as he took in the jewel of the Ibarra Nation. He touched the red Crusader cross sewn into his tabard, wondering just how duty and faith merged into this symbol.

At the far end of the catwalk, a door opened and a lone figure strode toward him.

He didn't have to look to know who it was. She was the only one that ever came through this way and she had introduced him to this spot.

"Roland?" Admiral Makarov gave him a half frown and sidled up next to him, playfully bumping him with her hip. "Shouldn't you be in armor? Sync rating and all that?"

"I have a little while before services. Every legionnaire and sailor will want to make their vows before this operation." Roland flipped a hand off the rail and Makarov slid her palm against his.

"The risks for this…we're almost going to Nekara blind," Makarov said.

"The great Admiral Makarov getting butterflies in her tummy?"

"Oh? And you're here because you think this'll be some kind of a cakewalk? I jumped to Mars and got you—

and the rest of our prisoners—off that planet because I had a plan, a plan worked out to the second and one you all almost fouled up because the number of prisoners we brought home was almost double what we anticipated. For this mission…no plan. Just jump in and hope we don't kick a hornet's nest of…I don't know, a billion Xaros drones that didn't get the annihilation signal. A star on the verge of going nova. A radiation field that will poison us all before we can recover the Ark. Use your imagination."

"We're going in on faith," Roland huffed.

"Hope," Makarov said and winced as she pulled a pin out from the back of her hair. Raven locks spilled onto her shoulders and Roland's heart skipped a beat. "Hope is not a planning method."

"You shared this with the Lady?"

"With Davoust. The Lady is…occupied with another matter. He noted my concerns and promptly dismissed them. The marshal has total confidence in her." Makarov glanced at a flashing message on the screen built into her sleeve and sighed. "Though he did accept my recommendation that we bring quadrium munitions in the off chance we encounter Xaros drones. Now my gunnery officer is on the verge of a conniption. Hasn't had time to calibrate the rail cannons."

"Quadrium?"

"Special munition. Disrupts Xaros systems. A Terran Union Strike Marine team encountered a drone in deep space not too long ago. Destroyed it, but better to have a tool and not need it than need it and not have it."

Roland gave her hand a quick squeeze and asked, "Do you think all this faith is…justified?"

"What?" Makarov pulled her hand away and glanced at the scars on the back of Roland's hand. "By the Saint, what happened to you?" She took him by the wrist and held his hand up for inspection.

"Lady Ibarra is…heaven help me, Ivana, I don't know what I can say. Lady Ibarra told me that you're different, that just because you—"

"That I'm a proccie? That I'm some sort of revenant of a woman that died during the Ember War? I know I'm different." She pushed his hand away. "You think that matters? That you being true born gives you some sort of insight into the Lady?"

"Lady Ibarra is…sick." Roland glanced at the ceiling, wondering if hidden cameras had captured what he just said. "Her mind is slipping away. Have you ever seen her lose control?"

Makarov looked away from Roland to distant Navarre.

"You have, haven't you?" Roland asked.

"There are times that her behavior has…come across as a little off."

"'A little off…'" Roland ran a finger across the scar on his hand. "She gave me this. She thought I was Ken Hale, who she hasn't seen in years. She wrecked some of the pews in the chapel in the process. This isn't the first time I've seen her lose control."

"Lady Ibarra's mind is trapped in that metal body," Makarov said stiffly. "Perhaps our minds aren't meant to survive that way."

"And if she's unraveling? Then what do we do?"

"Careful, Roland." Makarov turned to face him and took a step back. "What you're implying is—"

"I know." Roland tossed his hands up. "Treason? Me. The soldier that's fought for the Terran Union, the Nation, then the Terran Union, then the Nation again. What the hell kind of position am I in to suggest anything? I should just keep my trap shut, appreciate that the Ibarra Nation took me in. That you pulled me off Mars. That I have a life here. Even a future."

Makarov's forearm screen buzzed with a call and she slapped her hand against the screen to mute the alert.

"You have a reason to be concerned, I'll grant you that," she said. "But there wouldn't be a Nation without Lady Ibarra. Look around you," she said, motioning to the planet. "She could have executed the Union prisoners we captured off the *Breitenfeld* in retaliation for them murdering our own simply because they were procedurals in violation of a treaty we didn't sign. We could be at war with the rest of the galaxy right now, but she's kept us out of Earth's fight with the Kesaht as much as possible. Now we're poised to find a weapon that can end the wars once and for all. Where has she ever gone wrong? Tell me."

"You're right." Roland leaned against the handrail, his head low. "You're right. Lady Ibarra's results speak for themselves. Who am I to question it?"

Makarov put her hand on the Templar cross on his chest, then slid her fingers to the side and beneath it. She touched a pocket on Roland's chest, where he kept her favor: a cloth rank insignia that belonged to her mother.

Roland's chest tightened as he feared she was about to take it from him.

Makarov gave the favor a pat, then reached up and touched his face. She turned him to look into her eyes, dark as the void.

"We must always have faith, my champion," she said. "Saint Kallen is with us. We have the *Breitenfeld*. *Gott Mit Uns*, yeah?"

Roland's lips quivered at the mention of Saint Kallen. He couldn't bring himself to tell Makarov what he learned about the Saint and Stacey Ibarra.

"Without faith...we'd be lost," Roland said.

"I have faith in you." Makarov smiled at him. "In the Lady. In our Nation. Stay the course, yes?"

"Yes."

"Good. Now I have to put out a dozen different fires before this ship and my fleet are ready for war." Makarov kissed him on the lips and let her hand slide down to his Templar cross. She pushed him back and winked as she hurried down the catwalk, redoing her hair into a tight bun.

"I'll see you after the mission," she said over her shoulder, a particular lilt in her voice.

"After...yes, after!" Roland leaned against the railing and watched her go, then he looked back to Navarre and the cold pit in his stomach returned.

"What's going to come after?" he asked himself.

Chapter 8

Lettow shook off the effects of the jump gate and unbuckled his restraints. He moved quickly but controlled back to the *Ardennes*'s holo table as his staff and the ship burst into action.

"You all know the drill," he said to those assembled around the table, all in full void armor and with helmets on. The *Ardennes* always fought with the ship's atmosphere reduced to vacuum. Fighting in flammable oxygen and a medium to carry blast waves from explosions was ill-advised in any void combat.

"Fleet combat status. Deployed fighter numbers and—"

The deck bucked under his feet. He gripped the holo table edge, and a look of worry broke through his mask of command for a split second.

The holo came to life, the Crucible still active as the last of his fleet emerged from the wormhole. Blue icons spread out, forming a disperse wall with the *Ardennes* as the center point.

"Taking hits from—" The ship shuddered before his XO could finish and Lettow felt a strut beneath the bridge sheer loose, sending a new and constant vibration through his feet.

Red blinking icons filled in around his fleet. He zoomed in on one, a large crystal embedded in a dark gray block, the tip pointed at his fleet.

"Those are Toth weapons," Lettow said. "They seeded space with cannons to—" A bolt hit the ship's hull just outside of the forward windows, flashing the bridge. "Guns! Priority target all the weapon emplacements. I want fighters in the void now before the carriers take too much damage."

His fleet responded quickly, knocking out the cannons in short order, but for everyone they destroyed, two more fired from farther and farther away.

"Lost the *Jackson* and *Baron Richthofen*," his XO announced. "Severe damage reported from a dozen other ships."

"Keep moving and keep to the plan," Lettow said.

"Status on the Crucible assault force?"

"They report heavy resistance," his Strike Marine liaison said.

"Sir, if the enemy—"

"Don't, XO. We knew there'd be resistance. We're still in this fight," Lettow said. Fire from the crystal cannons petered out and he breathed a sigh of relief.

Lettow hailed the *Midway* and Admiral Ericson's head and shoulders came up in the holo.

"*Ardennes*, we didn't plan on a thorn bush right in the doorway," she said.

"We're through the worst of it," he said. "Break off and begin your ground assault. My task force will begin reducing their orbital struc…tures."

In the holo, a shipyard appeared around the moon. A belt around the entire satellite, an engineering effort that even Earth hadn't bothered to attempt. Kesaht ships—hundreds—emerged, pulled out of their moorings.

"Artillery ships, commence fire on the enemy. They're big and slow coming out of the docks, easy targets," Lettow said.

Massive rail-fired shells leapt from the artillery vessels, each built to be little more three-hundred-yard-long vanes connected to a power plant and minimal life support for the crews. Hits against the belt came quick, destroying dozens of Kesaht ships before they could join the fight.

In the holo, the *Midway*'s task force broke away and made for the Kesaht'ka.

"Sir," his sensor officer waved for his attention, "the planet's reading very high levels of radiation. There's no surface water and the ozone layer is…missing."

"Then how do the Kesaht manage to…what is that?" Lettow leaned over the edge of the tank as something massive orbited around the moon. His face fell as he realized it was a star fort, one many times the size of the Toth dreadnought that was the largest target he'd planned to engage.

Lettow straightened his back, his mind blank as he struggled to take in what he was seeing. The Kesaht hadn't overextended their reach, he realized; their home system was a fortress.

"Incoming fire from the fort!" his XO announced, and Lettow braced himself against the table. He looked to the Crucible and considered ordering a hasty, humiliating retreat.

"Forward!" he shouted. "Bring all firepower to bear on the fort. We'll show them what Union guns can do."

****

The grand hall aboard Bale's star fort was segmented into two halves, one with seats for the Ixio and the other bore padded couches for the four-legged Sanheel to rest upon. Despite many long years of integrating Sanheel and Ixio into an entity as simple and pure as the Kesaht, physiology still proved a marked difference between the two senior races of the Hegemony.

Bale stood on a stage behind a massive data globe as Tomenakai, one of his favorite Ixio, droned on.

"Assaults on the demons' colony New Rome have taken heavy casualties, but several outlying settlements were seized—"

"How many viable prisoners?" Bale asked.

Text scrolled past a semi-transparent patch covering one of the Ixio's eyes.

"Seven hundred and nine, though there was a reported revolt. Decimation of non-combatants is the normal protocol," Tomenakai said.

"Cease that measure." Bale's tendrils twisted against each other. "Return of prisoners is the highest priority for all deployed forces. I want them back here and delivered to me as soon as possible."

"Fighting for prisoners is...less than the strategic ideal," a massive Sanheel general said. "Once we dominate the system, the devils surrender easily enough. We grasp for the civilians first and they might—"

"So you understand my instructions, good. See to it." Bale looked at the data crystals protruding from his skull, the mark of the Risen Kesaht. All Risen were cybernetically enhanced to broadcast their psyches in the event of death. The recorded message would later be installed into a clone body, affording the Risen a form of immortality. Just how the alteration affected the taste of a Risen's mind was still a mystery to Bale.

How he obtained sustenance was still a mystery to the Kesaht. His reserves of sentient beings was kept hidden deep inside the last Toth dreadnought, the *Last Light*. He'd sent Kesaht raids to several different alien worlds before launching the assault on human space, each time to obtain subjects to test them for eventual Risen integration. The Kesaht never asked what happened to the failed attempts...not that Bale had bothered to even try and modify other species.

Running a star system and a war was hungry work. "Kricks?" Bale turned his tank to and fro. "Where is Kricks?"

"Here." A Vishrakath came up the stairs, the gray

flesh stretched tight over its ant-like shell looked ghastly in the light from the data globe.

"How much longer will your people play around the Solar System?" Bale asked. "It's time to bring Earth to its knees."

Kricks touched a claw to a badge on a royal purple sash, the only clothing he wore, and the data globe changed to the Solar System.

"We've maintained a steady bombardment of high-speed mass drivers," Kricks said. "Taking the Crucible at Barnard's Star has allowed us better target engagement. The main city on the moon Iapetus was destroyed nine hours ago. We still hold Barnard's Star, despite a projected Terran Union counter attack that has yet to happen."

"The devils aren't fighting for Barnard's Star?" Bale asked. "Curious…"

"A number of their Pathfinder and Strike Marine teams have been captured attempting to destroy that Crucible," Kricks said. "Vishrakath fleet losses were heavy."

"You have prisoners? What are you planning to do with them?" Bale asked.

"The Vishrakath don't bother with menials, but Bastion insisted we preserve some of them for negotiation—"

"Bring them to me, yes?" The tips of Bale's tendrils quivered with hunger. "Just…bring them to me. How much else is there? Don't you all need a break for a meal?"

"We've just begun, Lord Bale," Tomenakai said. "Still thirty-seven more discussion points remain."

Bale wanted to scream in frustration, but he had no lungs or mouth.

"A hive fleet is set to assault Mars," Kricks said. "And we've detected a shadow in the system's macro cannon coverage."

The globe switched to the Earth and its two natural satellites, Luna and Ceres. Just how the Xaros had moved the dwarf planet into Earth orbit was a discussion Ixio scientists would not stop bothering Bale with.

A red wedge appeared behind Luna, extending back for thousands of kilometers.

"An offset jump from a nearby Crucible could get a sizeable force close to the humans' home world," Kricks said. "But the data is fragmentary. Enough of a disruption field could displace the attacking force in full view of macro cannons on Earth or in its orbit. We'll have this back door, so to speak, fully identified in a few more days."

"And our fleet massing over Fairland will be prepared," an Ixio admiral said.

"Almost, yes?" Bale asked. "Almost have the humans on their knees…we'll need troops. So many troops to control the population. Rakka. Kroar. Vishrakath. All will take their share of Earth and its colonies…"

"Once we control the orbit over Earth and can bombard at will," Kricks said, "the war will be won. We can harvest the population at our leisure."

"And on that note, let's take a break." Bale's mind had gone cloudy with hunger. Nearly feeding on the girl had accelerated his addiction to mental energy, and if he didn't eat soon, he would grow…unstable.

Lights went red, and a low siren emanated from speakers in the ceiling.

"What is that?" Bale asked. "What's going on?"

"Quantum gate formation." Tomenakai went to the base of the data globe and worked the controls. The holo snapped to Kesaht'ka and several pulsing icons over the northern pole. The holo zoomed in on the icon closest to Bale's star fort orbiting the planet's single moon.

Terran Union ships emerged through the jump gates; dozens of ships bristling with rail cannons and launching fighters as soon as they cleared the white disks.

"No...no, how. How did they find us?" Bale nearly screeched. "I can't...I can't be here for this. One of you Risen needs to—"

"This is the safest place for you, my Lord," Tomenakai said. "You'll be vulnerable if you move to the *Last Light*. This fort can withstand any assault and our orbital platforms are already firing on them."

The auditorium doors opened and Toth warriors entered, all in crystalline armor. Risen admirals and generals tried to push past the Toth but were shoved back.

"Let...let the military leave!" Bale scratched at deck. "The planners and engineers stay here...I suppose."

Toth hissed and let Sanheel and Ixio squeeze past.

"And activate the...the thing that stops Crucible gates!" Bale ordered.

"The quantum wave inhibiter?" Tomenakai asked. "But then we can't bring our fleets back to bolster our defenses—"

"And it keeps more humans out! Why are you questioning me?"

"Inhibitor activating." Tomenakai touched his forehead in submission and went to a control panel.

Fear nagged at Bale's mind, the only emotion that could overpower his hunger. He moved closer to the data globe and watched as the battle unfolded.

His feeder arm emerged from beneath his tank and crept toward the back of Tomenakai's head. The Ixio turned around and his big black eyes narrowed at the tip of the feeder arm. Bale retracted the appendage with a snap.

"Just another sensor," Bale said quickly. "What's happening? Why are there so many Terrans in this system defiling our perfection?"

"A task force is moving to attack this fort, my Lord," the Ixio said, "but they're in for a surprise."

Bale sent a signal to his Toth bodyguard to prepare his escape pod.

****

Lettow bit his lip as another of his cruisers exploded. There'd been no sign of the *Last Light*, which had been his only bit of good news since the assault began. The dreadnought had been damaged in combat against the Ouranos, and his best guess was that it might have been moored on the far side of the belt around the moon.

"*Normandy* reports troops assault underway," his XO said. "Significant resistance around the dome cities and from Kesaht fighters. Many landers lost to kamikaze runs."

"Fanatics." Lettow tapped on the rail of the holo tank. "How much longer until the artillery ships have another volley ready for the fort? We're taking too much damage."

"Another sixty seconds," his gunnery officer said.

Fire from the star fort had proven infrequent but devastating to anything it hit. Just why something that size had only a few dozen weapon emplacements, which fired one at a time seemingly at random, was gnawing at him.

"Status on the Crucible assault?" he asked.

The Strike Marine liaison had her eyes on a screen in front of her.

"Same message," she said. "Significant resistance, but they're regrouping to…Sir, let me check something with the commo techs."

"That's not good enough, Marine!"

"Artillery salvo away," the gunnery officer said with a smile.

Lettow contained his anger with the liaison officer and watched as rounds converged on the star fort. The rounds stopped, blinking just shy of the hull.

"Admiral…the fort engaged shields," the gunnery officer said, his face gone white. "No effect. No effect on the fort."

As one, every energy cannon on the star fort opened fire, sending a deluge of bolts at the *Ardennes* and Lettow's assault element.

"They suckered me in," the admiral said, his jaw going slack. "They…"

"Admiral!" The Marine grabbed him by the arm. "The reports from the Crucible assault element, they're fake. The teams must have been killed or captured soon after they landed. We tried to authenticate, but we-we…we don't have the jump gate, sir. We don't have a way out of here."

A blast hit the ship and tossed Lettow against the holo tank.

Chapter 9

Santos felt the *Ardennes* shake through the torpedo he was loaded into, through his Armor and through his womb. He switched his HUD feed to the ship's battle tracker, and a mountain of data came rushing across his vision.

"Ah...this isn't the plan, is it?" he asked through the lance's IR channel.

"Assault on the *Last Light* is cancelled," Gideon said. "The ship's in space dock and hasn't joined in the battle."

Santos squirmed, feeling the amniotic fluid slosh against his skin as all of the ship's engines kicked on. The top of his head bumped against the womb and the inner padding closed in around him, cushioning him.

"Why are we accelerating?" Santos asked. "Our torp hasn't even launched yet."

"Stand by." Gideon's status symbol flashed on Santos' HUD as the captain connected to a higher priority channel.

The ship bucked against the torpedo, jostling Santos. The ship's data feed cut out.

"Ugh…Dragoons? What do we do now?" he asked.

"We're locked into a hypersonic torpedo loaded into a launch tube," Cha'ril said. "We don't have many options."

"This is a stupid way to die." Santos touched the inner wall of his womb. "Cracked like an egg in a carton. Won't even get to see the alien bastard that—"

"Stow it, kid," Aignar snapped. "Keep yourself together. How long did you last in the long dark back at Knox?"

Santos calmed down, remembering the tests where the cadre loaded him into a sensory deprivation chamber and didn't bother to tell him how long he'd be in there. If he panicked and demanded to be let out, he'd have been dropped from the program.

"I don't know how long it was," Santos said.

"This situation will get resolved pretty quick,"

Aignar said. "Either we're shot out to kill aliens and break things, or we won't have much of anything to worry about. Stay sharp."

As if on cue, Gideon returned to the lance network.

"Hold one," the captain said.

The torpedo blasted out of the *Ardennes* and external camera feeds fed into his HUD. His fleet was in ruins. Blasted hulls drifted in space, moving through wisps of flame from air bleeding out of ships. Bodies of sailors thrown out of disintegrating vessels speckled the void over Kesaht'ka.

The camera feed twisted as the torpedo maneuvered drunkenly, slaloming from side to side as if trying to find its own bearing. Santos got a brief glance at the *Ardennes*. The carrier advanced on a collision course with the massive star fort orbiting over the planet's moon. The light from afterburners of other landing torpedoes flared on and off.

"Where," Santos grit his teeth as acceleration sapped blood from his head even within his Armor, "where are we going?"

"Don't have the orbitals," Aignar said. "We…seem to be heading right for that giant planet that's coming right for us."

"Who's flying this thing?" Cha'ril asked.

"I am!" Gideon shouted.

Santos considered shutting off the camera feeds just as the torp angled toward a wrecked Kesaht ship. His eyes widened as the torpedo hit the hull and broke through. The dorsal half of the ship had been blown away, causing only minor damage to the impromptu escape pod.

The craft began undulating up and down, bouncing Santos against either side of his womb.

"Not the plan," he said between thumps. "Not the plan!"

Santos activated a rear camera and watched as a brawl between the Union fleet and Kesaht ships continued. Rail cannons crisscrossed with plasma bolts. Fighters swirled in a dogfight miles across, a melee he couldn't begin to figure out.

The star fort fired on the *Ardennes*, ripping off the prow of the ship but not stopping the carrier's advance.

"We're…we're losing," Santos said.

The torpedo leveled out and heat warnings popped up on Santos's HUD. They'd hit atmosphere.

"Marines secured a beachhead," Gideon said. "Link up with them soon as we hit dirt. I don't—"

A shell burst next to the torpedo's nose, showering it with shrapnel. It rolled to one side and spun out of control. Santos braced himself against his womb, feeling like he was in a barrel rolling downhill.

He felt warmth growing against his pod and heard armor plating rip off of the torpedo.

"Ejecting us!" Gideon's warning came laden with static.

"Saint Kallen," Santos swallowed hard, "if you're listening…"

The torpedo disintegrated around him and he went tumbling end over end through a cloud orange with the fire of burning debris. He twisted to bring his front flush with the onrushing wind, the distinctly un-aerodynamic properties of his Armor slowing his descent somewhat.

A flaming hunk of metal shot past him and he activated the jet pack bolted to his back.

"What's next? What's next?" He'd done only a single atmo landing in training and wished he'd paid more attention. "How long until I—that's right!"

He activated his laser range finders and a radar pulse found the ground. A distance and a time to impact popped up on his HUD.

Seven seconds.

He swung his feet toward the ground and fired his jet pack's boosters. Flame singed metal plating on the back of his legs as he wobbled with the sudden strain of the pack pulling him up while gravity and momentum pulled him down. His servos howled warnings, as if he were about to be torn apart.

Santos broke through the cloud layer and over a desolated city. His airspeed slowed and he felt a moment of hope.

Then his jet pack died.

Santos's arms pinwheeled as he fell. He crashed through a shingled roof and through three floors before landing hard in a pile of rusted-out pipes. He sat up, arm cannon charging. He rolled to his feet, pipes sliding off his armor and clattering to the ground.

The building went eerily silent as the last of the pipes came to a stop. Wind whistled through shattered windows. Dust swirled in the corners. He de-activated the mag locks on his smoldering jet pack and it fell with a clank into a pile of rusted metal.

A radiation hazard blinked on his HUD. No danger to him while he was suited, but an unsuited human would suffer effects after a few hours. Nothing unshielded could survive out here for too long.

"Kid," came from behind.

Santos spun around, knocking pipes against each other.

Aignar stood on the other side of a broken wall, his suit covered in dust.

"I've seen a sack of bricks land with more skill," Aignar said. "Atmo's frazzled like every planet the Kesaht attack. Can't tell if it's from the fallout or if they did it when we showed up."

Santos shouldered through a wall that crumbled like dry paper. Some of the outer façades were bleached white. Santos paused, his eyes on dark silhouettes of Sanheel centaurs stretched across the wall.

"What happened here?" he asked.

"Nuclear war." Aignar shot a pigeon drone out of the mortar tube on his back and the small robot popped rotors out and soared upwards. "Not a limited exchange either. Whole planet's irradiated. Lot worse than the EMP nukes used during World War III."

"Then where the hell have all the Kesaht come from?" Santos asked.

"That matter right now?" Aignar looked up. Long contrails of smoke and fire traced across the sky. "It's chaos up there. Never seen a mess like this before…got the captain and Cha'ril on IR…and something else. Come on."

The two ran down a dead street, blown sand congealed like snowbanks against buildings and rusted-out trucks with oversized cabs.

An empty temple-looking building exploded as flaming debris crashed through the domed roof.

"*—nar. Santos. Report in,*" Gideon's static-laced voice came over the IR.

"I've got him, sir," Aignar said. "My pigeon's got a lock on something strange coming in."

The two turned a corner and found the other pair in an intersection a few blocks away. Both looked slightly battered. Cha'ril's rotary cannon swung off a half-broken mount on her back.

"Any idea where we are?" Santos asked.

"About fifty miles north of the beachhead," Gideon said. "There's a dead zone between our forces and a domed city. Hard to know if anyone else from the *Ardennes* made it down."

"This signal mean anything to you two?" Aignar shared a telemetry recording across their network. "Picked it up from something moving under power in atmo near us."

"It's Toth," Gideon said. "I remember it from their incursion to Earth."

"A Toth signal in the middle of a battle? The only thing I think it could be is a search and rescue signal. Not like them," Cha'ril said.

"It would be for a VIP," Gideon said. "Our mission to destroy the *Last Light* is off, our secondary target is any Kesaht leadership. You know where that signal set down?"

"Tracks to a few miles east," Aignar said.

"Let's move. See if there's anything worth killing down here," Gideon said.

****

Lettow pulled himself up, broken ribs aching. The Marine liaison lay dead at his feet, visor smashed open and wisps of air leaked into the void.

In the holo, he watched his fleet wither under fire from the star fort. His carrier had escaped serious damage, almost like the Kesaht wanted him alive to see his ships die. But in this, he saw an opportunity.

"Conn." He slapped at the rail. "Conn, transfer maneuver control to me now!"

"Admiral?" An ensign stuck his head up out of his station to gape at the commander.

"Now!"

A new set of controls appeared on the holo tank. Lettow steered the ship at the star fort and redlined the engines. The *Ardennes* jolted as she accelerated forward. Lettow opened a ship-wide channel.

"All hands, this is Lettow. No time for excuses. All hands abandon ship. I repeat, all hands abandon ship. I'm taking her into the fort and I don't need any of you with me. Make for the beachhead. I'm ejecting all drop pods and troop torpedoes. It's been my honor to serve with you all. I'll buy you time to get to safety. Abandon ship!"

He keyed in an emergency code and launched every pod and torpedo as he promised.

Fire from the star fort cut out.

Ericson appeared in the holo.

"*Ardennes*, what's going on? Why are you on a collision course?"

"It's my fault," he said. "All my fault. I'll buy you some time, but you need to—"

Her image scrambled as a bolt from the star fort ripped past the bridge and wrecked his antenna array.

Lettow looked to the bridge. Each station was still manned.

"What part of 'abandon ship' didn't you understand?" he asked.

"You can't steer her on your own," his XO said. "We'll all go down together, sir."

"As you were, XO." Lettow winced, realizing he was hurt worse than he thought.

The ship took a hit to the aft, knocking out two of his engines. He righted the ship, still on course for the fort as it grew larger through the forward screens.

A hail came up, one without an identifier.

Lettow smiled and accepted it, the tank and suspended neural system of Overlord Bale appeared before him.

"Human captain…change course. Now! Do so and I will show your survivors some measure of mercy," Bale said.

The engines sputtered and died as another hit knocked out the ship's reactors. The ship's deck went still, but she was still heading straight for the fort.

"Can't do that," Lettow said. "This is the *Ardennes*; we have a motto to uphold. You want to know what it is?"

"Meat, if you do not change course, I will find your children and—"

"Resist, you walking colostomy bag. Resist…and bite!"

****

Bale's concentration floated in and out. Had he just spoken with an insane human admiral? Why was an Ixio tapping frantically on his tank? And just where did that scum get the nerve to smudge the inlaid gold patterns that he'd designed himself.

His consciousness drifted to an old memory, of being an immature Toth on the home world, devouring a *gishdan* bird with a broken wing he'd come across in an alley. The taste of raw flesh and hot blood in his teeth had been so exquisite…Then a flood of images of Bale descending from his great ship. Fear at watching the humans eradicate all life on the savior's planet…

Wait.

Bale snapped back and realized his feeder arm had stabbed into the skull of an Ixio. The alien head was tilted back, mouth gasping as neural energy sapped out of his body and into Bale's.

Bale drew a final taste and tossed the corpse aside.

The Risen, all the Risen that weren't fighting the human invaders, were staring right at him.

"I…I can explain," Bale said.

"His matrix didn't activate," Tomenakai said, backing away from Bale. "His mind is lost. He's dead. Forever."

"Maybe…maybe I can't explain." Bale glanced at

the data globe and saw the carrier *Ardennes* closing fast on the star fort. "Well, I can still fix this. Kricks, with me! And Tomenakai!"

Bale broadcast a command in Toth-speak and his warriors grabbed the Vishrakath envoy and the Ixio. They were carried out ahead of Bale as the Risen began shouting as their shock at seeing Bale murder one of their own wore off.

The overlord stopped in the doorway and nudged a warrior on the shoulder.

"Kill them all," Bale said. "I'll destroy their bodies before they can tell anyone else what happened."

The warrior snarled a question.

"Yes, of course you can eat their flesh. But wait until they're dead. They have been useful." Bale stepped out and the doors locked shut. He heard the screams as his warriors went to work. They didn't use their energy weapons, he noted as he listened to the massacre—such would foul the meat.

He quickened his pace to his waiting escape pod and sent an order to evacuate the only other valuable person on the star fort.

"Time to leave Kesaht'ka," he said. "Want something done right? Just have to do it myself…and do it someplace a little bit safer."

Chapter 10

A new sun burst in the sky, and Gideon's optics had to dim to compensate. The explosion lasted a few seconds, then faded out almost as quickly as it had appeared. An afterglow permeated through the clouds overhead.

"Something went boom," Santos said. "The star fort?"

"Likely…maybe we've still got a chance to pull this off. If we've found the overlord, then Earth can write this disaster off as some kind of a win," Gideon said.

"If this is winning…I'd hate to see losing."

Gideon tracked a lump of burning debris the size of a Kesaht tank as it rumbled through the sky over the dead city. Small explosions punctuated its descent, sending off sprays of burning metal and changing its inevitable course to the ground a few degrees with each pop.

His thermal optics caught a heat wedge at the top of a brick wall. The trace continued across the top of more apartment complexes, evidence of a ship that had landed close by.

"Eyes on," Cha'ril sent through the IR. *"Warehouse."*

The building walls flashed in his HUD as the Dotari shared the location.

Wind rushed over Gideon and Santos where they'd taken cover against a wall not far from the warehouse. His audio receptors picked up and isolated a sound that came and went with gusts. It struck him as a warning siren at first…then he realized it was a cry.

A child crying.

"Be aware, might have civilians on the battlefield," Gideon said.

A pic of the upper half of a Toth drop ship, shaped like a giant jewel, flashed across his HUD.

"Say again," Aignar sent. *"Did you say civilians?"*

A new voice came on the wind, one speaking words he couldn't make out.

"Contact!" Cha'ril sent, and gauss cannons snapped from her position to the west of the Toth lander.

"They're…cloaked!"

"Move out." Gideon powered up his gauss cannons and charged down the street toward the warehouse. He heard the clang of steel on steel and mortar work shattering as Aignar and Cha'ril fought.

Gideon lowered a shoulder and burst through the warehouse wall and slid to a stop.

A wide ramp had lowered from the ship, and a pair of Toth warriors stood in the rubble of the collapsed roof. One held a human girl in its claws, the other had an arm around the neck of a too tall green woman.

The Toth with the girl held her up as a human shield and slunk toward the one holding the green woman.

"What in the hell—" Santos drew down on the Toth through an open window.

"Our meat!" the Toth hissed. "Not yours. Back. Back or we'll spoil them both."

Gideon lowered his gauss cannons to one side and zoomed in on the Toth with the green woman. She was breathing hard, body rigid against her captor. Gideon sent a small charge to his rotary cannon.

"I know how to negotiate with Toth," he said.

The rotary gun snapped onto his shoulder and fired a single bullet. The round hit the Toth between the eyes and blew out the back of its skull against the lander. The green woman slipped out of the dead alien's hold and picked up a rock.

The other Toth hissed and put its claws to the girl's neck.

Trinia lifted the rock over her head and bashed the Toth in the face. It released the girl and whipped its tail around, catching the Aeon against the forearm. She swung the rock up and hit the Toth in the shoulder, sending it sprawling. She slammed the rock into its skull, crushing it with a snap. She went to her knees and hit the still dead Toth again and again.

Gideon grabbed her by the wrist.

"Think you got it," he said.

Trinia wiped a hand down her forearm, spreading a sheen of deep purple blood down her bare skin.

"Aunty!" The little girl clambered over the rocks and embraced Trinia. She must have been seven or eight, but looked like a toddler compared to the ten-foot-tall alien.

"Objective secured," Gideon sent over the IR. *"Santos. Perimeter sweep."*

Trinia ran her fingers through the girl's hair and looked at the insignia on Gideon's Armor.

"You're…the other kind. Terran Union?" she asked.

"Gideon. Armor Corps…I don't know what you

are," he said. "Or why you've got a little girl with you."

"I am Trinia, of…nothing. Nothing really. The Aeon are finished."

"Aeon…" Gideon said. The name jogged his memory of an incident report involving the Ibarrans and the Cyrgal that Ambassador Ibanez had sent him.

The girl began coughing and buried her face in Trinia's tunic.

"Sir, the radiation," Santos said.

"Yes, I can taste it." Trinia stood, clutching the girl in her arms. "The escape pod was automated. Nothing I or Maggie can use in there. Do you have shelter nearby? You can't get her into the pods with you; no way to refill your amniosis."

"You know a lot about my suit," Gideon said.

Trinia lowered her chin to touch the top of Maggie's head.

"She's dying out here. I'll last a few days longer, but we need to move. They'll come for the escape pod," the Aeon said.

Gideon looked over the ship, tempted to stay longer and pull it apart for any useful intelligence. Just how it had broadcast a distress call through the scrambled atmosphere would be useful intelligence. But the longer they stayed in the open, the more radiation poisoning the girl would absorb just by breathing.

Cha'ril and Aignar came to the broken-down wall, both stained with yellow Toth blood.

"Took care of the rest—what the hell," Aignar said.

"We have a beachhead nearby." Gideon stepped back and brought out the treads within his leg housings. His legs locked and folded forward to his travel formation. He extended a hand to Trinia.

"Get on. You know where the overlord is?" he asked.

Trinia stepped up onto the armored skirt over the treads and sat against Gideon's back.

"He's as far from the fighting as he can be, the coward," she said.

"Then you can tell me more as we move. Iron Dragoons, roll out."

****

Gold Beach wasn't a beach, nor was it gold. But it was the only foothold the Terran Union had on Kesaht'ka. Strike Marines and Rangers had secured what had once been a space port before the nuclear holocaust that ruined the planet. There was ample space for landers, and every drop ship and fighter that escaped the battle in orbit.

Gideon watched as a damaged Destrier transport hovered over a landing zone, wobbling as sputtering engines fought to keep the ship level. The anti-grav cut out and the ship dropped ten feet and belly flopped dangerously close to a pair of shore party sailors. The fuselage broke open and cases of gauss bullets spilled out like candy from a beaten piñata.

A woman with a mechanical brace on her arm rushed out of a field hospital: one of the few intact buildings now adorned with a tarp that had a red cross painted on it.

She adjusted a breathing mask over the bottom of her face.

"I don't need bullets!" She waved a fist at the crashed transport. "Don't need any more casualties either. You see the pilots walk away?"

"Not yet," Gideon said. He zoomed in on her face. "I know you?"

"Masako." She tapped the back of her head where plugs had once been. "I washed out on Mars. You sound like one of my cadre…that you, Tongea?"

"Gideon. Tongea's…not here."

"I'd love to catch up," she said, "but casualties

keep coming in."

"Wait. The girl."

"The child's stable. Resting. Seems happy to be around regular old humans, not frigging Valkyries like—"

Trinia ducked out of the door.

"I don't have wings or a spear," the Aeon said.

"And I'll be leaving." Masako hunched slightly and darted back into the field hospital.

Trinia squinted at the sunset and looked over the chaos of the space port.

"I have information you can use," Trinia said. "Who's in charge down here?"

"Follow me." Gideon waved her forward and the two walked down a row of cargo containers and ad hoc maintenance stations where pilots tried to instruct Strike Marines and anyone else nearby on how to rearm and refuel their fighters.

The Armor and Aeon garnered a number of doubletakes as they went by.

"Why did the Ibarrans want you on Ouranos?" Gideon asked.

"I spent many hundreds of years working with Qa'resh technology on Bastion. She wanted my expertise. She'd located what I thought was just a myth: a derelict Qa'resh ship left over from the time they ruled this galaxy."

"And if she doesn't have you?" he asked.

"Hard to say. She's more capable than I give her credit for. But her Armor abandoned me to the Toth…I wish they'd have killed me instead. Bale put me to work, forced me to make slave soldiers for him. I kept the work slow, but there was some progress."

"The Kesaht want you. The Ibarrans want you. What do you want?"

Trinia stopped in her tracks.

"You…you're asking that?"

Gideon's head snapped up as a Kesaht crescent fighter broke through the clouds. It trailed smoke from a wing and wobbled as it angled toward a cargo ship on the runway. Gideon raised his gauss cannons and loaded a pair of shells.

An Eagle fighter roared out of the clouds and fired a burst from the chain gun under its nose. The crescent ship broke in half, and the two parts spun out of control as they fell. One half landed on an empty forklift, smashing it to pieces. The other hit the transport and it burst into flames.

"You need to think worst-case scenario," Gideon said. "Our fleet's barely holding the orbitals above us. We don't control the Crucible. Our situation…is in doubt."

"We're not hopeless. Not yet," Trinia said. "A few hours ago, I was Bale's prisoner. Working just hard enough to keep that monster from eating Maggie. This is a step up. Believe me."

"There." Gideon pointed to a dilapidated building surrounded by Rangers and two lances of Armor. Antennae and satellite dishes had been set up along the roof edge.

"Uh, sir?" A Ranger with a skull face mask pointed at Trinia as they approached the headquarters. "She's...cleared?"

"She kills Toth. She's fine." Gideon continued without breaking his stride.

Inside, holo tables were set up along the walls of what had been a spacecraft maintenance bay. The Armor Corps commander, General Laran, stood in the middle, speaking with a Ranger colonel and a Strike Marine general. A map of the beachhead and the surrounding city projected out of Laran's helm.

"Our patrols along the outer perimeter have had limited contact with enemy ground troops," the Ranger said. "Hit-and-run attacks."

"What's this, Gideon?" Laran asked, pointing a finger at Trinia.

"I was a Kesaht prisoner until just recently," the

Aeon said. "You have time to mince words? Be polite? I didn't think so. I will help you so long as you promise to get Maggie back to human space and reunite her with any family you can find. Fair? Yes. Fair."

She looked over the map for a moment.

"I understand your symbols. You must take Hegemony City if you want to defeat the Kesaht. You know their Risen?" she asked.

"There were broadcasts a few hours ago," Laran said. "A good number of Risen died, one right after the other. We think we took out most of their military leadership with a lucky strike. The enemy's response has been uncoordinated and slow ever since that happened."

"Then you must act quickly." Trinia touched the domed city on the map. "A Risen's consciousness returns to Hegemony after they're killed. The cloning and reanimation center is beneath the step pyramid at the center of the city. Destroy it and they're mortal again. They'll fear death…and it'll weaken Bale's control over them."

"Or we seize it and bargain a peace settlement," Laran said.

"Hit it from orbit," Gideon said. "Seize the advantage while we still can."

"No good," the Strike Marine said. "The dome's

shielded."

Gideon looked at Trinia.

"I didn't know that." She frowned.

"We can't seize the Crucible," the Strike Marine said. "The assault force never even made it. Even if we could get off world, we can't leave this system. Not while the Kesaht control the gate. And no chance of reinforcements from Earth either. There's a disruption field emanating from the Crucible."

"If the disruption field is active, the Risen can't return to Hegemony City," Trinia said. "Scrambles the signal. Their leaders will be hesitant."

"The only thing that's gone according to plan is this beachhead," Laran said. "And if the Aeon is right, then we've got an opportunity. We need to strike hard. Strike fast. Because as soon as the Kesaht get their act together, we're in for trouble."

"An offensive?" the Ranger asked. "We barely know which units have even made it here."

"We'll manage," Laran said. "Muster every combat-rated soldier and Marine to sector Blue 1. Backfill the ones on the perimeter with support personnel not offloading supplies or treating wounded. Eight lances of Armor will lead the assault."

"And how will we breach the walls?" the Strike

Marine asked.

Gideon touched the vanes of his rail gun.

"And destroying this cloning center?"

Gideon touched his rail gun again.

"Always nice to find the simple solution," Trinia said.

"Get our troops moving," Laran said to the two colonels. "I'll have forward command. Gideon, with me."

Trinia wagged fingers at the map, rattling off information to the Strike Marine. She didn't give Gideon a second glance as he followed Laran.

Chapter 11

Admiral Makarov blinked hard as the aftereffects of a wormhole jump clawed at her body. White fractal patterns cleared from her vision as she keyed in demands by feel and memory for status reports from the *Warsaw* and the attending fleet.

"Scope reads clear," her gunnery officer called out.

"Launch ready fighters and maneuver to fleet formation phalanx-four," Makarov said. Ship icons on a screen attached to her command chair went from gray to green as more and more ships reported in from the wormhole jump.

Makarov looked out the front windows of her bridge. The band of a deep-purple nebula stretched across the void, while small pinpricks of stars glowed like distant lamps in a fog.

"Pulsar detection puts us in the Nekara system," her astrogator announced. "Passive sensors identifying planetary bodies now."

The admiral slapped the harness buckle on her chest and the straps over her shoulders and hips retracted into her seat. She swung out of the chair and found Lady Ibarra already at the holo table to the rear of the bridge. The growing picture of the Nekara system, the blue star and out system gas giants, reflected off her silver skin.

"We're close," Stacey said. Her mouth didn't move with the words, but Makarov heard her through her helmet's speakers. Stacey was the only one on the bridge not wearing a void suit or a helmet. The *Warsaw* made the last jump under combat conditions—atmosphere sucked out of the ship to mitigate the risk of fires and blast-wave damage from an enemy attack.

"Haven't found the inhabited world yet," Makarov said. "If there even is one. If the Ark is on a Kuiper Belt object or floating somewhere in the star's gravity well, we could be searching for a very long time, my Lady."

"This is Qa'resh," Stacey said, tapping her fingertips to her metal chest. "The Ark is Qa'resh. There's a certain...resonance...I feel when near that technology.

It's…calling to me." She reached into the holo field and twisted her fingers around to hold an imaginary sphere.

"Sensors," Makarov said, "turn scopes to sector nine-five. Declination two-zero-four off primary."

"Aye aye," the commander replied.

A moment later, a green and brown planet appeared in the holo field, a fraction off where Stacey had her fingers.

"Nitrogen, oxygen atmosphere," Makarov said. "Surface pressure is a few percent off standard. Temperature and every other factor is within habitable parameters. An ideal world to support life and colonize."

"But there's no sign of any, is there?" Stacey asked. "No radio energy. No heat from massive cities. Nothing."

Makarov swiped two fingers down the axis of the planet and pulled up sensor data. Stacey was right. The planet was dormant.

"This may not be the place." Makarov bit back a frown. "You said the Qa'resh sent a probe here and sent a message back to old Bastion, correct? This is the most likely place it would have found life…Wait."

The image of the planet resolved further. A wide band of an earth-colored ring formed around the planet, canted across the equator.

"That's...odd," Makarov said. "Rings always form level to the—"

A second ring appeared, perpendicular to and intersecting with the first, a massive X over the planet.

"They're not rings," Stacey said. She pinched the nexus between the two bands and a small icon flashed between her fingers as one of the *Warsaw*'s powerful telescopes focused on the point. Stacey opened her fingers and the icon grew larger.

A window opened, and inverted pyramids floated in the space. The bases of the structures were flat and long, and irregular spikes hung from the triangle faces. A central spire twisted out from the apex, pointing to the planet below. Dozens more of the structures stretched out through the image.

"The rings are...the rings are those pyramids," Makarov said, and a tendril of fear slunk around her heart. "There must be thousands of them."

"Millions." Stacey drew her hand back to her lips. "They're miles high. Bigger than even the Cyrgal ships or Toth dreadnoughts."

"If they're hostile...I don't know if we could defeat a single one of them," Makarov said.

Stacey's doll face turned to the admiral.

"It's not cowardice, my Lady. It is the truth. To

build a ship like that is beyond us. If that is Qa'resh technology, then—"

"That is not the Ark," Stacey said. "Not even Qa'resh technology. Look at them, Makarov. No energy signature. No power. They're off-line…or abandoned." She tapped out commands on a keypad and bands of the planet popped off the holo as the fleet scanned the planet below.

"What are they?" Makarov pulled a pyramid out of the holo and examined it further. "It's even larger than the star fort over Navarre. The engineering to build so many is—"

"Irrelevant. We're here for the Ark, nothing else." Ibarra touched a strip of telescope feed taken off Nekara and swiped through it slowly.

"Shall we send a pioneer team to examine one of the pyramids?" Makarov asked.

"No. Have the *Breitenfeld* unload the Keystone gate and begin construction. Maintain strict radio silence…dormant ships aren't a threat to why I'm here." Stacey swiped the other direction on the feed strip and held a fingertip to the holo. The image changed to an infrared image and concentric circles appeared within a jungle. At the center was an ivory building with discordant protrusions.

"There you are," Stacey half-whispered. "At last."

Makarov thought she would feel a sense of relief knowing that the Ark had been found, but her apprehension only grew.

"*Breitenfeld* acknowledges the order," Makarov said. "Void construction teams estimate eighty hours before the Keystone will be ready to get us back to into the Crucible network and back home."

"Good." Stacey stepped back from the holo table. "Inform Marshal Davoust that I am on my way to the Ark. His legionnaires will establish an outer cordon while the armor and I go inside to take control."

"And if the pyramids activate? Become hostile?" Makarov asked as Stacey went to the elevator doors.

Stacey Ibarra said nothing, but she tapped her fist to her chest over where her heart would have been if she still had one. She gave Makarov a nod and got into the elevator.

"I tell Roland to have faith in the face of doubt and now look at me," the admiral muttered to herself. "I'm not going to tell him he might have had a point. I'm just not."

Her executive officer, Andere, and other staff officers approached the holo table and Makarov focused her attention on her fleet and on constructing the

Keystone jump gate that would get them all home.

She had a feeling the next hours would pass slowly…all too slowly.

****

A pyramid ship hung in Roland's vision. He was in armor, his suit folded onto itself in a long rectangle, bolted to the deck of a Destrier transport along with the rest of his unit and the Nisei and Uhlan lances.

Details of the pyramid ship's dimensions appeared as he zoomed in on the structure.

"That…is really big," Roland said.

"Amazing observation," Morrigan said through the lance's internal IR channel. "I can tell you're an experienced soldier."

"We're all thinking the same thing," Nicodemus said. "I'm not even sure if the massed rail cannons of every armor on this mission would make a dent in that thing."

"A dozen of us can slag a Kesaht battleship," Morrigan said. "We can do more than scratch their paint…whoever 'they' are."

"No activity since we jumped in," Roland said. "Maybe we got lucky and they'll stay asleep, or they're all dead. When did old Bastion last have contact with this place?"

"Mission brief says several thousand years," said Martel, the lance commander. "But for two rings of that many structures to orbit through each other and stay in the sky for that long…there's something or someone tending to them. Marshal Davoust has us making landfall under anti-grav engines. Slow atmo entry to reduce thermal signatures."

"Long and slow," Morrigan said, a sigh to her words. "Good thing we're all cozy in transport config."

Roland felt footfalls through the Destrier's deck. A launch alert icon appeared on his HUD and he dismissed it with a flick of his eyes. He felt hydraulics activate in the large transport and activated cameras on the outside of his armor.

Lady Ibarra's honor guard passed by him, heading to the crew compartment in the fore of the ship. Roland pulled his arms and legs close to his torso, feeling the slight current of amniosis against his bare feet and hands.

Stacey stopped next to Roland and waved her guards onward.

Roland's mood darkened as Stacey looked over the rows of armor, all folded into transport configuration. She sat cross-legged against Roland's armor and he felt the ship rise off the *Warsaw*'s deck; a hum through his womb told him the ship was moving under the anti-grav engines.

"*Roland,*" Martel sent to him. "*Why is the Lady—*"

The channel cut off, replaced by a slight hiss of static.

"Hello, my Black Knight," Stacey said, referencing the dark matte color of his armor and a nickname he picked up fighting Kesaht on a bridge.

"My Lady," Roland said.

"You've been…quiet?" She reached to one side and ran her fingers over the red Templar cross painted onto his shoulder actuator.

"I spoke with Admiral Makarov about…my hand. Little else."

"You're not lying to me. Should I be honored or offended?"

"Templar do not lie to our leaders."

"There are lies of commission, Mr. Roland, and there are lies of omission. A fine line if ever there was one. Does not telling the whole truth constitute a lie? Should we tell everyone everything we know at all times? That would be a bit bothersome, no?" Stacey held out a hand and the cargo bay lights reflected off her shell.

"I will stay true to my vows, my Lady. This mission is vital to the Nation."

"Why can't you just…do you know how annoying

it is to speak to you? Straitlaced. Duty, duty, duty. Why can't you just talk to me like a real person?"

"You are...Lady Ibarra."

"And I'm not a real person. Not real like you. Or anyone else in the Nation but my bastard of a grandfather. Of all the people in the galaxy to keep a Qa'resh ambassador shell, it had to be him. Couldn't have been Pa'lon of the Dotari. He wanted to die surrounded by fat grandkids on his home world. I can't tell who's the more selfish, him or Marc Ibarra."

"I'm sorry, my Lady. I don't understand."

"Roland, we are here for the Ark. But what if...there was something else? What if I found something that could put me back into my old body? Would I still be your 'Lady' then?" She tilted her head back slightly to touch his armor.

A slight chill flowed through the amniosis.

"It would not matter to me," he said. "But...I believe you were injured? Which is why you—"

"Trapped. Yes. But to feel my old self again...even if it was for a moment before it all ended. The bullet clipped my heart. There wasn't much time left for me. Grandpa and Jimmy had one chance to keep me alive and they took it. Even though I don't know if this is living."

She tapped the tips of her fingers against her thumb.

"Do you ever feel like you're not alive when you're plugged in?" she asked Roland. "There's no pain for you. No fatigue. Is it like being in a dream?"

"I 'feel' my armor. It is an extension of myself. I am Armor."

"Yes, that's the way it has to work for you…hmm…" She traced a line from the tip of a thumb to her wrist, then up and down each finger. "I feel this. It's like I'm in my old self…but I see the silver and I know it's a lie. My soul is here, but my heart is not."

"Are we really here for the Ark, my Lady?"

"Yes," Stacey said firmly. "That is all that matters. Make no mistake of that, you understand. If we find something else…who knows? In this form, I will be Lady Ibarra forever. If I could return to my body for a few seconds before I died…that would be the height of selfishness, wouldn't it? I'd abandon you all just for…nothing, really. To surrender to death. Suicide is simple cowardice."

"You are my Lady," Roland said. "No matter what. I don't agree with what you've done…but I can understand why you did it."

"I don't deserve you." She shook her head. "Any

of you. Armor was always better than me, or Grandfather. I knew that when Elias tried to destroy Malal. He knew what a monster Malal was…but I saved that monster. Because we *needed* Malal. Didn't matter if we destroyed the Xaros Masters, their drones would still have killed us all."

"I don't understand."

"Elias was the hero. He was stronger than I was. All the Iron Hearts were. They saw annihilation coming and fought to the end. I saw the same fate and made a deal with the devil to keep myself—and everyone else in the galaxy—alive. Seemed like a good idea at the time. Did you know that I—what's this?"

She drifted off for a moment, then a faint glow formed behind her eyes.

"Lady Ibarra? Are you all right?" Roland asked. When there was no answer, he tried to open another channel but was locked out.

Roland wondered if this was another of her episodes and began to unlock the safety protocols keeping him in transport configuration.

Stacey's chin dropped to her chest, then reared back and struck Roland's armor.

"Fools!" she shouted, so loud Roland's ears rang.

"My Lady?"

"Our old friends in the Terran Union have

attacked the Kesaht in their home system. My link to their armor, the component you were looking at with your techs, sends data through the Crucible gates from time to time. I can connect to individual Armor when needed. Alerts will come in when there are casualties."

"Casualties? The Iron Dragoons, are they all right?"

"You care?" Stacey put the base of a palm against her temple and her eyes glowed faintly.

"They…no, my Lady."

"So much to sift through…they're losing. But they have a foothold on the Kesaht's planet. They left Earth nearly undefended. Stupid, stupid move, Garret. Should've waited for me. Should have waited. I have nothing from your Dragoons. Not that I'd mind seeing Gideon die; he's cost us dearly."

"When we're finished here, will we help them?"

"When we have the Ark, nothing else will matter." She stood up. "The Kesaht won't be the first to see what the Ark can do. We have scales to balance, Roland. Blood debts to pay." Pressing a finger to her lips, she said, "Hush hush" and walked away.

Roland's communication systems came back online.

"Roland?" Nicodemus asked. "What was that all

about?"

"She…she asked me not to say." Roland's heart felt heavy as he replied, unsure if he was telling a lie by omission or commission.

"Such is her privilege," Martel said. "Run targeting diagnostics. We've got a good eleven hours until we make landfall. Use them wisely."

"Yes, sir." Roland wrapped his arms around his body within his womb, the chill of Stacey's presence still with him.

****

The drop ship shuddered as it entered Nekara's atmosphere. Ochre clouds filled the view ports as Roland watched the first licks of flames against the craft's heat shield. The deck bucked hard enough for him to feel a slight disturbance within his armor's womb. His lance stood at the four corners of the cargo bay to distribute their weight equally.

Making the descent in walker configuration bothered Roland; standard operating procedure was to go down strapped to the deck in their boxed-up travel config. But if their VIP was in jeopardy, there was no time to unlimber.

He turned his helm to Lady Ibarra and her entourage in the middle of the cargo bay. Holo screens floated around Stacey, the rapid-fire switch of information from the holos reflecting off her silver face. She wore a standard set of matte-black legionnaire power armor, leaving only the metal of her face and hands exposed as she swiped through the incoming feeds. A half dozen of her honor guard formed a circle around her, their boots mag-locked to the deck, ceremonial halberds braced to keep their balance during the descent.

Roland pulled up his HUD, but the only thing he could access was the drop ship's telemetry. They were still on course to a narrow isthmus. He activated an IR receiver on one side of his helm, hoping it would tap into stray data going to Lady Ibarra.

"Stop it," Nicodemus said over a two-way channel.

Roland shut off the receiver. Nicodemus, his assigned partner for the mission, was a few yards away from him, his Armor still as a statue, his gaze locked on the ship's ramp.

"Why are we going in blind?" Roland asked. "The Legion set down half an hour ago, but we've got nothing from them…this isn't how we operate."

"You'd rather ride a torp into the dirt?"

"If it means going in with my eyes open, then yes. Load me into a torp."

"This isn't an assault, Roland. This is a deliberate operation with tens of thousands of troops and a logistics train from the fleet to the excavation site. Slow and purposeful," Nicodemus said.

"But why no—"

"We are the Lady's Armor. Our only concern is her immediate safety, not the location of the other lances or where the Legion's set up."

"How can we protect her if we don't know what's happening down there?" Roland asked. "What if the Qa'resh left behind defenses or—or the Terrans beat us here and—"

"Don't tempt fate. Lady Ibarra's in contact with the landing party through quantum dots. If there's something we need to know, she'll tell us," the older armor soldier said.

"Will she?" Roland asked, regretting the words as soon as he said them.

Nicodemus half-turned around, his helm's optics on Roland. "Why were we chosen for this honor, Roland? Of all the lances in the Nation, why are *we*—Martel's own Templar—to accompany the Lady?"

Roland bit his lip, unsure what answer to give. Should he tell Nicodemus of his doubts about Stacey now? The thought almost sickened him. That she could be monitoring this conversation was a possibility, armor-to-armor, tight-beam IR or not.

"She's…giving us a chance to redeem ourselves," Roland said. "After we failed to bring back the Aeon from Ouranos."

"We cannot let her down again. We cannot." Nicodemus turned back to the ramp.

"Forgive me, sir."

Nicodemus raised a hand slightly, then let it settle back against his side.

"Brace for landing," came from the pilot.

Roland looked out a porthole. There was nothing but an abyss of tan cloud cover and a darker band of the world's sea on the horizon.

"Lock and load," Colonel Martel said.

Roland cycled gauss shells into the twin-barreled cannon mounted on one forearm. An ammo belt connected to the rotary cannon as it hinged up from his back and snapped next to his helm. The barrels spun with a quick function test. He put one hand to the grip of his Gustav rifle mag-locked to his armor, but he didn't run a charge through the vanes of his rail gun. The strong magnetic fields would wreak havoc on the lander's systems.

"Most of us were Iron Dragoons...once," Morrigan said. "If the good colonel would allow us a slight indulgence? An old lance tradition?"

"The chant is older than Gideon's command," Martel said. "It fits."

"I am Armor," Morrigan said.

"I am fury," Nicodemus intoned.

"I..." Roland struggled to get the words out, thinking of Aignar, Cha'ril, and even Gideon fighting the Kesaht at that very moment. "I will not fail."

Thrusters boomed from the lander and deceleration tugged at Roland within his womb. His feet pressed against the inner wall for a split second before the ship landed hard. The ramp fell open with a clang, and Nicodemus and Morrigan were the first out.

Roland stomped out and into a thick, desert-colored fog. He unsnapped the Mauser and held the barrels with his other hand as he took up his assigned position to the right of the ramp. He made out shadows of nearby structures: short pyramids with a small dome in place of the upper half and a mountain in the distance.

"Going to infrared," Roland said, anticipating that the optics switch would let him see farther. Instead, the new feed was a wash of red and static.

"What the hell?" Morrigan asked.

"UV's no good either," Martel said. "Stay with your standard optics."

Roland went back to spectrum visible to the naked eye. The surroundings were a soup of fog and muted sound, like they were in a snowfield. He heard Lady Ibarra and her entourage making their way down the ramp and a brief conversation between her and her bodyguards.

Shadows moved in the distance.

"Contact." Roland spun up his rotary cannon and aimed his Mauser.

"Now, now," Stacey said as she walked up beside Roland. She stood slightly taller than his knee servo.

Roland took a step in front of her, shielding her as the shadows materialized into humanoid shapes.

"*Ferrum!*" came from the fog.

"*Corde*," Roland replied and shut down the rotary cannon and lifted the barrel of his Mauser. He'd wondered why the operation order included an old-fashioned spoken challenge and password. Now the instructions made perfect sense.

Marshal Davoust, his power armor's faceplate bearing a red Templar cross and five stars, came out of the fog, heavily armed legionnaires following him. The marshal didn't salute Stacey as he approached—spotlighting senior leadership in a potentially hostile environment was a dangerous move—but gave her a quick nod.

"My Lady." He removed his helmet, revealing a bald pate streaked with sweat. "We've established a perimeter around the Ark. There's some sort of mineral in the fog that's attenuating our IR comms more than we can compensate for. We're still radio silent. All contact is through quantum dot."

"And the structures?" Stacey asked.

"No activity from them or the pyramids in orbit." Davoust swallowed hard. "But…but there's something you need to see, my Lady."

"Have our scouts found the entrance to the Ark?" She looked toward the mountain peak looming in the distance.

"Still searching," Davoust said. "Drone range is limited, but they've cleared over half the outer hull. The lower edge is covered in the…I don't know how to explain it. Follow me, please."

Stacey flicked her fingers back the way Davoust came.

"Perimeter," Martel said over the lance's channel, his voice tinged with static in the close range.

Roland went into the fog, stopping a few yards to

one side of Stacey and Davoust as they spoke to each other in Basque. He kept a slow pace to match the shorter legs of the un-armored party.

"Comms range is garbage," Morrigan said. "You go too far into this soup and you'll have to send up a flare for anyone to find you again."

Roland thought back to the ocean of Ouranos, where he'd had to throw Marc Ibarra out of the shallow depths to find their way to Trinia's island. He smirked, remembering just how much the older Ibarra had complained about the maneuver.

Davoust led them to a building, one of the squat pyramids with a dome in the place of the upper half. The walls were covered in what looked like thick vines, each the width of a man's arm. The vines, all a dirty-metal color glinting from within, crept out of the packed earth and up the sides, reaching a few feet over the top onto the alabaster material of the roof.

Roland switched between his optic filters as he examined the vines, but they appeared dormant.

Stacey held up a hand and one of her bodyguards gave her a leather pouch. She removed what looked like a flint and it glowed to life and floated around her hand. She waved her palm over the vines and an afterglow emanated along the path.

"It's…not Qa'resh," Stacey said. "Not exactly. I can feel something there…"

The crunch of boots against sand sounded through the fog. Roland brought his rotary cannon online and turned toward the noise.

A half dozen legionnaires came out of the fog, gauss rifles in hand and dirt clinging to their legs. An officer went to Stacey and Davoust and a brief conversation followed.

"Track up," Martel said through the lance channel. "Crunchies found something Lady Ibarra wants to see in person."

Roland sent a mental pulse through his umbilical, and armored panels snapped to the outside of his legs and treads shifted out with the whirl of gears. His hip gyros extended and his upper body shifted back as his legs went flat to the ground. His treads bit into the dirt and the legionnaire officer climbed onto him.

"Secure," he said, and Roland thought he recognized the voice. "Head north. Fifteen degrees."

"What am I looking for?" Roland drove forward, the sensation of moving on his treads sending a prickle through his legs. Armor used their travel configuration when speed was of the essence, but the dust the tracks kicked up could give away their position to a watching enemy.

"You'll know….you'll know it when you see it." The officer gripped the rail-gun housing on Roland's back with one hand and then crossed himself.

Roland continued past more of the structures, all with the same vines gripping their base and walls.

"You sound…are you the same Union Armor I ran into on Oricon?" the officer asked.

"Major Aiza?" Roland asked.

"That's me. Glad I didn't have my men drill you with anti-armor grenades," Aiza said. "Nice having you with us. Worst ride's better than the best walk, yeah?"

"Union and the Nation should never have been at each other's throats," Roland said. "The Kesaht threat is reason enough for us all to be on one side."

"Yeah, you used to be Union. Why don't the dogs on Earth get that?"

Roland thought to Gideon, a soldier determined to kill aliens on the field of battle with the fury and determination of legend. Why his old lance commander had been so incensed and ready to kill Nicodemus and Roland when the two crossed blades on Nunavik had grated against Roland's mind for weeks.

"Hatred runs too deep for some," Roland said. "They see us as traitors."

"Or abominations." Aiza shifted uncomfortably. "Terrans get any of us procedurals born after that damn Hale Treaty…it's a death sentence. Who kills someone just because of how God brought them into the world?"

"You still wonder why the Union's against us?" Roland asked.

"Not hard to see why. But you left them."

"I did." Roland tried to zoom in on new shapes wavering in the fog. "Templar fight for all of humanity. The Union…the Union turned away from that. What's that in the distance? Looks like…Xs?"

"That's it. Slow down," Aiza said, hopping off before Roland came to a stop. The lance transformed back into their walker configuration.

Stacey waltzed past Roland and rapped her knuckles against his leg. He followed, Gustav in hand and rotary cannon sweeping from side to side.

She made her way up to one of the X shapes, each nearly ten feet tall and made out of a dark rock that looked like basalt. It was embedded in the ground, and a single strand of the same vines wrapped around the end of each segment. More of the Xs spread out into the fog, all spaced too far apart to be much of a defensive measure.

A breeze picked up and a bit of cloth flapped around the other side of the X.

Roland stomped ahead of Stacey.

A corpse was tied to the X. Humanoid, but far larger than the average man. A tattered, decayed robe hung from the body, the flesh the same dirty-metal color as the vines. Its head hung low from the shoulders.

"My, my. This is like a *crux decussata*. Romans had more than one cross for crucifixion…" Stacey went to the foot of the X and looked up at the corpse's face, hidden from Roland's view. "It's not flesh, is it?"

"It reads the same as the vines. Inert. Inorganic. Could it be a statue?" Roland looked back at the other Xs and made out more bodies attached to each one.

"If this is a statue," Stacey said, leaning close to the foot bound against the cross, "it would put da Vinci to shame." She looked up at the face and froze, then backed away, her hands slapping at pouches on her belt.

"What's wrong?" Roland stepped between her and the body.

"Anthalas," she said. "This is just like Anthalas. Look at the face. Look at it!"

"My Lady, are you—"

"Look!"

Roland touched the side of the corpse's head and it wobbled slightly. Placing a finger just beneath the chin, he raised it slowly. Empty eye sockets stared into Roland's optics. The face was contorted, frozen in a moment of pain and terror, lips curled back over teeth. Roland could have sworn he heard a rasp escape the open mouth.

Sparks of light flashed in the sockets.

Roland snapped his hand back and the head swung down, tearing loose from the neck and crumpling against the ground in a cloud of dust.

"They're all different," Major Aiza said. "Every one of the X crosses has a body. Seem to be the same species."

"This…this was to be expected," Stacey said. Even with her expressionless face, Roland could feel the fear behind her doll eyes. "This place would have his touch."

"Who, my Lady?" Davoust asked.

"Malal," she said. "It could only be him. He…no. To the Ark. To what we came for."

****

The Ark formed as Nekara's sun burned away the fog. The ship had no symmetry that Roland could make out. The pearlescent hull soared into the sky, ending in sharp points and ridges, like a great conch left behind as a momento of an extinct ocean.

The air settled as the armor and Stacey's entourage approached. Roland couldn't hear the waves from the nearby ocean or noise from the defense perimeter the legionnaires built around the Ark just fifty yards away.

A chill breeze wafted over the Ibarrans, cold enough that the bodyguards adjusted their armor against the sudden change.

Roland craned his helm up, trying to find the apex of the Ark in the low clouds.

"It's bigger than anything in our fleet," Marshal Davoust said. "Bigger than even the Vishrakath's asteroid ships. How we'll ever get it off world will be a—"

"This ship came here of its own power," Stacey said. "It will leave the same way."

Davoust put a hand to the side of his helmet.

"There's an entrance three hundred meters to the east," he said. "Along with some…artifacts."

"Keep moving," Stacey said.

Roland looked back to the field of crucifixions. His optics counted thousands, and from what he'd overheard between Davoust and Stacey, the entire Ark was surrounded by more.

Millions more.

The lower hull of the Ark was covered by vines

that reached several stories up the hull. The vines clung to the milky-white metal, the same material he'd seen on the Oricon station—where he'd been captured by Nicodemus—and the Qa'resh research station on the dead planet Nunavik.

Rudimentary patterns appeared in the vines as they moved closer to the entrance. They were twisted into rows of what Roland first thought were lines of music. The image shifted to a humanoid shape in a simple robe, staring at the sky. The alien had narrow, almost fey features with sharp ears and tiny bone protrusions at the chin.

"I've seen this kind of art before," Roland said. "Trinia's people, the Aeon; they had carvings like this."

"These were not Aeon," Stacey said. "They were victims of a different form of extinction. The Aeon died to hope, died to their own hubris. These people…were slaughtered."

"Not mass suicide?" Nicodemus asked. "There are aliens that chose to extinguish themselves before the Xaros armadas got to their planets."

Stacey stopped at a mural, one depicting a throng of the same aliens around the Ark. A lone figure hung over them, arms outstretched and rays of light emanating from its body.

"What do you know of the Qa'resh?" Stacey asked.

Morrigan glanced at Roland, then tilted her head toward Stacey.

"They saved us from the Xaros," Roland said. "Sent the probe that contacted…contacted Earth and helped us retake the planet." Roland was careful not to mention Marc Ibarra.

"True. They set up Bastion and helped us win the Ember War," Stacey said, "but there's more to them than that. Much more. A truth they didn't share with the galaxy as they posed as the savior of all intelligent life against the Xaros threat.

"They were an ancient civilization. One that flourished and took control of the Milky Way many…many years ago. They had wormhole jump drives to cross the stars, technology millennia ahead of where we are today…but they had a problem. One that vexes us—well, most of us—the same as it did the Qa'resh."

She looked down at her metal hands and continued.

"They died. No matter what they learned, the technology they possessed, they still died. And for those as powerful as the Qa'resh…this was a problem they could not abide. They did not believe in an afterlife. They wanted immortality that they could grasp and control. So they set out for a solution. And after a time, one of their number found a solution."

"The one called Malal?" Roland asked.

"Indeed. He discovered that sentient minds—minds with imagination…soul—could tap into an energy within the quantum fabric of the universe. The ability to conceive of a future, make decisions that affected the quantum state of—I can only explain it in Qa'resh mathematics. Suffice it to say that a living, intelligent mind possessed an iota of power to reshape reality. And Malal learned how to harvest that energy."

"Harvest?" Nicodemus looked back to the crucifixions.

"The procedure proved to be quite fatal," Stacey said. "Through this soul energy, Malal discovered a dimension where existence was perpetual. A true heaven where entropy and death were impossible. But the energy required to open a gate to that dimension was immense. The universe would decay to the point of energy death before the Qa'resh could open a doorway and escape fate if they stuck to more conventional physics. But if enough souls were harvested…they had their way out."

"The Qa'resh didn't offer themselves up, did they?" Roland asked.

"Why would they? They were supreme. But there was a galaxy full of sentients available to them. So…Malal began harvesting soul power. World after world. All fell victim to Malal's promise of eternal life. It seems the fear of death, the annihilation of self, is a constant for any species."

"How many?" Roland asked. "How many did Malal kill?"

"All of them." Stacey clasped her hands behind her back. "Malal killed every last sentient in the galaxy…that wasn't Qa'resh. Some were duped into giving up their lives willingly. Others were taken more suddenly. I saw it happen to the Toth just after the Xaros were destroyed. Humans and all the others we know today weren't developed enough to be worth the effort."

"And Malal's people agreed to that?" Morrigan asked. "Just okayed an apocalypse?"

"They did." Stacey nodded. "Some developed a conscience during the cull, but when so many trillions had already been killed…it would've been a waste to stop so close to the ultimate goal."

"Trillions?" Roland asked. "It couldn't have been—"

"Trillions more followed," Stacey said. "During the harvest, Malal…his true nature came to light to the other Qa'resh. It wasn't that he killed so many for their benefit; it's that he enjoyed it. Delighted in the suffering. As the time of their apotheosis came closer, the Qa'resh decided they didn't want to spend eternity with a monster."

"Did they let Malal in on this decision?" Roland said.

"They did not. Malal continued his work, shared his technology with his kind…and then they imprisoned him on Anthalas. Malal's laboratories remained. His harvester ships continued their trek from planet to planet. The Qa'resh used the life force of countless innocents and they went on to their reward: eternal life. But one—one close to Malal—felt a tinge of guilt. She half remained in our reality to make sure Malal never escaped his prison and to watch new civilizations—the ones the Qa'resh didn't murder—rise across the galaxy.

"Then came the Xaros. The Qa'resh tried to stop them, but the drones were too many, and the Xaros Masters were safe in their world ship. Eventually, the Qa'resh had to bring Malal back into play if we wanted to survive the Xaros, and I was the one that brokered the deal."

"What…was done?" Nicodemus asked.

When Stacey didn't answer, Roland went farther

along the Ark's hull and found another giant mural, this one of souls leaving the aliens' bodies and reaching toward the figure above the ship.

"The Qa'resh promised Malal he could join them in paradise. All he had to do was help us defeat the Xaros. Which he did. But the dimension gate had grown cold. He needed more soul energy to join his brethren," she said.

"The Toth," Roland said, turning to look at Stacey. She nodded quickly.

"The Toth. I delivered Malal to their home world and watched as he devoured their billions. It was a bargain, really. Malal took care of two different enemies. All it cost was the near total extinction of a race of slavers and murderers," she said.

"Not total enough," Morrigan said.

"No. One overlord survived and he escaped to turn the Kesaht against all of humanity." Stacey tapped a fingertip against her cheek. "Karma? Our sins come back to haunt us? Do we deserve to suffer for putting our survival over the Toth's? Who can decide these things?"

"The Toth are evil," Martel said. "They deserved it. Sacrificing another people, like the Ruhaald or the Kroar…that would have been wrong."

"Well, Overlord Bale certainly disagrees." Stacey turned from the mural and walked toward Roland. "I'll deal with him soon enough. Loose ends have a way of unraveling entire tapestries, don't they?" she asked him.

Roland's communication suite fuzzed out and a single channel opened, one without a designation.

"Don't they?" Stacey asked over the private line. "Keep walking."

Roland kept pace with her as they continued along the hull.

"Am I a loose end, my Lady?"

"Only if you choose to be one, my Black Knight. What did you notice about our discussion back there?"

Roland glanced at the mural of the souls departing as they passed it.

"Only the armor asked questions of you," he said. "Davoust and the others…nothing."

"Because they aren't made to question me. Blind obedience has its perks, but it is not how our Nation must survive. What would happen if every soul on Navarre and our colonies was utterly devoted to me?" she asked.

"You could—it doesn't matter. I am Templar. And so long as you—"

"Don't you hide from me!" Stacey's cry sent a stab of phantom pain through Roland's ears. "Don't you cower behind your vows and your Crusader cross. Answer. Truthfully."

"You could be a tyrant," Roland said. "With the procedural tubes, you have almost unlimited manpower at your command. And with the Ark—"

"A god. A god empress that can burn the galaxy at her whim, and my children will leap into the fire at my command. You wonder why I have you—you who raised arms against the Nation and betrayed one master already—so close to me, don't you? What's the answer?"

Roland felt a touch of ice in his chest, one that had nothing to do with Stacey being so close.

"You know my vows as a Templar. All your armor is Templar. We will not let innocents suffer. We fight for humanity against the darkness, the evil that destroyed Earth. We will never waver from this…and you know it."

She nodded.

"Our loyalty to you is never absolute. If you step out of line, we will—"

"You *must*," she said. "You must put me down. I know what's happening to me, Roland. I know I'm slipping. If my mind…if I become a monster like Malal, then you and the Templar must end me. You understand this?"

"That won't happen," Roland said.

"Your convictions are that weak?"

"You will stay strong. The Nation needs you. The

Union—even if they won't admit it—needs you. Are we here, at this Ark, so that you can destroy the galaxy in a rage?"

"Hardly."

"Then my faith will be rewarded," Roland said.

"*Faith*, such a word. Not one for the pragmatic. But do you understand why I keep the armor so close? Why I keep you so close? Because I believe in you, my Black Knight. I believe you will do the right thing when the moment comes. Promise me. Promise you won't let me slip away to madness."

Roland's heart tightened. He felt shock at the request, and unworthy of such a mantle. But if she was on the verge of losing all control, especially with the Ark within her grasp…

"I serve the Nation, my Lady. I will…I will protect you."

"Now you understand. Good. Good. Your gauss cannons can do the job. Shatter me into a billion pieces and stop this body from ever putting itself back together again. Then I'll know if there really is a ghost inside my shell."

"I understand," Roland said.

They walked past a mural of a single alien face, the eyes soft with love and a faint smile to the lips. Even across the boundaries of biology and culture, Roland grasped a message of bliss from the art.

"My Lady, what happened to Malal?" Roland asked.

"He got exactly what he deserved, but not what he bargained for," she said. "Which is what I fear we'll all get in the end. The wheels of justice grind slowly, but they grind exceedingly small."

****

Three aliens were crucified before the Ark's entrance. Each wore tattered remnants of robes and gold-embroidered sashes. Jewels and platinum studs stood out against desiccated flesh. The airlock to the Ark stood several stories high, the gleaming alabaster of the Qa'resh ship unmarred by the vines or passage of time.

Stacey stood a few feet from the doors, her arms loose at her sides, head bowed slightly and eyes glowing.

Roland and his lance formed a semicircle around her, giving them full view of the crucified and the legionnaires behind them, all working to construct hasty defenses around the Nation's leader.

"Wonder if the grand pooh-bahs were the first—or last—to sacrifice themselves," Morrigan mused aloud.

"Better question is why," Nicodemus said. "Those murals back there? Looked like they were supposed to die in a moment of rapture, not tied to a cross and…ossified."

"Lady Ibarra witnessed Malal consume the Toth over the course of minutes," Martel said. "What's out there doesn't fit what we know about the Qa'resh. Something went wrong here."

"Something wrong with the Ark, perhaps?" Roland asked.

"There's nothing wrong," Stacey snapped. "It's dormant…just waiting for the right command. Thankfully, I have the keys to the kingdom. Rather, *I* am the key. Hamish!"

The bodyguard hustled toward her and removed a pouch from the small of his back. He handed it over to Stacey.

She unsnapped the lid and removed a small rod made of linked cubes.

"The Qa'resh on Bastion were terrified of this place," she said and one of the cubes lit up. "They sent a probe to this sector hundreds of years before they ever discovered Earth. The probe here sent back one message—just one—and it was enough for the Qa'resh to quarantine this star system and everything around it for a hundred light-years."

She twisted the rod and a second cube turned on.

Roland felt a vibration through his suit and lines of light traced up the Ark's doors.

"What was the message?" Morrigan asked.

"I don't know exactly, but I knew it had something to do with Malal." Stacey raised her hand and the rod floated a few inches over her fingertips. "The Qa'resh are very specific, loved their quantum designations for things, left no room for error. I dealt enough with Malal when he was their prisoner to learn his name in their language. The probe must have found the Ark, and the Qa'resh knew it belonged to that monster. No reason to search nearby for intelligent species to fight the Xaros because Malal had already killed them all."

The last cube in the rod pulsated.

"Now…for my next trick," Stacey said.

The rod spun around, and the doors opened with a hiss of blowing sand.

Roland aimed his Gustav heavy rifle into the abyss behind the doors. A single dish-shaped platform hung in absolute darkness just beyond the threshold.

"At last," said Stacey as the rod floated down into her grasp. "Years of scouring the galaxy for any clue to where to find this ship…and the means to operate it. Malal left behind a ship that will…will…"

Her head turned to one side, and one eye glowed faintly.

"Fools," she said. "You fools, you should have waited and now…"

"My Lady?" Roland asked.

Her gaze snapped to the entrance.

"Nothing. Nothing of consequence for us," she said. "Marshal? My lance will accompany me into the hull. The environment can't support human life."

"And of the excavation efforts?" Davoust asked.

"You doubt me? Of course you don't. See that we're not disturbed," Stacey said. "Inform Admiral Makarov that I've made entry."

Davoust beat a fist to his chest in salute.

"Shall we?" Stacey went to the threshold and paused, one foot inches away from crossing into the ship. "Roland…hold my hand."

Roland tapped the side of his helm.

"I'm sorry, my Lady, my receptors must be off."

Stacey lifted her arm.

"Portals," she said. "The Qa'resh and their damn portals. Hold my hand so if the inner workings are off, I won't be alone."

Roland gently pressed his armored fingers around her hand, and they stepped through together.

The saucer wobbled slightly as he shifted his weight onto it. Sound cut off and the abyss seemed to press in around him and Stacey.

"Doesn't seem so—" He turned and found only darkness. "—bad?"

Morrigan, Nicodemus, and Martel materialized and rushed onto the saucer, each with their heavy gauss rifles in hand.

"I hate Qa'resh tech," Martel said. "No offense, my Lady."

"None taken," she said. "It's so cold in here…can you sense it?"

"Atmosphere's thicker than outside, and it's pure nitrogen. Temperature's far below freezing, minus thirty," Morrigan said.

"Preservation conditions," Stacey said. "You all will be fine in your suits. Ambient temperature is high enough to keep my shell operating."

She put a palm to the saucer and branches of brass-colored light cut through the material. She raised her hand and a golden lattice came up with it. Stacey reached into the lattice, moving small beams of light and connecting them to different nodes.

"The code's off…somehow," she said. "But I can access enough of the systems from here. Enough to get us to the command throne."

"Throne?" Roland asked.

"Their word, not mine," she said. A tiny sun formed next to her face and she flicked it with a fingertip.

The darkness began fading away, ever so slowly.

Stacey dropped her hands and took a step back from the lattice.

"The Terran Union attacked the Kesaht home world," she said. "They're losing. Badly. Most of their fleet has been destroyed. What forces made it to the ground are under siege."

"How...how do you know?" Nicodemus asked.

Stacey glanced at Roland, who said nothing.

"I still have my sources in the Union," she said, tapping the side of her head, "and a quantum-dot bulk-information connection."

"Are we going to help them?" Roland asked.

"They're not our concern." Stacey raised her chin toward the waning darkness, and Roland made out shapes in the distance. What looked like bookshelves the size of small buildings held stretched ovals, all packed into rows.

The distant objects appeared to be moving, but Roland felt no sensation through the saucer.

"What of the Iron Dragoons?" Roland asked. "My—old lance."

"Aignar is still alive," Stacey said. "The Dotari and…two others. Odd."

"Gideon fell?" Nicodemus asked. "He's my enemy, but he deserved a better death than to fall against the Kesaht."

Roland's stomach squirmed. If Gideon had died, then the situation for the Terran Union must have been even worse than what Stacey had described. He wanted to beg Stacey to stop this mission and help the Union, but he knew that would be futile. She was close, so close to the goal she'd worked toward for so long…there was no stopping her now.

"Will you leave me again?" Stacey's voice came through a private channel. *"If a portal opens to your old friends, will you abandon me the same way you did when you went to your brother in Terra Nova?"*

"What are you saying?" Roland asked.

"I need you, Ken. Don't leave me again."

"Lady Ibarra, your mind is drifting. We need you to come back." Roland looked at her, but she was as stoic as ever. The darkness around them slipped away, and the rows of ovals glowed with internal light. The saucer continued upwards, toward a crystalline globe that glinted and rotated oddly, shifting its axis every few seconds.

"Do you all know what those are?" Stacey walked

to the edge of the lift and swept her hand across the expanse. "Soul energy. I've seen them before, in Malal's laboratory hidden in deep space."

"From the dead outside?" Morrigan asked.

"Not just them," Stacey said. "You're looking at the combined energy of billions and billions of living beings. This Ark harvested hundreds of worlds before it came to Nekara. It would have kept going, but then the Qa'resh had what they needed. It must have deactivated when they imprisoned Malal. This ship had more than enough energy for that demon to open the gateway to the dimension with the rest of his kind…but the Qa'resh had him devour the Toth instead."

"They didn't trust him," Nicodemus said. "What could Malal have done with this ship?"

"I'll show you," Stacey said. "I'll show the whole galaxy."

"Wait…this ship runs on souls?" Roland asked. "How are you going to—"

Stacey held up a hand.

"The dead cannot be brought back to life. Once I have this ship under my control, and the galaxy is safe for humanity, we will have no more use for it. I'll drop it into a black hole, erase the last trace of Malal's legacy," she said.

Dread gripped Roland's heart.

"This Ark is done harvesting the innocent," Stacey said. "I will make it into a great hammer of justice, redeeming all who were sacrificed. It is the least we can do."

Roland lowered his Mauser to one side. Could Stacey be trusted with that much power? Could anyone?

The light from the globe grew brighter.

"Hold on," Stacey said. "This will feel…odd."

The light overwhelmed Roland's optics and he felt like he was going through a Crucible gate. His mind recoiled as something—something cold and evil—reached through the light and caressed his neck.

Chapter 12

Stacey and her Armor were still on the saucer, but it was at the bottom of the globe. The structure was transparent from within, and the other crystal edges appeared to be solid beams of golden light.

Stairs of ruddy white crystal, too tall and too wide to have been made for a human, extended up to a dais where a fractal throne sat. Next to the throne was a glowing sliver, one that bobbed up and down.

"Yes," Stacey said as she struggled up the first step. "Yes, it is here, just as I hoped. Just as I prayed."

"I assumed a command bridge would be on a ship," Morrigan said.

"No!" Stacey waved a hand excitedly. "No, don't you know what that is? It's a probe. A Qa'resh probe. It can transfer my mind out of this metal and back into my body. It could be the last one!"

She started up the stairs, struggling to find a gait over the too-tall steps.

"Marc Ibarra had the fragments of one in his cell," Roland said. "He told me they all deactivated after the Ember War."

"My Lady," Martel said, putting a foot on the base of the steps, "perhaps caution is warranted."

"This ship changes everything, my knights. I'm done waiting!" Stacey made it to the top, and white light reflected off her shell, like motes of falling snow. She reached a hand to the probe but stopped short of touching it.

"But we're not here for me," she said. "We're here for the Nation."

She bent her fingers to the throne and it glowed from within.

"Yes…yes, let's get to the point." She hefted herself up onto the throne and put her hands onto the armrests, nearly stretching to fit the frame of the being the seat was meant for.

The floor vibrated against Roland's sabatons. He turned away from Stacey and backed against the bottom of the stairs with his lance.

"It's…it's incredible." Stacey's head tilted to one side and light built around her from within the throne. "This ship's been here for thousands of years…waiting…waiting for its master to call it back to—"

She shook her head quickly then tried to lift one hand off the throne, but her shell wouldn't budge from where it met the crystalline material, as if it were locked in place.

"Something's not right." She turned her gaze to the floating probe.

"My Lady?" Roland began up the stairs slowly.

"Who…who are you?" Stacey asked the probe.

Thick, dead-gray vines crept around the back of the throne and wrapped around her wrists. She struggled forward, but a vine gripped her around the neck and yanked her back.

"No!" Roland bounded toward her.

The probe's light went from silver to a fiery red.

"Don't! Don't do this to me!" Stacey shouted.

The probe hinged a tip toward her chest and shot into her heart.

Stacey screamed. Her voice pitched higher and higher until she froze, head locked back in agony.

Roland's armor froze mid-step. He tried rebooting the neural controls, but his HUD went red with errors. Stacey's scream came through his plugs and his mind went white with pain.

****

Stacey emerged from white so intense, it drowned out all other sensations. The light dimmed and she felt cool rock beneath the palms of her hands. She breathed and blinked hard to push away the afterglow.

"What is this?" she asked...and felt her mouth move. One hand went to her face and she felt the give of flesh. She touched a loose jumpsuit on her arms and ran her hands down her flanks, marveling at the sensation of being in a flesh-and-blood body.

She was in a small, oblong room made up of pitted rock, like the inside of a lava tunnel. There were no markings anywhere, but she realized where she was.

"Oh, no...no, this can't be."

There was a rustle behind her.

She turned slowly and found a man sitting on a bench carved out of the wall a few yards away. A glowing line in the floor separated them both. The man was hunched over; oily black hair hung down around his head and pale skin stuck out from beneath the strands.

Stacey touched the wall, feeling the tiny ridges cut against her skin. The pain didn't wake her up from what was an old, recurring nightmare.

+You know him.+

The voice came from nowhere, old and kind.

"This is a lie. It is a lie because this is the past, and I will not—"

The man looked up. Once-handsome features were slightly elongated, twisted into an almost demonic mask. His eyes were dark pits that stared into her soul.

"Say my name," he rasped.

"Let me out!" She banged a fist against the rock. "Let me out or—"

The rock enveloped her hand, locking her in place. The floor flowed over her feet and ankles, nearly crushing them with their grip. The cave billowed out and snagged her other arm, then flowed around her back and over her body. Only her face was left exposed.

The man stood, his limbs just long enough to register as *wrong*, as inhuman.

+You know him!+ a new voice shouted, and Stacey winced.

+He is in your mind. In your matrix. Name this being,+ said another new voice.

"No…no, you're not real…" Stacey struggled as the man stepped over the line and went to her.

Black talons morphed out of his fingertips and he caressed her face.

"I would have burned your worlds," he said. "Why? Why would I have done this? I am love. I am the light. I am the peace that all life deserves."

Stacey's mind went to where she heard those words and the cave wavered, shifting into a Qa'resh structure.

The man looked over one shoulder.

"My people...my people live?" he asked. "Their emissary gave us nothing. Tell me more, child. Tell me my name. My true name so that my children can know who redeems their souls."

Stacey focused on the twisted face, keeping her mind still. Whatever had her was reacting to her thoughts. She needed time—time and a bit of breathing room.

+SPEAK!+

Stacey gasped in pain.

"Malal!"

The cave vanished in an instant and she fell. She didn't feel when she hit a basalt floor, but the air chilled and her breath fogged.

A thick line of blood ran across the floor and over her hand.

+She is here. She is always here.+

Stacey pulled her bloody fingers into a fist, feeling the warmth and slickness against her skin.

"No, no...please, not this."

A bare foot with uncut nails set down next to her

hand, blocking the flow of blood.

"So much pain," Malal said. "So much fear. Why don't you come to me? I will take it all away."

Stacey looked up and saw the body of a woman with black hair crumbled on the deck of the Crucible's command center. Blood soaked through her uniform from a bullet wound, the pool of red growing with each heartbeat.

"Stop." Stacey tried to look away, but Malal grabbed her by the collar and lifted her up like she weighed nothing at all. He carried her to the body and rolled it onto its back with his foot.

Stacey—a mortally wounded Stacey—flopped to the deck. She mouthed words as blood trickled from her lips.

Stacey stared down at her dying self and all the suffering of the day she died came back to her.

"Give us what we want," a woman said.

Malal put Stacey's feet to the ground and wrapped an arm around her throat, the smell of ammonia and decaying flesh filling her nose. He whipped her around and a middle-aged woman of mixed descent approached, a smoking gun in one hand.

"Where is Malal?" she asked. Stacey knew her, knew her well. The woman had been in her grandfather's employ for decades and had been close to Stacey, almost like an aunt.

"Shannon," the gun-wielder said. "Shannon killed you. No one...no one can save you here, little girl."

Shannon pressed the muzzle against Stacey's chest, just over her heart. Flesh seared and Stacey cried out in pain.

"You want this all again?" Malal whispered into her ear. "You can have it. For eternity. Over and over again. You're in our world now, Stacey Ibarra."

"No! You can't—you can't have him!"

+GIVE HIM TO US!+

The gun fired.

Malal's grip vanished and Stacey collapsed. The basalt of the Crucible was gone, replaced by the alabaster of Qa'resh material.

Gold and glass struts rose out of the floor and up to a platform. She remembered a view port to one side but didn't look to it. A portal, one big enough to let a Mule fly through it with room to spare, glowed on the platform.

A humanoid alien, its head equine but with the mandibles and multifaceted eyes of an insect, stepped around the portal.

"This...this is the last place you saw the redeemer," the alien said. "But...you're fighting the memory. Stopping us from seeing where he is."

"What are you?" Stacey struggled to her feet, her gaze locked on the alien, the only Qa'resh she'd ever laid eyes on.

"We are Malal's children," Malal said from behind her.

"We have been waiting for him," Shannon said as she blinked into existence at the base of the stairs. "Waiting to be carried to paradise, just as Malal promised. We gave our souls…but we must have been unworthy, impure. Where is the redeemer? Where is our reward?"

"I wanted this," Malal said, looking to the portal. "Why? What did I need there?"

Stacey looked down at her hand and saw the blood—her blood—on the fingers. She flexed it open and the stain faded away.

"I'm in the probe…aren't I? Grandfather described it like this," she said.

"I did?" Marc Ibarra—clad in his silver body—touched her chin. The cold numbed her skin and she sneered at him.

"I need…you need to see something," Stacey said. "Very important to understand why Malal…found you unworthy."

+WE ARE WORTHY!+ a chorus of voices

shouted.

Reality fizzled around Stacey and she went to her knees, her mind ablaze with incoherent noise and images.

She braced against the floor, nothing but an invisible wall over infinite darkness.

"You need…need to see," she managed. The blackness morphed into white sand and she gripped it in her hands, concentrating on the sensation of the grit between her fingers.

She looked up to a sapphire sea with waves locked in mid-crash. She turned her head to a towering suit of armor standing guard in front of Trinia, the galaxy's last Aeon. She focused on the armor, and the insignia changed.

+WHERE IS MALAL?+

The words rocked Stacey and she doubled over, her arms over a now bleeding wound in her chest.

"Let…stop hurting me!"

+SHOW!+

The hot knife in her breast receded.

Stacey shuffled through the sand, stopping to rest against the armor. She looked up at it, changing the helm's shape to match a non-Ibarran design.

Noise rose in her mind, a background rumble of thousands upon thousands of voices. One word jumped to the fore over and over again.

Geist.

"That's who you are?" Stacey wiped blood from her mouth. It froze against her silver shell and snapped away as her knuckles flexed.

"We are his chosen people," the Malal apparition said. "Geist. Our purity will join his perfection."

+GEISTGEISTGEIST—+

"Please…" Stacey stumbled, but there was no pain this time. Sand cracked as the cold of her body froze it against her bare feet. The memory of flesh was gone, only the purpose she knew from the prison of her mind remained.

"Too strong." Malal reached toward her and his arm stretched with nightmare logic.

Stacey grabbed him by the wrist and resisted his pull.

"You want answers," she said. "You'll have them."

Malal vanished into smoke.

Trinia knelt to one knee, her face still and lifeless. A necklace of jade flakes dangled over her collarbone.

Stacey squeezed the center flake between her thumb and forefinger. The golden lattice of Qa'resh language formed a wreath around the necklace.

"What are you doing?" Malal leaned over Stacey's

shoulder.

Stacey pulled on the necklace and it came away from Trinia's neck. Stacey backed up, her eyes locked on Trinia and the Armor with Terran Union markings.

"Help," she said, gripping the flake in her hand, and the lattice flared.

"Lies." Shannon stepped from around Malal and aimed the same gun that mortally wounded Stacey years ago.

"Stop the Geist. Help me!" Stacey snapped the flake in half and reality crumbled.

****

Roland's HUD flickered on and off and his optics cycled through different spectrums. His hands went to either side of his helm, trying to stop the spinning he knew existed within his own brain.

Stacey was in the throne, the vines still gripping her in place. The probe slid out of her body and hovered in front of her face, emitting a riot of color that reflected off her silver shell.

"What…what was that?" Morrigan asked. "You all felt it? Saint Kallen was with us. She…"

"She needs our help." Nicodemus started up the

stairs toward Stacey. "These Geist…must be who has our Lady."

"No." Roland put a hand out to stop him. "You saw what she—the vision. We can't help Lady Ibarra yet. You all saw Trinia, didn't you?"

"On Ouranos," Martel said. "I saw one of us with her."

"It wasn't us." Roland touched the Templar cross on his breastplate. "Fleur-de-lis."

"Iron Dragoons," Nicodemus said. "Terran Union armor. Why would Saint Kallen show us that?"

"Because the Terran Union—because Gideon—has Trinia," Roland said. "They're on the Kesaht planet, all under siege. She wants us to…" Roland hesitated, unsure if now was the time to tell his lance the truth about Saint Kallen and the visions. The others' faith was stronger than his, untainted by knowledge.

Nicodemus, Morrigan, and Martel, warriors he respected and had fought beside, looked at him, and he knew what he had to do—even if it meant betraying them.

"Saint Kallen wants us to rescue Trinia," Roland said. "Bring her here and free our Lady from whatever prison she's in."

"Trinia knows Qa'resh technology," Morrigan said. "That's why we went to Ouranos to get her in the first place. There's no one else in the whole galaxy."

"The Union's fighting for its life against the Kesaht," Martel said. "In the time it will take us to get there, it might all be over."

"We are Armor," Nicodemus said. "We act. We seize victory. We do not hesitate."

"The fleet in orbit," Martel said, looking up. "If we send it to rescue Trinia, the legions will be vulnerable. The world was dead when we arrived…something's awoken."

"I can convince Makarov," Roland said. "Besides, what risk wouldn't they take to save our Lady?"

"Trinia," Martel said, leveling a knife hand at Roland. "She is your mission. Not the Union soldiers."

Roland tilted his helm to one side ever so slightly.

"No." Martel snapped his hand into a fist. "Saint forgive me, I'm wrong. Trinia…and whoever you can save. We are Templar. That the Union hates us doesn't change that they're human."

"Who stays?" Morrigan gestured to Stacey. "Who goes?"

"If Gideon does have Trinia," Nicodemus said as he tromped down the steps, "then we should send those he's most likely not to try and kill on sight. No matter if we come to rescue him or not."

Roland looked to Morrigan, Gideon's old lance mate and the one who shoved him into an escape pod and ejected him onto Ceres when the Ibarrans first defected. Nicodemus and Gideon had already crossed blades once, and Nicodemus had lost that fight. Martel was the head Templar, and a lightning rod for everything Gideon considered treason.

Roland…he had beaten his former commander and left him helpless.

"No good options," Martel said. "Roland. Nicodemus. Go. Return with the Aeon. You will not fail."

"Sir." Roland beat a fist to his chest and went to the disk.

Morrigan and Martel extended the blades of their swords and jabbed the tips into the floor. They took up the honor guard position at the base of the stairs, just like the armor that guarded Saint Kallen's tomb on Mars.

"Good luck, boy-o," Morrigan said. "May the blessing of light be on you—light without and light within."

The disk moved and light enveloped Roland and Nicodemus.

Chapter 13

Within one of innumerable small temples surrounding the Ark, a glow rose from the metal vines covering the inner walls.

Vines snaked out, coiling together into a sphere of moving threads. The vines retracted, leaving a dull humanoid shape behind. Red lines glowed across the body's skin and it tightened into well-defined male form and a face with sharp features. Ruby eyes opened.

Doors on opposite sides of the chamber opened, and two Geist arrived, both with female proportions.

"This…" the male said, reaching forward with one hand, "this is a step backwards from perfection." The filaments making up his body flexed and reshaped, adding lines of muscle and protruding veins.

"Malal tests us again, Pallax." One of the females approached and ran a hand across his chest as her body resolved into nude curves.

"We abandoned the flesh, Seru." He took her by the wrist and stared into her pale-blue eyes.

Her mouth pulled back into a smile, and the tiny wires shifted, revealing clenched teeth that didn't move as she spoke.

"But not its pleasures, my love."

"The human-not-human in the temple," the other female said. Her body was slimmer, with hair that spouted off her scalp and bent into locks the width of a pencil. "This Stacey Ibarra…her mind is damaged. We should have been able to draw everything from her once she joined with the emissary."

"She's strong enough to keep the emissary from flaying her mind." Seru swiped a finger across Pallax's mouth. "Capable and willful. I hate her already…but I can break her mind. Won't take long."

"The others will awaken soon enough," the slimmer of the two females said. "They were promised paradise upon awakening…not replacement bodies. The thralls will be difficult to manage."

"Malal tests us," Pallax said. "He sent a final test to us. This is truth. The minds of the others will accept this. What are the humans doing now, Noyan?"

"Ships…moving through a construct in orbit," the slim female said. "Their troops…smaller than the metal walkers…they are flesh and bone."

"Then let us elevate one," Pallax said. "The theosar will bring them to the Geist, then all will know everything. Dispose of the intruder."

"Don't deny me a toy. This Stacey…her construction is of Malal's exalted people. Strange…" Seru leaned against a wall and the vines reshaped into a seat. She crossed her legs and tapped fingertips across her chest. "Harvest one of her flesh thralls. They may know something I can use to crack her mind."

"Impetuous as ever," Noyan said as she snapped her fingers and screens appeared over the walls, all showing the Ibarran troops arrayed around the Ark. "We had so much time to contemplate perfection and you're still the same…These heretics are well armed. We need a prisoner, just one. If we push them, they may damage the temple—or harm the prophet in the holy of holies."

"Then bring forth the scythes," Pallax said. "We just need a head."

"My theosar works best with living subjects, my darling." Seru blew him a kiss. "Get me one to play with, won't you, Noyan?"

"I shall." Noyan turned a hand over and a shadow formed in her palm. "Ready the pilgrim fleet."

"It will draw from the offerings," Pallax said. "They still have ships in orbit. Let us lie in wait just a little bit longer. Who knows what they'll bring back for us. This Aeon sounds interesting…"

"The scythes are difficult to control without the tamers…but I see your wisdom," Noyan said. "Let the hunt begin."

Chapter 14

President Garret's hands kept trembling. He bit his lip and willed his digits to still, but they wiggled of their own accord these days. He gripped the edge of his coat, tempted to reach for the pills in a pocket, but he couldn't do that just yet. Not in front of the war council.

A moon with a bulge around the equator hung in front of the Terran Union's senior leadership. Plumes of dust rose from glowing craters along the bulge.

"The mass driver strike threw Iapetus off its axis," General Kaufman said. "Every macro emplacement is off-line. We're still trying to figure out how the Vishrakath got three warheads through our defenses. Current best guess is they stacked off-set jump points behind each other, staggered the munition velocity, and—"

"Rescue. The rescue efforts," Garret said.

"Elements of 12th Fleet responded immediately. Titan station as well…three thousand seven hundred and twelve souls rescued…so far," Kaufman said.

"There were over a quarter million on that moon." Garret leaned against the holo rail and shook his head.

"It was a failure. No denying it." Kaufman raised his chin slightly. "But it is the only successful mass driver strike the Vishrakath have had since they began bombardment nearly three weeks ago. We've integrated new artillery ships into the defense grid. Proximity warheads have a near perfect intercept rate and have reduced our volume of return fire by—"

"Does the public know yet?" Garret asked the lone civilian in the room.

Chambers, the head of Union Intelligence, tugged at her cuffs, a tell any intelligence professional should have been able to control.

"It's slipped through the censor controls," she said. "We delete any images that make it onto the net, but word of mouth isn't something we can control. I suggest you make a formal address in the next three hours before the story blossoms into a full-blown panic."

"You think it won't?" Garret scratched his face

and realized he hadn't shaved in days. "Civilians think they can sleep safe in the bunkers. They see what one mass driver hit does and the illusion of safety will be gone. It's one thing to hear about the kiloton effective yields the Vish rocks can drop on a city. Another thing to see it."

"Then cancel the assault on Kesaht'ka," Kaufman said. "Send that force to the Vish-held systems where they're opening the offset wormholes and—"

"We've been over this!" Garret slammed a palm against the rail. His hand shifted back and forth, and he shoved it into his pants pocket. "We won the Ember War with a bold, decisive attack. It worked because the Xaros weren't ready for us to show up on their doorstep. Same difference. The Kesaht don't know we've got their home address. We'll knock them out of this war. That'll make the Vishrakath realize they're about to face our entire might and they'll fold. We push the Vish back and they'll come at us even harder. Was I not clear?"

"Crystal, Mr. President," Kaufman said. "The attack on Kesaht'ka continues, though the communications we're getting aren't responding to crypto challenges. Keeper thinks interference from—"

"I have a speech to write." Garret tucked his other hand beneath his armpit and stormed out.

Chapter 15

Armor techs worked around Roland's suit within the *Warsaw*'s cemetery as a robot arm hoisted a jet pack onto Roland's back and the frame locked on with a snap of bolts.

Roland ran the pack's integration sequence and monitored his HUD as his onboard systems meshed with the new addition.

"Attention on deck!" came from below the catwalk running parallel to his suit's waist.

Roland made manual adjustments to the stabilizer gyros and a fuel nozzle connected beneath the left jet.

"Chief? I need my IR transmitter boosted. The Kesaht always scramble the atmos…Chief?" Roland leaned forward slightly, searching for his tech crew.

Admiral Makarov came down the catwalk, her hands clasped behind her back.

"I sent them away." She stopped, facing to one side, not looking at Roland.

"I didn't think I'd see you before we dropped," he said. "We're one gate—"

"I know damn well where I'm supposed to be, Roland. The admiral should be at the helm of her ship, readying a blind assault into a heavily fortified system that already chewed up the best fleet the Terran Union could muster. Yet here I am, down here with you…"

Roland paused the final steps of the jet pack's installation and the cemetery went silent.

"What's wrong?" he asked.

"You," she said as she turned to him and put her hands on the railing. "You come out of the Ark and tell us Lady Ibarra is trapped in some sort of Qa'resh technology. That Saint Kallen…" she paused and narrowed her eyes, "*Saint Kallen* appeared to you and the rest of your lance and ordered you to go and rescue the Aeon from the Kesaht. Or from the Terran Union. That's what Saint Kallen told you?"

"That's…how we understood it," Roland said.

"Marshal Davoust had no problem with this?" Makarov flung a hand up next to her face. "Just send our warships away. Leave him and the Legions practically undefended while *I* take *my* fleet and *my* ships and *my* sailors into a warzone to carry out a mission given to us by a long-dead armor soldier." She crossed her arms over her chest. "That sound about right to you, Roland?"

Roland nodded.

"And you're—this doesn't bother you?" Makarov's jaw clenched.

"The mission isn't the problem," Roland said. "You took the *Warsaw* on a suicide run over Mars to save me and the rest of the Union's prisoners. Long odds aren't the problem. The problem is your doubt. You doubt what we're supposed to do. That's what's driving you crazy."

"Don't think we've been together—dating, whatever it is we are—long enough for you to know me that well," she said as she turned away.

"Am I wrong?" Roland asked.

Makarov rubbed her face.

"You're not like the other commanders," Roland said. "Lady Ibarra told me you were…different."

"Different in that I somehow have decades of command experience up here," she tapped the side of her head, "yet am barely out of my twenties. I don't even know how old I actually am. Did I come out of the procedural tubes a week before we met? Years? Am I different in that I'm some sort of a contrived person?"

"You can question Lady Ibarra," Roland said. "She...wanted you to be more independent than the others. You can doubt, and that freedom is what's bothering you. We're to save Lady Ibarra. No one else in the Nation will even blink at acting for her."

Makarov let out a frustrated hiss and beat a fist against the railing.

"Do you know who inherits command of the Ibarra Nation if anything—God forbid—happens to her?" Makarov asked.

"Her grandfather...is out. Davoust?"

Makarov shook her head slowly.

"There's Admiral...no. Wait. Really?"

"We begged her to generate a successor." Makarov sighed. "Bring forth someone with her vision and her intelligence from the crèches...but she wouldn't do it. The other flag officers didn't press the issue, but I did. In private. That's when she named me her successor. That decision makes more sense now. *I* was always the successor."

"And now you're at the head of a fleet on the way to the Kesaht home world—"

"I am not afraid! Lady Ibarra isn't gone, is she? She can be saved?"

"If we rescue Trinia…"

"Put yourself in my place, Roland. As heir apparent, as the one who must lead our Nation if we lose our great Lady, as commander of this fleet…tell me what my doubts should be."

Roland shifted within his armored womb. She could project gravitas when she needed to, even though he was the one in the giant suit.

"One with a history of conflicting loyalties comes out of the Ark, saying that Lady Ibarra is locked inside a Qa'resh machine, revealing that Saint Kallen has shared visions with Armor, and now she wants us to save an alien scientist and the Terran Union forces on the Kesaht home world. That—"

"Not just any Union force," Makarov interrupted, brandishing a finger at him. "Your old lance. Your old commander, the one named Gideon. The same one that killed Ibarran Armor on Nunavik and tried to murder Lady Ibarra. Do you see the issue, Roland?"

"You fear I'm just trying to save my former companions. That I'm trying to put the Nation into the middle of the fight against the Kesaht, the alliance the Union wanted from Lady Ibarra. That I'm still loyal to the Union."

Makarov's eyes softened and her lips pressed into

a white line.

"You have your doubts about Lady Ibarra," she said quietly. "I know you do. This is your chance to call the whole thing off. Save Ibarran lives. We don't need the Ark to survive, Roland, but if we charge into a massacre, the Nation may not recover. It's…"

She put a hand to her chest.

"I wish I was like the others—no conflict, purity of intention. But my command instincts tell me one thing: these blasted…emotions are tearing me apart," she said. "Just tell me the truth. Are we going to save Lady Ibarra, or is this a trick? I don't believe you're so selfish or manipulative as to…but I have responsibilities. For our Nation. For us all."

Roland reached a huge hand to her, the whirl of gyros the only sound in the cemetery. He turned his palm up and stopped a foot from her chest. Makarov put a hand on his metal finger.

"We will save her," Roland said. "Lady Ibarra…her ends are just. Her life is worth far more than mine. By my Armor and my honor, I swear I am true to the Nation. True to the Templar. True to all of humanity. This fight is a long shot, but we need to take it. Better to try to win it all than hesitate and lose everything."

"L'audace, et toujours l'audace," Makarov said.

"I don't speak Basque, Ivana."

"'Audacity. Always audacity.' It's French, you knuckle-dragger. You still have my favor? My mother's rank…the only tangible thing I have from her?"

Roland tapped his breastplate. He had the bit of cloth inside his skin suit. Regulations be damned.

"Why did I work myself into knots over this? Are you really going to engineer a betrayal of our Lady, me, the Nation…while you've got a *momento mori* to our parents? If you're that evil, then what hope does the Lady have?"

Roland ached to tell her the truth about the visions, unsure if that would help convince Makarov…or anger her because he'd withheld that truth.

"It must be hard to trust me. I've been on both sides of the battle," he said.

"The insignia on your armor doesn't make you who you are," she said. "You bring Lady Ibarra back to us, you understand? I don't think I'm ready to lead the whole thing. Being a fleet commander is hard enough."

"I'll do it for you," Roland said, tilting his helm slightly.

The screen on her forearm buzzed and she ran her hands over her lightly armored vac suit, checking seals, and then removed her helmet from her hip.

"The Keystone's ready for us. We've got a few

jumps before we arrive in the Kesaht system. Once we get there, I'll do my best to convince any Union force that we're there to help. Still...they may not be happy to see us—you in particular."

"Enemy-of-my-enemy sort of thing," Roland said. "I hope."

"I don't have time for hope." She locked her helmet on and it hissed as the suit pressurized. "I come to battle with guns for the Kesaht and a ticket off that planet. The Union wants to play stupid, I'll leave them to their own devices. Good hunting, Roland."

"And you, Ivana."

Makarov touched her fingertips to her visor and blew him a kiss.

Roland felt a warmth in his chest as she left, one that replaced the nagging dread he'd had since he left Stacey in the Ark.

Chapter 16

Santos checked his battery charge for the dozenth time: still near a hundred percent full. Made sense, as he'd hot-swapped for a fresh stack just before he and the rest of the Armor had set out from Gold Beach.

He sat against a wall, Mauser rifle clutched in his hands. Even in his suit, he felt fatigue in his limbs. A data packet pinged on his HUD, and he opened a new operations overlay.

Simple enough: he would still take up rail-gun firing positions just outside a wide empty zone surrounding Hegemony City. A pic of a shield generator built into the lower edge of the dome flashed, and he acknowledged that he had his target identified.

A team of Pathfinders rushed past him, their

image wavering as their cloaks struggled to compensate for the rapid movement.

"Irks me to have crunchies out ahead of us," Aignar said.

"I thought Pathfinders loved this sort of thing," Santos said. "Being the eyes and ears of the main force. Not like we're going to sneak up."

"There were nine Pathfinders when we left Gold," Aignar said. "Six just went by."

"Can we hurry up already?" He looked to one side, where Gideon and Laran were in consultation with each other.

"Santos, you have the easiest assignment," Cha'ril said. "Point and shoot. Your target isn't even moving. The rest of us will keep any enemy from bothering you."

"Any easier and we'd have to write it out for you in crayon," Aignar said.

"And I appreciate the vote of confidence," Santos muttered. "I just…I'm ready to go!"

"This is a shoestring tackle of an operation, kid," Aignar said. "We're not getting a second chance at this."

"I am Armor," Santos said. "I am fury. I will not fail."

"Better not," Cha'ril said. "You screw up and one of us will have to drop anchor and fire. We don't have the batteries for a shot and a long fight. You do. Lances behind us will take care of the Risen building."

"Get set," Gideon said. "Friendly force tracker pulse coming."

Infrared relays built into the lances' suits and the power-armored Rangers and Strike Marines sent location data across the web formed by their IR comms.

Santos swallowed hard as he realized just how many warriors were taking part in this assault. Thousands of individual soldiers and a few dozen Armor. If this was enough to bring the Kesaht to heel, then it would be a battle to be remembered long after Santos was gone.

Dad said he never got nervous before a fight, he thought. *I'm starting to think he's a damn liar.*

"Hold up," Gideon said. "Waiting for Strike Marine snipers to get into over watch."

"Them and their pea shooters," Santos said. "Tiny little rail guns compared to what we've got."

"You want me to tell that to the sniper watching over you?" Aignar asked.

"No. No we need to be nice to the crunchies," Santos said.

Laran looked to the horizon then waved at Gideon. A wide comet tail broke against the sunset.

"Go. Go!" she shouted.

"What about the—" Santos didn't have a chance to finish before Gideon grabbed him beneath the arms and hauled him to his feet. Santos got his legs moving, barreling forward at a sprint, his boot heels cracking pavement with each strike.

"A Kesaht battleship broke through our fleet," Gideon said. "Get fire on the dome, and bring the shields down before the ship can hit us from low orbit."

"Can't be accurate from that range." Santos scanned the ground ahead at the firing point, looking for a place to drop anchor. "They miss and—"

"They could hit the unshielded city!" Cha'ril shouted. "Which is why we need the shields down now. Stop thinking and start functioning!"

Santos slid to a stop and pressed his left heel against the road. A diamond-tipped spike snapped from the housing in his foot and punctured the concrete. The drill in his leg bore down, sending loose rock spraying through the light coating of dirt across the road.

"Ah…crap!" He picked up his anchor foot and retracted the drill. "Hit a void. Relocating." He looked around and ran toward a building, knocking the wall and roof aside with wide sweeps of his Mauser heavy rifle. He checked that he had line of sight on the distant dome.

The city was atop a slight rise, a dead zone of

cleared buildings a few blocks from where he was all the way to a several-story-tall wall that made up the edge of the city. The thought of crossing that kill zone while under fire felt daunting. But he had his Armor and his rail gun to put things in his favor.

"Dropping anchor!" He stomped a heel down and the drill spun into solid rock. "Good point!"

"Wait, you detected a void?" Gideon asked. "Like a tunnel?"

Santos extended the twin rail vanes of his rail gun out of his back and angled them toward a disk the size of a barn on the outer wall.

"Nice of them to give me a bullseye," Santos said.

"Santos, what did you—contact!" Gideon shouted and Mauser rifles fired.

The wall ahead of him collapsed and a Sanheel leapt over the rubble, a spear clutched under one elbow. Santos tested his anchor's grip; it was solid as the last of the drill worked into the bedrock.

He snapped his rifle up and hit the Sanheel in the chest. The round blew out its back and the Kesaht stumbled forward. Santos caught the dying alien by the throat and tossed it to one side.

Through the collapsed wall, Santos saw more Sanheel and Rakka foot soldiers clambering out of an open tunnel once hidden by metal sliding doors in the floor of an adjacent building.

"Cover! Need cover!" Santos shouted.

Rotary cannon fire peppered the Sanheel as Gideon kicked down a wall. The smaller bullets sprang off Sanheel armor and ripped through the brutish Rakka.

Gideon emptied his Mauser, killing three Sanheel, and then grabbed it by the barrel. He swung it like a club, crushing the sternum of a Kesaht centaur as it jumped out of the tunnel.

"Take your damn shot!" Gideon bellowed.

Santos primed the rails and electricity crackled down the lengths.

A thunder crack slapped dust across his vision as a nearby Armor from another lance sent a hypervelocity bolt at the city. A line of ignited oxygen traced from a shield emitter to the right of Santos's target to a firing position off to his right.

The shield wavered, green waves like an aurora washing over its surface.

A green reticule blinked over his target.

"Rail shot!"

The building blew apart as a wave of overpressure from his bolt shattering the sound barrier hit his surroundings like a giant fist. Santos began retracting his anchor, waiting for all the dust to clear to see if his rail gun had brought down the shields.

"No…"

The disk he'd fired on was lit with energy, a shield swirling over it. The force field over the dome was still active.

His vision jumbled as a Sanheel blindsided him. The alien, bleeding freely from its eyes, ears, and mouth, pinned him to the ground with its weight. A wretched howl came from open jaws and blood dribbled onto Santos's optics.

He swung a hand and connected with nothing but air as the Sanheel reared back. It drew a dagger and lifted it over its head. The edges lit up with power, and Santos got the distinct impression it could pierce right through his breastplate and the womb beneath.

The Sanheel's head vanished into a cloud of red mist. The crack of a Strike Marine sniper rifle followed a split second later. The dead alien went limp and slouched to one side.

"God bless the Marines. Especially the snipers," Santos said as he popped to his feet.

"Help!" Cha'ril called out.

She fired her Mauser one-handed into the open tunnel, and her other arm gripped Gideon by a carry handle behind his helmet.

A lance had impaled his torso and electricity snapped around the haft where it penetrated the Armor.

"Brace for impact!" General Laran broadcast.

There was a whoosh of air as an energy bolt streaked overhead and impacted behind Santos. The ground roiled, sending him into a wall. A column of smoke and ash rose into the sky, melding into the darkening sky as night came for them.

Marine and Ranger IR beacons on Santos's HUD blinked off.

Santos spun around. The Kesaht battleship was still distant on the horizon, but growing larger with each passing second. A point of light emerged from its prow.

"Retreat!" Laran ordered. "All forces ret—"

Another bolt hit even closer. The blast wave picked Santos up and hurled him to the ground. Debris rained down around him as he fought his way out of rubble. He got clear and saw both his rail vanes sticking out of a wrecked building.

"Santos!" Cha'ril stood, broken masonry sloughing off her back. The haft of a Sanheel spear still stuck out from Gideon's chest. She'd covered the captain with her own Armor to protect him from the blast.

"Gideon!" Santos crunched through broken rocks

and got to his lance commander. He reached for the crackling spear.

"Wait. Don't!" Cha'ril tried to stop Santos, but he gripped the spear before she could intervene.

His arm flared with sympathetic pain as the spear sent a jolt up his Armor. He tossed the Kesaht weapon aside and Gideon sat bolt upright.

"—port! Where is...I was off-line." Gideon's helm ticked from one side to the other.

"General?" Cha'ril touched the side of her helm and looked back to a wall of fire a hundred yards away. "She was there."

"I've got anchor!" Aignar called out. "Reading rail shot."

"Sir, what do we do now?" Santos asked as he looked around but couldn't see Aignar.

"Fall back." Gideon lurched to his feet and touched the hole in his chest. Speakers on either side of his helm whined with feedback as he cranked up the volume.

"Fall back! Get to Gold Beach!"

"What?" Santos pointed at the intact city. "This was our only—"

The blast of a rail cannon felt like a summer breeze compared to the energy strike from the Kesaht battleship.

"Incoming!" Aignar shouted.

Another blast wave hit Santos from behind, slapping him to the ground like a toy. He got onto his knees, his HUD awash with static.

"Getting tired of that." He looked to the horizon, and the Kesaht battleship was an expanding fireball. "Good shooting, Aignar."

No response.

"Aignar?"

Where once had been a decaying city was now a hellscape of small fires and ash.

"Go." Gideon emerged from the gloom, Cha'ril by his side. "Get back to Gold Beach."

"We do that and we...we've lost," Santos said.

"Can't breach the city. We need a new plan." Gideon reached out and clamped a hand against the bottom half of Santos's helm. He pulled the younger Armor's optics close to his own.

"Retreat. You understand me?" Gideon snarled.

"Yes, sir." Santos pulled back and took off at a jog. "What about Aignar?"

"Off-line," Cha'ril said. "He...he was over there." She pointed to an impact crater.

"Laran is dead," Gideon said. "Command falls to me. I have to do what's right for every survivor, not just our lance. Get our people back to the beachhead. Pick up any wounded you can. We'll search for the missing later…if we can."

Santos stopped, his sensors active for any trace of Aignar, but he came up empty.

A pit opened in his stomach, and it grew deeper as he and the remains of the assault force limped away. Broken and beaten.

****

Santos rolled to a stop just outside the field hospital inside Gold Beach. Medics rushed over to him and unloaded the wounded Marines and Rangers strapped to the skirts on top of his treads. He handed over the last, a Ranger he'd carried in his arms missing her lower leg and most of an arm.

Santos watched as the wounded went into a tent set up outside the building, and he wondered just how much radiation the casualties would take. If they survived surgery…it may have just bought them another day or two of pain-filled life.

He was about to transform his treads back into legs, when he saw just how much blood had pooled against his Armor.

He leaned over to one side and scooped up a handful of soil and rubbed it against the stains.

"Stop." Cha'ril walked over to him, her legs similarly stained. "You'll look weak. Blood doesn't bother us."

Santos transformed back into his walker configuration.

"I can't believe we made it out of that," he said, and a realization hit him. "Aignar! Aignar's still out there. We need to—"

Cha'ril bumped her knuckles against his chest, sending a thump that went through his womb.

"General Laran is out there too. So are *four* full lances of Armor. They may be listed as missing in action, but they are *not* coming back, Santos."

"Don't say that. We are Armor, we can take the rads and—"

"We are not invincible. Aignar is gone. Captain Gideon needs us right now. Needs us sharp. Needs our iron in this fight. You understand?"

Santos lowered his synch rating and pulled into a ball within his pod, a mountain of fragmented memories from the fight at the city gates and the retreat back flooded through him. He tried to remember the moment Aignar died, but it wouldn't come to him.

"Aignar saved us," she said. "Rail'd that ship and killed it. It would've picked the rest of us off if he hadn't dropped anchor and turned himself into a target out in the open. He died for us, Santos. He did it so we can keep fighting, you understand?"

Santos stretched out and reconnected fully to his Armor.

"Sorry, Cha'ril, just took me a moment. Captain Gideon…he took charge after Laran died. He was…really rose to the challenge."

"A clear, confident voice goes a long way in combat," the Dotari said. "We're lucky he was in charge. Now let's go live up to his expectations. Yes? Kid?"

"Don't." Santos shook his helm. "Aignar called me 'kid.' Don't. Not right now."

"We need fresh batteries and ammo. Let's go find some."

Chapter 17

Garret lay back on a narrow cot set up in his office beneath Camelback Mountain. His shirt was untucked, one shoe half off. He crunched three pills between his teeth and the hand holding the open bottle fell against the cot bar.

"Lousy...day," he mumbled as the drugs took hold, smoothing out his thoughts and letting him drift off to sleep.

Or that was the plan. The very specific plan he'd given his Secret Service guards when he told them no disturbances for four hours. When the door burst open and the head of his detail jammed a hypo against his neck, he knew something had gone terribly wrong.

The substance in the hypo sent an electric jolt

through his body and his entire mouth tasted bitter. His detail hauled him to his feet and began re-dressing him.

"Wha…" Garret drooled as his eyes struggled to focus.

A guard held a metal tube under his nose and his sinuses felt like he'd snorted fire.

"Ah, Jesus, not that crap." Garret beat weakly at the men holding his arms.

"He's up," the head of his detail said and pulled a data slate with a red and white striped case from his coat. The screen snapped on, and Keeper, the controller of the Crucible over Ceres, came up. She looked like an elderly woman, but she carried herself with strength. That she was actually the mind of a dead Strike Marine named Torni trapped in a Xaros drone was known by only a handful of people in the Terran Union.

"Mr. President, we've a situation," she said. "A Vishrakath hive fleet came through a wormhole near Mars. They've already launched attacks on Olympus and Deimos."

"No…you said that's impossible," Garret said.

"The Crucible over Mars has been emitting a disruption field for almost a month now. The field will fluctuate as the gate recharges from dark energy and—my theory is that they've been able to monitor the fluctuations from the gate on Novis. I should've planned on this, but after the Ibarrans came through that gate, we've—"

"Mars! The Vishrakath are on Mars." Garret broke out into a cold sweat, and he wasn't sure if it was from the counter-narcotics or mounting terror.

"The planet's holding, but Mars is the lynchpin of our macro cannon grid. If they manage to disrupt it, then—"

"Earth is vulnerable," Garret finished. "Recall the assault from Kesaht'ka. Winning there won't mean anything if Earth is lost."

"That's…I've lost contact with Admiral Lettow."

"You what? Then…dear God." Garret looked at the pills spilled on the floor; a deep ache yearned in his chest. He grabbed his head of detail by the shoulder. "Get the war council together. Now. Then convene the senate. We may have to consider…surrender."

"No," Keeper said. "We still have enough macro cannons to—"

Garret flung the slate into the corner and wiped his head down with a towel as he stormed out of his room.

Chapter 18

Marc Ibarra walked down a narrow hallway cut through solid rock. He moved with a false air of confidence, a small matte black case clenched in one hand. If his chrome body could still exhale air over lips, he would've whistled as he tapped in an access code on a door panel.

A vault door opened with the squeal of gears and Marc set off into a small room with a single box in the center. He waited for the door to close behind him, then ran a small data line from the case to the box.

Lights flashed across the box and a holo menu appeared on the top side. Marc ran his finger down a long list and stopped one space below the last entry. He double-tapped and a hidden field blinked twice.

He stepped backed and waited. And waited. Frost crept out from where his feet touched the floor.

A lens flared to life and a holo of a gaunt, sunken-eyed President Garret appeared in front of Marc.

"Finally!" Garret reached for Marc's arms, but his grip passed through the metal man. "We've been trying to reach you for hours. Earth is under assault. We need your help. Now!"

"Wait. What? I thought you just sent a fleet to the Kesaht home world to end this whole thing."

"We lost contact." Garret pulled a small bottle from a pocket and twisted the top off. He swiped at someone as they reached for his pills. He stuffed two into his mouth and chewed hard. "The attack failed. All ships lost. What can you send to help?"

"What do you mean 'the attack failed'? That was the bulk of your reserves. If that's lost, then how are you going to stop—"

"I don't give a damn about stopping anything but the mass drivers the Vishrakath and the Kesaht are slamming into my planets!" Garret swallowed and wiped a sleeve across his mouth. "Iapetus is gone. Our macro cannons aren't going to last much longer, and Mars is about to fall. We need you, Ibarra. We need your help, god damn it. Do you know how many lives have been lost? I don't want to surrender Earth, but I may not have a choice."

"I don't…" He looked around the small room. "I don't exactly have the keys to a fleet on me."

"Then get Stacey!"

"She's away. Which is why I called you in the first place. I can send her a message, but I'm not exactly much of an influence on her these days. If you can get word to her, with the same intensity and near-panic—okay, total panic—she might be convinced to help you."

"You got me out of the situation room for this?" Garret's left eye twitched. "Some hope is better than none. Where is she?"

"Nekara," Marc said. "You can reach it through the Keystone at—"

A button on the quantum box pressed down of its own accord and Garret vanished. The button snapped up and the matte case went flying into the wall.

Air behind the box wavered then peeled away to reveal a legionnaire in combat fatigues and a pack on one hip. He held a gauss carbine trained on Marc's chest.

"How…long have you been there?" Marc backed up to the vault door.

"Many hours," Medvedev said. "I activated the Karigole cloak as soon as we realized you were on your way here."

"I can explain." Marc held his palms up. "I…I'm just worried about our Lady and her expedition. I thought the Union could—"

Medvedev switched his carbine to high power and a dull whine filled the room.

"Okay, I'm not entirely sure what she'll find on Nekara, and if the Union could send some help, then—"

"Stop her?" Medvedev raised an eyebrow. "That's what you said to Garret."

"Context!" Marc grabbed the vault handle and flipped it up, but the door didn't move. "I'll explain everything to our Lady as soon as she gets back. Let's just forget all this and you can go back to hiding in the corner, yeah?"

"The Lady left specific instructions for what to do if you tried anything." Medvedev put a finger on the trigger.

"You can't shoot me with that! What…what if you miss? The bullet will bounce all over and then you'd be in a world of trouble. I'm looking out for your welfare, so I'll just be go—"

Medvedev fired a single round that hit Marc in the stomach. Cracks broke through his body and it collapsed into a pile of shards like a shattered window. The legionnaire went to the remains and nudged the toe of his boot through the pile.

****

Admiral Valdar of the Terran Union Navy sat on the bunk of his Ibarra Nation prison cell, feet off the floor and tucked under his knees. He pulled a thin blanket tighter around his shoulders and shivered as his breath fogged. Ice clumped in his beard and tiny specks of frozen condensation clung to his eyelashes.

Freezing to death, he realized, was a horrible way to die.

In the other cell, a plastic box sat on the floor was encased in ice, where the guards had delivered it without a word to Valdar. Whatever was inside had sucked all the heat out of the cells within minutes.

Valdar's teeth chattered and he realized all feeling had leeched from his face. He didn't call out for help; he. He wouldn't give his captors the honor of hearing him beg.

A chrome arm shot out of the box, sending shards of ice bouncing off the bars.

Valdar reeled back against the wall, watching as a

jagged figure emerged from the box. Ice cracked and fell from the rest of the body as it stumbled into the bars between the two cells. The ice man wiped his hands over his face, smoothing it out into features that Valdar recognized.

"Oh, hi, Marc."

Ibarra shook his head from side to side quickly, then flicked loose bits of ice from off his body.

"Here again, fine. Fine. I've been in worse places…Valdar?" Marc cocked one eye to the admiral.

"C-C-Can you do something about the cold?"

"I'm good as new." Marc tapped his chest with a clink. "These Qa'resh ambassador bodies run off ambient heat. Ingenious; never need something so banal as food or electricity to—are you freezing to death? So sorry. The temp should regulate itself as soon as…"

Marc looked up at the lights.

"As soon as!"

There was a whoosh as hot air came through the vents.

"Service here is awful," Marc said. "How's the food? Not that I care, but you deserve better than white bread and hot dogs."

Valdar scrubbed his beard and brushed out ice.

"What did you do?" the admiral asked. "We had

intelligence you were in and out of favor with Stacey. You seem to be back on the outs."

"I may have committed some light…treason. Again." Marc bumped his fists against each other with the faint ring of a bell. With one hand clenched on top of the other, two fingers popped out at odd angles. The fingers moved to new angles. Then to a third. Then back to the first.

Valdar, a blue Navy sailor in his early career, recognized the semaphore signals.

N-O-D.

Valdar nodded.

"I'm so glad you're finally here, Valdar. We never really had the chance for a real heart to heart. What with you hiding out on the *Breitenfeld* around Saturn while I was working to help the Union before our little spat over the Hale Treaty." Marc leaned forward, shielding his hands beneath his chest from the watchful eyes in the lights. His signaled a new message, one at odds with his words. "I'm going to tell you exactly how stupid the Terran Union is and I'll start with President Garret."

Valdar kept his eyes on Marc's hands, taking in the silver man's real message one letter at a time.

Chapter 19

A jump gate opened near the Lagrange point beyond the dark side of Luna. The Toth dreadnought, *Last Light*, slipped into the Solar System and her engines flared to life. The massive plumes of plasma fire scored Kesaht klaw ships emerging behind the miles-long vessel.

Bale perched atop the command throne of the ship's bridge, his claws scratching at gold-weave carpets around him.

"Faster! Faster! Before they fire their macro cannons!" the overlord shouted.

"We'll be in the dead zone in just a few more minutes," Tomenakai said. "We could reduce our acceleration. It would stop damaging the support fleet we—"

"But Lord Bale's safety is paramount," said Charadon, a Toth warrior with scales white with age. He swiped at the Ixio, who slunk away from the angry Toth.

"Access the Crucible gate over Ceres," Bale said. "Send a message to the Vishrakath assaulting Mars. I wish to speak with our allies." He nudged a limp corpse at the foot of his throne. Kricks had proven more forthcoming with Vishrakath battle plans and communication codes once Bale had consumed his mind.

"Yes, master," Charadon hissed and used his tail to whack a menial on the back of its head.

A holo globe projected out of Bale's throne and a bloated Vishrakath queen in a fog of green smoke appeared.

"Bale? Your assault is four hours late. My brood has lost nearly fifty vessels!"

"Mother Gale Sting, I presume?" Bale asked.

The queen scratched stunted forelimbs against her mandibles.

"How do you even know my brood call? That is not for lesser species." Venom dripped from her mouth and Bale realized she was particularly angry.

Bale tapped a claw tip against Krick's sunken cranium. He was glad the cameras didn't show the envoy's fate.

"I have my means, brood mother. My fleet will take close anchorage over...Fermi City, a densely populated section of Luna. The humans lack the will to sacrifice those lives to a miss from their macro cannons. My ships will clear a corridor for my *Last Light* to orbit to the Earth-facing side...and then bombardment will begin. When will you neutralize Mars? I did give you a head start."

"You let us lead the assault and we took the full brunt of the Union's counterattack," Gale Sting said.

"And now Earth is nearly defenseless. You served as excellent bait."

The brood mother hissed and spat curses that didn't match any translation protocol.

"Incoming fire detected," Charadon said.

"Do hurry, insect," Bale said. "Just remember to stop shooting mass drivers once they surrender. No point in killing off potential slaves or ruining a habitable planet more than necessary." He cut the transmission. "Any danger to me?" Bale asked.

"This is the last of the grand ships," Charadon said. "Her capabilities are still a surprise for the meat. Macro shells are intersecting in space around the jump gate...We are clear."

"And the Kesaht ships?" Tomenakai's hands

whipped through a data globe. "The...the portal opened in the wrong spot. Our fleet will be at the mercy of their cannons for nearly fifteen minutes."

In the globe, a straight line cut through the Kesaht fleet, annihilating two cruisers and damaging more ships as a macro shell ripped through the hulls like a bullet through glass.

"Acceptable," Bale said. "Tomenakai, order the Klaw ships and Crescent fighters to scour Luna's and Ceres's surface of all weapon batteries. Raid leader, keep us close to Fermi City and have our shields up. I do hope the Union decides to break their own rule about civilian casualties. To see a shell bounce off our shields and impact the city...ah, to know the look on their faces."

"Yes, master," Charadon said.

"The rest of our ships?" Tomenakai asked.

"Have any that survive form a perimeter around my ship," Bale said.

Tomenakai was silent as he issued orders. A few minutes later, the Ixio studied a real time projection of Earth, then ripped his gaze away from the Kesaht fleet as it was savaged by macro shells.

"My Lord Bale, you said the human world was desolated. Worse than Kesaht'ka, destroyed by human cruelty, and that is why they came for your home...why they annihilated your people."

"I did?" Bale asked. "I mean, of course I did. Don't be fooled. To set foot on that planet is a death wish. We'll remove every human we can…for their own good. Raid Leader, prepare a culling force, just like the old days. I want true born humans, Trinia gave us the genetic markers to look for. I want a thousand to feast on soon as Earth surrenders. Last time I ate this well was when things got out of hand with the Karigole." His tendrils twitched, anticipating an epic meal.

"'Ate'? Lord Bale?" Tomenakai glance between the Toth over lord and the data globe as more Kesaht ships died to Union guns. "I thought what happened in the war room was some sort of…sort of…"

"Oh that," Bale's claws snapped with annoyance. "Stress eating. It does happen when I get a bit peckish. I was going to reveal that particular aspect of my existence to the Risen…eventually. A necessary evil due to human treachery. Well, that's a lie. Toth upper castes have lived like this for so many centuries."

Tomenakai touched a control panel below the data globe and keyed in a command. He opened a synaptic link from his Risen crystals to the Crucible and dropped the disruption field around Kesaht'ka.

"And your fellow Ixio, I was a bit rushed when I

tasted his meat," Bale's feeder arm snapped out from under his tank. "I would like to savor that one more time."

Tomenakai ducked under Charadon's grab and ran for the doors. A Toth warrior levelled a crystal pole-axe at him as more moved to block the Ixio's escape. Tomenakai ran faster, and impaled himself against the spike at the tip of the warrior's weapon.

It wasn't the first time he'd died, but hearing Bale curse out his warriors did lessen some of the sting as his brain died and his mind broadcast to the Crucible and back to Kesaht'ka.

Chapter 20

Major Aiza of the Ibarran Legion shuffled his feet in the Nekara dust as Sergeant Jaso finished burying a sensor. A fog had rolled in, leaving the crucified as looming shadows all around them.

The rest of his team formed a loose perimeter as the sergeant worked.

"I don't like this place," Saunders said. "Ghosts are watching us."

"We've done archaeotech grabs before," Aiza said. "You've been in…unusual places before."

"Not someplace haunted." Saunders flicked a thumb against his gauss rifle's safety.

"I swear these dead are watching us," Maddinger said, motioning to a corpse hanging from an X. "How long they been here? Shouldn't they have rotted away by now?"

"Jaso, are you done with painting the Sistine Chapel on that sensor by now?" Aiza asked.

"Motion detectors keep giving me an error message," Jaso said. "There's some sort of constant vibration throwing off the calibrations. Like we're on top of buried utility cables or something."

"The marshal wants a trip wire to tell him if anything moves out here, not excuses." Aiza felt sweat run down the back of his neck. Even in temperature-controlled power armor, the stress was getting to him.

"There." Jaso tapped his forearm screen. "Getting a reading from Ivey and Weber on the perimeter."

"What're you talking about?" Ivey said from behind Jaso. He jerked a thumb at Weber. "We're right here."

"Then…" Jaso did a double take at his screen and scrambled to his feet. He flipped his gauss rifle off his back and charged it to high power.

"Pull in, close perimeter," Aiza said. He put his back to the rest of his team as they drew back to the sensor. He opened a channel. "Ground command, team seven has…I've got static. Weber, get me a link."

The team commo specialist hit a button on his belt and an antenna extended out of the back of his armor.

A rattle rose through the fog like a snake's warning.

"There!" Jaso pointed at a shadow as it flit between the crucified.

"Some sort of an animal?" Ivey asked.

"Sounds good to me," Aiza said. "No first contact bull with an animal. You see it, you shoot—"

There was a rush of air like an arrow passing and a crack.

Weber let out a cry and Aiza turned to see him being dragged into the fog by a black stalk bristling with spikes. Weber vanished into the fog and his screams cut out with the crunch of breaking power armor.

"Light it up!" Aiza fired from the hip and sparks flew as gauss bullets hit a cross in the fog.

"Stop—stop moving." Jaso looked at his forearm screen and shot a hand to his right. The legionnaires opened fire.

Aiza checked the compass built into his visor and set a bearing back to the Ark.

"Fall back," he ordered. "Conserve ammo or we'll—"

A shadow flashed across his eyes and blood splattered against his visor. He wiped it away and saw Ivey and Maddinger standing still, arms lowering their rifles.

"Move, move, legion!" Aiza nudged Ivey and his head fell off, blood spurted out of neatly severed arteries, and his corpse wobbled on its feet.

Maddinger slid apart, cut from shoulder to hip.

"Jaso?" Aiza heard the sergeant screaming in the fog. He whirled around, utterly alone. He shifted his weight forward to run, but something grabbed him by the shoulder.

A dead alien on a cross had one hand on him, its eyes dead and face slack.

Aiza shrugged hard and ripped the corpse's arm out of the socket. Dust fell out of the tear like sand down an hourglass. Terror overwhelmed his training, and he dropped his weapon as he backed away, eyes locked on the dead alien as it lurched at him, one hand still bound to the cross.

His heels bumped against something and he tripped back, landing flat on his back. Weights slammed down on his forearms, cracking the armor as they pinned him to the ground. Two long, spiked tendrils held him firm.

Aiza fought, but he could manage little more than thrashing his legs and bumping his head against the ground.

The rattle grew louder and Aiza froze as a thickset

jaw moved into his vision. The creature looked down at him, silver eye slits set deep in a wide onyx skull. Triangular teeth jutted from the jaw, some dripping red with human blood.

It leered closer to Aiza's face, and the eyes flashed.

The stalks on his arms wrapped around his wrists and the creature bolted away, dragging the screaming legionnaire behind.

****

Seru regarded the human splayed out in front of her, his limbs stretched to an X by ropes of tightly woven cubes. She stood half again as tall as Major Aiza, now stripped of his power armor.

"What a disappointment to find flesh beneath your exquisite exterior." She bowed slightly and lifted his chin with sharp fingers. "Do you cling to your rotting shell because you choose weakness, or because the curse this—" she prodded his chest, drawing points of blood "—is all the prophet will allow you? Perhaps you're unworthy. Are you fodder or is the prophet the only one that's transcended? So many questions…"

Seru gripped Aiza's face and turned it up to hers.

His eyes widened, alive with fear.

His jaw tried to open, but she held it shut.

Seru released him, her face contorting as he spoke.

"*Kallen, ferrum corde...*"

"No time for this. No time to wait and test your answers for truth." Seru went to a wall made up of the same linked cube strands, each the width of Aiza's arm. The strands flexed against each other, and a gap opened. A glowing cube a half-inch across floated out and Seru plucked it from the air.

"No time...so we have something special." Her mouth pulled into a smile, revealing clenched and pointed teeth. "We reserved the theosar for the best of our culture. The most loyal. Transcendence without the loss of higher functions. Don't worry...your soul will still join with Malal. One day."

She set the cube a few inches in front of Aiza's forehead and it levitated when she released it.

"The sensation is extraordinary, but worth it in the end. Trust me." Seru's lips mimed a blown kiss, but Aiza felt nothing.

The cube floated toward his face and he tried to look away.

"Noooo," Seru grabbed his chin and turned him to the cube.

It hit his skin with a hiss and Aiza went into convulsions. The light spread through his face as it melded into his flesh. He gagged and became rigid. His face froze in a silent scream and his flesh turned dark gray. Circuit-like lines spread from the cube, running through his eyes and down his veins.

Aiza collapsed, chin lolling against his chest. The strands let him go and he flopped to the floor.

"Oh dear, I do hope you're not permanently broken." Seru crouched down, face close to the ground.

Aiza flipped to his back, mouth locked open. He sat bolt upright and his hands went to his throat. His skin had gone dark gray, the lines of circuitry shining.

"You don't need to breathe anymore." Seru's eyes flashed. "We've transformed your worthless flesh into living metal. You'll thank me soon enough. We brought our entire race to greatness…some more willingly than others. Now…whom do you serve?"

Aiza stood, body rising like strings were guiding him.

"I am Major—"

Seru jabbed fingernails into the top of his head and motes of light flowed through her hand and into Aiza. The Ibarran's eyes filled with white.

"Such a strong will, but that can be torn

away…Now, whom do you serve?"

"My soul for Malal," Aiza rasped.

"Very good. Very good. Now come with me, thrall. You'll tell me all there is about the prophet, the Ibarrans, and the entire rest of the galaxy. Tell me, how many races need Malal's grace?"

****

Marshal Davoust bounded up the metal stairs of the barricade Ibarran pioneers had assembled around the Ark. Aides loaded down with communication gear followed him, along with the biggest, meanest legionnaire bodyguards the procedural tubes on Navarre could put out. More than once, the marshal thought Lady Ibarra should've restarted the doughboy program, but she had little interest in having the Nation's fighting done by such simple constructs.

"What is it?" he asked a soldier on the battlements.

"Reports of movement out there." The legionnaire said, motioning his rifle toward the fog. "But we're not picking anything up on optics."

"Could be our sensor teams?" He glanced at a

clock displayed on the inside of his visor. "They're due back. Status?"

An aide with a small forest of radio antennae on her back shook her head.

"None have reported back in," she said.

"You hear that?" the legionnaire asked. "Coming from out there…sounds like a bag of dirt hitting the ground."

Davoust turned up his audio receptors and the soldier was right…irregular thumps from the surrounding crosses. Then the sound of shuffling feet.

"Armor to me." He slapped his thigh to get his staff's attention.

A faint tremor caused pebbles to shimmy across the ground.

"Is it the Ark?" Davoust looked up the pearl hull and frowned.

"Down!" a bodyguard shouted and Davoust was shoved off the battlements. A black streak ripped through the top of the defenses, killing the legionnaire and knocking his staff off like bowling pins.

The scythe dug its claws into the dirt as it slid to a stop. A giant panther's body with a blunt dragon's snout. A pair of thick, spiked stalks bent out of its back like double scorpion tails. It looked right at Davoust, silver eyes gleaming as it hunched back to pounce.

It leapt at him, claws raked down…and missed his face by inches, slamming into the ground.

The scythe snapped its head up and back, staring at the red Armor holding it by the tail. The Uhlan jerked it back and it twisted in midair, grasping at the Uhlan with all four limbs. The Armor caught it by the neck with his gauss cannon arm. Double barrels blasted up and out the scythe's back, blowing dry bits of its body that landed around Davoust like old corn husks blown by the wind.

The Uhlan slammed the scythe into the Ark's hull, and it went into convulsions like it had touched a live wire. It slipped out of the Armor's grasp and slashed its tail at the Armor's helm.

The Uhlan caught the blow with his forearm and the tail wrapped around his arm. The Uhlan slammed a foot against the scythe's flank and ripped its tail clean off. The monster showed no sign of pain as it pounced toward him, catching a hooked fist to the side of the face that sent it to the ground. The Uhlan stomped its head, crushing it. He ground his heel from side to side and the scythe went limp. Steam flowed out of its body and it seemed to deflate, then disintegrate into tiny cubes.

A bodyguard lifted Davoust up to his feet. Only then did he hear the gauss fire.

The Uhlan banged a fist to his chest and walked up to the barricade. His rotary cannon spun to life and opened fire.

The marshal grabbed a bar jutting out from the wreckage that marked the scythe's passage and pulled himself up.

Figures shuffled out of the fog, heads hung low and shoulders hunched. He zoomed in and saw they were the same bodies that had been crucified.

Scythes loped through the crowd, closing like a wolf chasing down prey. Gauss cannon shots from armor knocked them back, and the scythes retreated back into the mist.

"Air support." Davoust called, drawing a pistol from his holster and put the other hand against the small of his back as he took careful aim at the oncoming horde. He made three shots, each exploding craniums at over a hundred yards.

One of his bodyguards glanced at the marshal, and then at the optics on the guard's own rifle.

"Orbital, engage final protective fire," Davoust said through his quantum-dot connection to the commander of the *Gilcrest*, a strike carrier in orbit directly overhead.

"Shrikes vectored," the captain replied. *"Go for rail*

cannon bombardment?"

"Stop asking and start shooting. Judicious aim is appreciated." He ejected his pistol magazine and slapped in a fresh one and resumed his firing stance.

Saint Kallen, return our Armor with the Lady's salvation…soon, please, he prayed and opened fire.

Chapter 21

"And that's why we never should have let soccer come back from the dead." Marc cocked his head to one side, his blank expression focused on Valdar.

The admiral put one hand to his temple, wobbled from side to side, then collapsed to the floor.

"Really? You're going to pass out to keep from talking to me?" Marc whacked the bars with the back of one hand. "Valdar? Come on, man, get up. Valdar?"

He grabbed the bars and gave them a quick shake. Marc looked up at the lights and waved.

"Hey! Tweedle Dumb and Tweedle Dip Shit, got a man down in here! Maybe you should've kept the heat on while I was recovering from a gauss shot. Get in here before I have to explain to Lady Ibarra why you let the hero of the Ember War die while you sat there with your thumbs up your—"

The cell block door burst open and three guards entered. Two in simple fatigues, Medvedev with his gauss carbine behind them. Marc raised his hands and backed up as the legionnaire drew down on him.

The other two guards hurried into Valdar's cell. One keyed a mic attached to his uniform and spoke Basque, then leaned over the admiral and put two fingers to Valdar's neck.

"Pulse is fine." The guard said, looking over his shoulder to the other.

Valdar's hand snapped up and grabbed the mic.

"Florence. Sigma. 4-6-1!" Valdar shouted.

The three Ibarrans went soft-eyed and Medvedev dropped his weapon.

"Give me a second." Marc put his hands over his face and his body shrank several inches.

Valdar poked the nearest guard in the face.

"What did I do to them?" he asked.

"One…second." Marc's voice fluctuated several octaves.

Valdar got to his feet and went for the pistol still holstered in the guard's belt.

"No," a woman said and Valdar stopped. Stacey

Ibarra looked up from Marc's hands, her nose tilted to one side. "No, let me take it from here," Marc said in his granddaughter's voice.

Valdar tapped the bridge of his nose and "Stacey" snapped "hers" into place. Marc wagged fingers at the guards' mic. Valdar held the key down.

"Dawning. Yellow. Rochefort," Marc said as Stacey.

The guards snapped back like a switch had been thrown. The one in the cell door put his hand on his pistol grip.

"The prisoner will—"

"That's no prisoner," 'Stacey' said. "That is Admiral Valdar of the Ibarra Navy."

"My Lady?" Medvedev picked up his gauss carbine. "How…why are you—"

"Seize him!" 'Stacey' pointed at Medvedev and a guard slapped the weapon out of the legionnaire's hands. Medvedev started to protest, but a shock baton to the ribs sent him to the floor.

"He is a traitor." 'Stacey' shot a finger to Valdar's bunk. "Put him in that cell and keep the privacy filters on. Don't believe a single word he says. Now let me and Valdar out; we have to deal with that scoundrel Marc Ibarra's vile treachery."

"Yes, my Lady." A guard dragged a groaning Medvedev into Valdar's cell.

"Kick him," 'Stacey' commanded and there was a thump of boot against flesh. "Harder. Okay, that's enough. Come, Valdar. We've much to do now that you're on Team Ibarra."

Valdar took a tentative step out of the cell.

"Guards, I need your data slates," 'Stacey' said and took the devices from both men. "Stay here for an hour with the privacy filters up. That one's rascally. Can't have him get away."

"Yes, my Lady," the guards said together.

Marc motioned for Valdar to follow him and the two left the cell block.

"What the hell is going on?" Valdar asked as Marc tapped out commands on the slates. The admiral followed the disguised Ibarra as they went past several elevator doors.

"We have a number of subconscious commands in our procedurals," Marc said. His Stacey disguise grew several inches, but he shrank back down once he saw his reflection on a door. "You triggered a fugue state, made them highly susceptible to commands for a few minutes. All the guards on that mic's network are now laser-focused on the knuckle dragger. They won't respond to anything but your command to watch him for hours. Buys us all the time we need."

"If you can do that, why the hell did you leave Stacey in charge for so long?"

"I'm not the top lobster of this hierarchy, Valdar, and Stacey is no fool. That word combination triggered several fail safes throughout Navarre's network—this elevator—which means she was just waiting for me to try and use it. The entire commo grid just went down, her way of stopping me from messing with more of the Nation's head. Which works out in our favor."

Marc stepped into an elevator and slumped against the wall when the doors closed. He reverted back to his normal form, that of an older gentleman clad in chrome.

"Uh…that's exhausting. These ambassador bodies match self-image. It takes a good deal of concentration to keep up."

"Ibarra, we're out of our cells, but now what?" Valdar watched as floor numbers ticked higher on the elevator consol.

"You're a what? Forty-five chest? Size ten shoes?" Ibarra's brow furrowed as he tapped on a slate.

"My crew." Valdar tried to grab the slate, but Marc slapped his hand away. "The rest of the sailors from the *Breitenfeld*. What about them? I'm not leaving without them."

"I'm good, Valdar, but I'm not that good. The rest of your people are on Zelara, not even in this system. Let's worry about saving Earth from the Kesaht and the Vishrakath first, yeah?"

"How are we going to—"

"Go time." Marc said, shifting back into Stacey. "Act in charge."

The elevator came to a stop and the doors opened, revealing a half dozen Ibarran legionnaires in full power armor. One handed a plastic case to Valdar, took a step back, and beat a fist to his chest in salute.

"Is my shuttle ready?" Marc asked in Stacey's voice.

"Yes, my Lady." A legionnaire stepped to the side and motioned to a small shuttle idling at the edge of a hangar. "We're unable to contact your honor guard for escort. The network is off-line for some reason. Shall we—"

"Not necessary." 'Stacey' strode forward, catching Valdar flat-footed. "Admiral Valdar and I have a mission that is vital to our Nation. Double top secret. Not a word of this to anyone. In fact, you never saw us. Understand?"

The legionnaire looked to his fellows and said, "Saw who?"

"Exactly. Come on, Valdar. You can change on the way." 'Stacey' got into the passenger compartment of the small shuttle. "Take us to the *Yalta*," she told the pilot and activated the privacy screen and shut out the cockpit.

Valdar sat in the only other passenger seat and opened the box. He lifted up an Ibarra Navy uniform as the shuttle buttoned up and took off. The afterburner engaged and pressed him to the back of his seat.

"You can't be serious." Valdar touched the admiral's insignia on the collar.

"Every sailor in the Ibarra Navy reveres you as a hero," Marc said. "Taking orders from you will be an honor. You know how to drive ships and fight space battles, not me. You also have a number of access codes that'll get us to the fight faster. Hurry up and change. No time to be bashful."

Valdar unzipped the top of his dirty and worn Terran Union jumpsuit.

"Semaphore?" He raised an eyebrow at Marc.

"We're old farts, Valdar. We didn't teach our procedurals to signal each other with flags. I figured you might remember your blue water Navy days. Good thing you did, otherwise, my charades were going to be a bit too obvious for the guards not to notice."

Valdar shrugged his shoulders out of his jumpsuit.

"What'll we do when we get to the *Yalta*?" he asked.

"Just follow my lead."

"You have a plan?"

"Yes. Mostly. More of a vague idea that I'm making up as we go along."

Valdar stopped changing and gave Marc a hard look.

"I got us this far, didn't I?"

Valdar grumbled and put on his new uniform.

****

"Admiral on the bridge!" an armsman announced as Valdar, wearing a full Ibarran uniform, stepped off a lift, a short female legionnaire in power armor behind him.

Captain Zahar of the *Yalta* sprang to his feet and stepped away from his command chair.

"Valdar?" Zahar reached for his forearm screen but stopped when "Stacey" Ibarra removed her helmet.

"He's with us now," Marc said. "Take all orders from him, Zahar. I need you and your fleet to make ready for a Crucible gate jump."

"Of course." Zahar touched his lips. "It's just

that…we're the ready reserve…for your mission to Nekara."

"All a brilliant ruse of my own design," Marc said. "I'll explain it all in good time."

There was an awkward pause and Marc gave Valdar a tap to his lower back.

"Captain, set the fleet to pilum formation and ready boosters. Bring this ship to the fore and get us through the Crucible," Valdar said. "Open a channel to gate command from my holo tank."

"Aye aye." Zahar nodded and turned away, then began issuing rapid fire orders to the bridge crew.

Marc put his helmet back on and went with Valdar to a lit holo table. Valdar touched panels, trying to familiarize himself with the layout.

"Ibarran ships aren't that different than Union," Marc said. "Though our sailors are more likely to swear in Basque."

"Is that why I can't read any of the displays?" Valdar frowned.

"I'll fix that." Marc tapped on a screen and the language switched to English.

"*Yalta* is a battleship…more rail batteries than the *Missouri*-class I've done maneuvers with." Valdar swiped through ship icons in the tank as the fleet re-formed into a long spear formation with the *Yalta* at the front. "Two strike carriers...not a lot of fighters. Cruiser and frigate heavy compared to a Union task force."

"Is there a problem?" Marc asked as he brought up a display to one side of the tank and opened up a star chart.

"Commanding a fleet in battle isn't like driving a car, Ibarra—"

Marc cleared his voice and waved fingertips over his female visage.

"I mean...my Lady." Valdar had to force out the title. "Please give me a moment to familiarize myself with my new command."

Marc tapped two fingers to the side of his forehead then pointed at a new screen as it popped up in the tank in front of him. An elderly woman with short blonde hair canted her head slightly as she looked at Marc.

"Stacey?" Keeper asked. "Now is a hell of a time to—"

Marc touched the screen on one side and swiped it to Valdar.

"Keeper, this is Admiral Valdar of," he took a quick breath, "the Ibarran Navy. I understand you could use some cavalry."

"Wait. No. Valdar would never do that," Keeper

said.

"I didn't."

"No, he didn't," Marc said.

"But you just said that—" Keeper flinched as light from an explosion flashed across her head and shoulders.

"I know what we said." Marc's fingers tapped furiously on a panel and a text message popped up on Keeper's screen. "But what we said is not what we're saying. If you know what I say."

Keeper's brow furrowed as she read the text.

"You two are insane," she said.

"Clear us for Ceres gate transfer and we'll join the fight over Earth," Valdar said.

"No, not Earth. I need you on Mars," Keeper said. "The Vishrakath have the planet blockaded. I need those macro cannons back online and intercepting mass drivers on course to Earth."

A situation map over the Solar System came up in the holo tank.

"But Earth—" Valdar gripped the handrails tight as he took in the current state of the battle.

"The main force of the Kesaht armada is still out of range," Keeper said. "We can hold the line long enough for you to get Mars back into the larger fight. We are hours from losing cities to a mass driver strike. Millions of lives,

Valdar. I need you to save civilians. We'll lose soldiers and sailors…but that's the choice we have to make."

"That's the right call, Keeper." Valdar touched the mass of Vishrakath asteroid ships arrayed around Mars. He double-tapped a massive ship nearly the size of Deimos. "There's the hive queen. Can you get us to cross their T?"

"How close?" Keeper asked.

"Close enough for a knife fight," Valdar said.

"The firepower on that ship is—"

"Can you do it or not?" Valdar snapped.

"For you…yes. But the margin of error on a maneuver like that is extreme. Even for something this desperate. You want to blow them to hell, not smash into them face-first."

"I'm glad my intent is clear," Valdar said.

"I can give you a small jump window," she said. "Anything more and the enemy might try to piggyback off your jump."

"Thank you, Keeper."

"Godspeed, Admiral." The screen blinked off.

"You're going to *what?*" Marc asked.

"We don't have time to bring in your—our fleets on the far side of Navarre or your out system ships. Earth needs a miracle. Just wish I was aboard the *Breitenfeld* to deliver it," Valdar said.

"The *Yalta* is a fine ship," Captain Zahar said, "and our crew is second to none. We're honored to have you aboard, sir."

The corner of Valdar's lip tugged to one side.

"I'm sure this ship and her crew will distinguish themselves," Valdar said.

"Perhaps…a fleet-wide address?" Zahar asked. "Our inter-ship comms are unaffected by the shutdown. To escort you and the Lady into battle is…a fine moment for us."

Valdar looked back at Marc.

"My presence is to be kept secret," Marc said. "Can't highlight this ship for enemy attack, can we?"

"No, my Lady." Zahar put a hand over his heart. "Admiral, this may be the last best time to speak to your sailors…perhaps explain the mission." He held out a small comm link.

Valdar took it and pressed a small button. A bosun's whistle piped a general call and a red light pulsed on the comm link.

"Ships of the…" Valdar glanced at Zahar who held up several fingers, "Fifth Fleet, this is Admiral Valdar. This is not the mission you expected, but it is vital. Earth is under threat. The Kesaht and Vishrakath have the system under siege and our home world—Ibarran or

Terran Union; we came from Earth—has hours before the defenses crumble and millions die to bombardment. No matter the differences between us—we are all still human. And to save lives is far nobler than rigid obedience to the patch on a uniform or the colors on a flag. We will break the aliens over Mars, then we will chase down the remnants and teach the rest of the galaxy that Earth and the Ibarra Nation will unite against a common foe. The *Breitenfeld* does not fight beside us this day, but may God still be with us. *Gott mit uns.*"

Valdar keyed the link off and turned back to Ibarra, who gave him a tepid thumbs-up.

"Captain," Valdar said, "order all rail cannons loaded and charged. Gunnery officers are to fire at will on the Vishrakath hive ship until instructed otherwise. Volume of fire is more important than accuracy."

"Exactly how close will we be to the target?" Zahar asked.

"We may trade paint." Valdar removed his void helmet from off his belt and put it on. "Ready ship for combat conditions."

"Aye aye." Zahar turned to the bridge crew. "Sound zero atmo alert and set combat condition one."

Through the forward windows, rail cannon batteries angled up from the hull, vanes crackling with electricity as the ship bore down on the Crucible.

Valdar went back to the holo tank and watched as ready icons sprang up across the Ibarran fleet.

"This'll work?" Marc asked.

"Or we'll die trying."

Chapter 22

Tomenakai tried to scream, but his mouth was full of fluid. He beat against glass walls of a narrow tank holding his body. He struggled to sit up, but his limbs seemed to have a lengthy latency between his attempts to move and their response.

Hands pulled him upright, and electric blue fluid dripped off his face. He felt the tug of cables against the back of his skull. The flesh of his new clone body was raw and puffy.

"Stop!" Another Ixio cupped his face with her hands. "Stop all this squirming or you'll ruin your new synaptic pathways. You've gone through this before."

"Bale…Bale has gone mad." His mouth was numb, but his tongue felt fat. "The other Ixio, the grand council on the Star Fort…"

"So tragic to have so many Risen killed at once," the female said. "None have recompiled yet. The buffers overloaded when the humans—"

"Wasn't the humans." Tomenakai leaned against the side of the tank and grabbed the nurse by the neck. "Who are you?"

"Rillia, second class reanimation—"

"Give me…give me your communicator." He reached for the ring at the top of her long neck, but his strength gave out.

Rillia took hers off and snapped it onto Tomenakai's neck. He tapped at holo keys and opened a channel to a Sanheel he trusted, then he opened monitoring channels to all the rest he found on the network.

"Tomenakai." Admiral Garvan appeared, projected directly onto the Ixio's retina by the communicator, tugging at his tusks. "If you're here, then…is Lord Bale uninjured? Victorious? We'll have the humans dead by—"

"No," Tomenakai said. "Don't call Bale 'lord' ever again."

"That's sacrilege." Garvan's thick lips pulled into a frown. "Another Sanheel would rip your Risen implants out for that."

"Listen...just listen." Tomenakai laid out everything from Bale devouring a Risen Ixio's mind to ordering the murder of the others aboard the star fort and the Toth's actions on Earth.

Garvan, to his credit, didn't interrupt.

"Impossible," the Sanheel said. "Lord Bale would never do that to us. He saved the Kesaht. Gave us the Risen technology and—"

"It's all true, Garvan. Once the rest of the Ixio reload into their clones, they'll tell you the exact same thing."

A new Sanheel broke through the link, High General Braxis.

"Lies!" he shouted. "The humans have set foot on our sacred soil, and I will not believe some Ixio that would have me abandon my holy duty."

"Braxis, the Ixio and Sanheel are one." Tomenakai's head drooped as he spoke, his strength fading. "Kesaht unity...was from before Bale. Don't go back to the old ways."

"I command the forces defending Hegemony Dome," Braxis said. "I will kill every last human at our gate and set their heads on pikes as tribute to Bale. You...you, I will keep alive so he can punish you himself."

More Sanheel broke through, shouting. Tomenakai wobbled and sank back into the tank, his ears full of discordant voices.

Rillia removed the communicator ring and Tomenakai slipped to sleep.

Chapter 23

Gideon's Armor sat on a crate, hunched over and back plating splayed open. Trinia, field expedient goggles made from a cut down Eagle canopy, worked an arc welder against the captain's inner womb.

Ranger Colonel Gutierrez held a small holo projector in his hand. The face of a helmeted woman in a Navy void suit floated between the two humans.

"That Kesaht battleship was the last cap ship to try a run on our lines," Admiral Ericson of the carrier *Normandy* said through the holo. "Klaw ships and their fighters are still harassing us, but my destroyer pickets hammer them every time they get in range."

"What are they waiting for?" Gideon asked. "If every Kesaht ship massed and tried to overwhelm what we've got left over Gold Beach, how long would we last?"

Ericson, a veteran of the Ember War and one-time executive officer of the fabled *Breitenfeld*, turned her head aside.

"I could buy you all an hour," she said. "If that."

"The Crucible gate dropped its disruption field," Gutierrez said. "Any chance we could make a run for it?"

"The bulk of their fleet's between us and the gate." Ericson shook her head. "Suicide. And we don't control a single command node in the gate. If any of our ships survived the gauntlet, which we won't, they could open a gate into a star just for the laughs."

"Word from home?" Gideon asked.

"Keep this close hold," Ericson said furtively. "Earth is under siege. Vishrakath over Earth. Kesaht making a slow orbit around Luna. It's only a matter of time until our defenses break and we start losing cities."

"God damn it." Gutierrez looked away.

"The Kesaht could stomp us out at will," Gideon said. "Why haven't they? They dropped the disruption field. Reinforcements could come for us from other Union systems."

"You don't know Bale." Trinia stood up, examining a charred piece of equipment. She tossed it at Gideon's feet. "He's vindictive. Cruel. The longer we're here, the longer we cling to hope. Once he forces Earth's surrender, or destroys it outright, he'll return and broadcast video of your planet in flames. When your spirit is broken, then he'll take your surrender…and feast on your sorrow."

"Sweet Lord." Gutierrez swallowed hard.

"Armor dies hard," Gideon said. "That—or victory—is the only way our battle ends."

"So we have…eight hours?" Ericson asked. "You ground pounders have a miracle in your pocket to take down dome shields? I could take the *Normandy* on a death ride. See if all engines burning on a collision course will get the job done. Worked with the *Ardennes* and the star fort."

"I sent our Pathfinders into the subway system under the city to try and find the tunnel network the enemy used to hit us before the last attack…None have reported back," the Strike Marine said.

"We got some telemetry data from our rail hits," Gideon said. "See if we can find something there we can use, some variance frequency we can hit and punch through. The shields some of the Sanheel and Toth use are vulnerable to staggered hits…"

"Give it to me," Trinia said, her head buried in Gideon's back. "Soon as I repair your stabilizers."

"That's something," Ericson said. "My crews are

holding, but I see the cracks. We need some good news, and soon."

"I need to walk the lines," Gutierrez said. "Can't have my Marines think I've forgotten about them."

"Go. I'll join soon as I can," Gideon said.

"Keep me up to date. I'll let you know when another crisis is on your way." Ericson's holo fizzled out.

Gutierrez slipped his helmet on and left the command center, a trio of bodyguards with him.

"You're lucky," Trinia said, motioning to the burnt-out bit of gear at his feet. "That component saved your life when the electro-spike breached your chest cavity."

"Do I need it?"

"No. It's not a system that I designed for your suit. I don't actually know what it does, but it was linked to your sensors and your neural input links," she said.

Gideon nudged it with his foot and flakes of ash fell away.

"Let me sew you back up." The Aeon slammed a panel shut. "While I have you here, I need a promise from you."

"Ask."

"My people...have customs. Even though I am the last of us, I cannot let our passage from life be marred by…sin, you would say. We do not end our lives by our own hands willfully. Ever. When the Kesaht come for us, if all is lost…" She hefted his rear plates shut and activated the mag locks. She rapped a tool against his Armor twice and Gideon stood up and faced her.

Trinia guided his hand up to her neck and put his fingers around her throat.

"They will enslave me. Force me to create abominations that will stain the stars for years and years. I want you to promise that will not happen."

"That's what you want? The end of hope?"

"Say you'll do it. Don't abandon me like the Ibarrans did."

Gideon pulled his hand back slightly then bent it into a fist.

"I'm not like them. If it needs to happen, it'll be quick."

Trinia closed her eyes and bowed slightly.

"Captain?" Cha'ril sent over IR. *"We need the Aeon. Santos is feeling weird."*

"Get your tools and follow me."

****

Gideon looked over the trench gouged out of the

dead city. Mechanics and supply soldiers in light armor worked to make the trenches just a little deeper, building dug outs to shelter artillery attacks, and brace the trench walls with bricks repurposed from crumbling buildings.

He thought back to the trench lines on Hawaii where he'd earned scars down his face from a Toth warrior. This battlefield was different. Back then, there'd been a decent chance of repelling the Toth assault. Here, on Kesaht'ka, everything they did reeked of desperation.

"It was *me*," Santos said as Trinia examined a data slate connected to his helm. Cha'ril was within earshot, her attention more on the No Man's Land beyond the trench. "I saw me and Trinia. And I felt…like I was supposed to help. It was like a vision or something."

"Stress," Gideon said. "This is the first time you've been plugged in and in a fight for so long."

"I don't think so, sir," Cha'ril said. "Gershwin and the rest of the Eisenritter lance experienced it too."

"But not you?" Gideon asked.

The Dotari shook her helm. "And not me."

"There's nothing here," Trinia said. "He scans normal."

"Sir…" Santos pulled the plug connected to her slate. "I heard rumors that…that sometimes Saint Kallen would appear to—"

"Don't." Gideon took a step toward him and leveled a knife hand at his chest. "Don't you dare. Lies and superstition. All of it. That 'saint' is just a pile of bones in a—"

Santos grabbed Gideon by the edge of his breastplate.

The captain looked down at the hand touching him, then back to Santos's helm.

"Behind you, sir," Santos said and released his hold.

Gideon turned around. A crowd of sailors, Rangers, and Strike Marines had gathered. All were on one knee, rifles held in one hand as they genuflected. One man, unarmed, stood with his head knelt in prayer. A chaplain.

"What is happening?" Trinia asked.

"We are Kallen's avatar," Santos said quietly. "Doesn't matter if I believe it or not. They do. It was…was her spirit that carried us through the final battle of the Ember War. Steeled the Armor on the Xaros world ship."

"Carius didn't need a Saint," Gideon said. "I knew him."

"Kallen was an *Iron* Heart," Santos said. "We are *Iron* Dragoons. The soldiers see her in us. Believer or not, morale is hurting. We need something, captain. They need hope. Where's the harm?"

"The harm is in joining a damn cult," Gideon said. "But you have a point about morale. Go on. Play icon."

Santos took a half-step forward, waiting to see if Gideon was serious. When the captain didn't stop him, he went over to the chaplain.

"Trinia." Gideon said, turning back to her and Cha'ril. "Does the Dotari …does it have that component that got fried by the Kesaht spear?"

"I can check." Trinia frowned and pulled the data line to bring the plug to her hand.

"Friendlies coming through!" came from down the trench line, echoing from defender to defender. The call for a medic followed a moment later.

Gideon went down the line, ignoring soldiers as they crossed themselves and reached out to tap his legs for luck.

A team of Strike Marines hurried out of the ruins to the trench, a litter carried between two of them. The Strike Marines were filthy, their power armor caked with dust and blood. They brought the litter up first, and defenders lowered it to a pair of waiting corpsmen.

The wounded was missing arms below the elbow and legs below the knee, a blood-stained bit of ripped cloth over where his jaw should've been.

"Aignar?" Gideon went to the edge of the trench and bent down. "Aignar, can you hear me?"

He raised a stump and waved it slightly.

"Low grad radiation poisoning." A Strike Marine Corpsman slid over the ramparts and put a hand on Aignar's shoulder. "We had to cut him out of his suit, but he's been responsive since then."

"Let's get him to the field hospital," another medic said and grabbed the litter handles.

"Booker, go," Lieutenant Hoffman said from the top of the trench and she grabbed the other set of handles without a word.

Hoffman crouched slightly and used his power armor's strength assist to jump across the gap and land next to Gideon. He removed his helm, hands shaking.

Gideon saw a pair of dog tags wrapped around the Strike Marine's hand.

"I thought Aignar was…well done, Marine," Gideon said.

"He'd…he'd better be worth it." Hoffman wiped the back of a hand across his mouth and put his helmet back on. The rest of his team followed him away from the trench, all but one, the tallest of the group, one with a scimitar sheathed on the small of his back.

"This city reeks of death." The tall one looked up

at Gideon, and he saw a scaly alien face within.

"We'll need you back on the line…when you're ready," Gideon said.

"Valdar's Hammer will be ready when the enemy comes." The alien beat a prosthetic fist to his chest and followed after his team.

"Is that a miracle?" Trinia asked from behind Gideon.

"Duty is duty," the captain replied. "We don't leave wounded behind. Aignar's just too tough to die."

"I did a scan on the Dotari's suit," she said. "She's missing component CD-999B. Santos has one installed." She tapped her data slate. "Yours was damaged, and I removed it."

Santos knelt as the group of defenders filed past him, each touching his Armor.

"It's…all a lie." Gideon's fists tightened so hard, the servos squealed.

"Are you going to challenge their faith?" she asked. "Now?"

Gideon didn't answer.

"Then I suggest you let it go. You're the ranking Armor. Don't you have a battle in the material world to worry about? Fight for the spirit now and what will you win?"

"You make too much sense," he growled.

"You pick up a few things over the centuries…"

"See to Aignar. See that he wasn't hurt too badly when they removed him from his womb." Gideon turned and made his way down the trench line.

She tapped the data slate against her thigh and sighed.

"Humans are always such a mess."

Chapter 24

Santos waited near Cha'ril as a tech with a bad limp and a bandage wrapped around her lower leg unfastened a power cable from the leads on the back of the Dotari's armor.

"What are you doing?" Cha'ril asked. "I'm at forty percent on my reserves."

The tech knocked on the battery stack.

"And this one's down to single digits. Our only field reactor went boom during the last strafing run. This unit's solar panels burned up in atmo. I charge you up for more than eight hours of sustained combat at a time and then I don't have—"

"I understand," Cha'ril said. "Santos. Your turn."

"No need." He tapped a shoulder where his rail gun vanes should've been. "I'm good for eight. No worry about me pulling deep for a rail shot."

An alert pinged on his HUD, a nearby trench reporting enemy contact. Alerts from adjacent units pinged soon after.

"Let's go." Cha'ril took off at a run. "I can't raise the captain." She glanced up and slid to a stop. "Oh no."

The night sky was alive with star bursts, sudden meteor showers of shells tracing brief lines through the upper atmosphere. An explosion cast momentary shadows across Gold Beach.

"There's a fight up there," Santos said.

The snap of gauss rifles picked up.

"And we're down here." Cha'ril ran on and turned hard around a corner.

A motley crew of Rangers and sailors fired from their trench into the surrounding darkness beyond their line. Santos launched an illumination shell from his mortar tube and made for the back of the trench. His rotary cannon spun to life and he locked it to his shoulder.

The shell burst and lit up the trench and the surroundings. Santos caught himself before opening fire.

There were men and women out there. Not the hulking and hunched-shouldered Rakka he was expecting. A human wave advanced on the trench at a slow jog, each carrying a crude club or axe in their hands. They wore little more than rags, and their alabaster skin was almost unnatural in the harsh light.

He spotted a few of the brutish Rakka mixed between lines of humans, all carrying whips and beating at anyone that came within range.

"What is this?" Cha'ril asked.

"You two going to help?" a Ranger shouted up from the trench. A corpse of a sailor, his head crushed, lay jumbled together with one of the too-pale humans.

"Heaven forgive me." Santos fired his rotary gun, sending quick bursts into any Rakka he saw, killing it and several of the new enemies as well.

Gauss fire dropped off down the line as a wave reached the trench. The Kesaht's humans sprang into action once they realized there was an enemy within swinging distance. Their crude weapons were useless against the power-armored Rangers in the trench, who proceeded to crush skulls with their rifle stocks or use their fists and augmented strength to beat their attackers to death.

Lesser armored sailors and techs scrambled out of the trench and retreated.

"No time for mercy." Cha'ril's rotary cannon went full cyclic, spitting bullets as fast as her barrels could spin. Santos joined her, cutting through the wave like wheat to the scythe.

"*All Armor,*" Gideon came weakly through the IR. "*Move to sector red five.*"

"We're holding back the tide here," Santos sent back. "We move north and—"

A grainy image came up on his HUD. A picture captured from orbit. The gates to Harmony City were open and Sanheel were pouring out. A second picture flashed; the mass of centaurs had grown and stretched toward the Union's lines.

"These are a diversion." Cha'ril's rotary gun snapped to a halt and she ejected a spent ammo canister. "Move. Move!"

Santos followed her. The flash of battle in the skies above grew more intense, and he realized that the Kesaht had launched a final attack that neither he, Cha'ril, nor anyone else would survive.

"We'll make them earn it," Santos said.

"My hatchling," Cha'ril said. "Man'fred Vo, my love. I just want to see them one more time."

Santos thought of his father and wondered how he would learn of his son's fate.

****

Cha'ril's Mauser snapped, muzzle blaring a flash of light that lit up the battlefield like a strobe light with each bullet she sent into the Sanheel charging at her. Rounds ripped off legs, ore through flanks, and each single shot killed at least two of the densely packed aliens.

She gripped the rifle by the red hot barrel, with her cannon hand, firing gauss shells while the rifle was braced across her chest as she slapped a fresh magazine into the Mauser. She backed up as a group of Sanheel hopped over their fallen and scrambled toward her.

She killed the lead alien and shifted her aim to the next, when a bolt hit her in the shoulder, twisting her back and into a wall.

"Think I'll make it easy for you!" She parried a thrusting spear tip with her rifle and swung hit the Sanheel in the head with the backswing, crushing its face. She dropped her rifle and grabbed the dying alien and flung it into a Sanheel with golden tusks and feathers worked into its dreadlocks.

A spear nicked her neck servos and she swung at her attacker, retracting her fist and stabbing with the punch spike housed in the forearm. The spike pierced its sternum and exited out its back.

The sound of Mauser fire assaulted her speakers and once she pushed off the dead alien impaled on her arm, all she saw was dead Kesaht.

Gideon and Santos, their rifle barrels smoking, were half hidden behind a broken wall.

"I had them." Cha'ril picked up her weapon.

"Fall back." Gideon motioned her toward him. "This line's lost."

"There is no place to fall back to, captain," she said as she jumped over the wall. A Kesaht fighter dove at them, firing twin bolts of plasma that stitched down the street. Cha'ril spun around, stopping between the rows of deadly energy as the fighter roared overhead. She shot from the hip and blew the fighter into fragments.

"The hospital," Gideon said.

Santos skidded to a stop, his helm to the sky.

"Look." He raised his chin.

Lines of fire arced toward Gold Beach, an orbital bombardment that the Armor was powerless to fight.

Santos stood up straight and held his rifle low across his waist.

The ground trembled as the first shell landed and a flash of light went up…from the north. More hits pounded a rhythm through the earth, all striking beyond the Union's crumbling defenses, but landing along the Kesaht's advance from their domed city.

"Bad shots?" Santos asked.

"Something's coming in." Gideon pointed to the sky. Twin gouts of flame broke low over the city, like sudden angel wings.

"You two deal with that," the captain said. "I think the command post is under attack."

Cha'ril checked the bullet count on her Mauser: two rounds. She'd loaded an older magazine. She touched the bottom of her torso, where spare mags were attached to her Armor, and found nothing.

"I'm low," she said to Santos as they ran past Union troops carrying wounded back toward the field hospital.

"I'm out." Santos locked his rifle on his back and unsnapped his MEWS from his thigh. The weapon morphed into a gladius.

The thump of heavy weapons fire carried through the air. They were about to turn a corner, when a Sanheel body went flying past them and landed with a crunch.

Cha'ril raised her rifle and stepped around the corner.

Armor, clad in matte black, swung a katana and chopped the head clean off of a Sanheel. A kick sent the body into a pack of Rakka. Fire inside a building full of dead aliens and a handful of Union Marines lit up three more Armor suits, all killing Sanheel.

Cha'ril froze, unsure of exactly what she was seeing. Then she recognized the markings on the Armor. Templar crosses.

Ibarrans.

She aimed her rifle at the nearest Armor and was about to fire, when Santos slapped her muzzle down.

"What the hell are you doing?" he asked.

"They—they're here to—"

"Here to help." The nearest Ibarran stabbed a dying Sanheel through the back. He flicked blood away, then sheathed the weapons with a smooth, practiced motion.

"Araki, Nisei lance, Ibarra Nation. Where is the Aeon?" he asked.

"What?" Santos asked.

"Tall. Green. Female. I doubt you've come across more than one in this hell hole." He lifted up a hunk of broken wall and a dust-covered sailor scrambled out.

"Yeah, we've got one of those," Santos said. "What do you want with her?"

"Shut up, you idiot." Cha'ril brought the stock of her rifle to one shoulder, muzzle to the ground, but the weapon was at the ready. "They're Ibarrans."

"And we have an Ibarran fleet." Araki pointed to the sky. "One with room for more than just one Aeon.

The Kesaht ships seem more interested in fighting each other than dealing with us. We took the Crucible with barely a fight."

"You…came for us?" she asked.

"The Lady sent us for the Aeon. She didn't mention the Union, though Admiral Makarov and the Black Knight made clear that we're to remove you all from Kesaht'ka…unless you want to stay?"

"She's at the field hospital," Cha'ril said. "Now how are you going to get us all off this rock?"

"Really, Cha'ril," Santos said to her, "I thought we'd play a little hardball with where Trinia was at."

Araki tilted his head slightly and a stubby antenna mounted to his helm lit up. His gauss cannon arm shot up to one side and fired, blowing through a wall and killing a Sanheel cowering on the other side.

"Fall back to the landing pads for evac!" the Nisei broadcast from his speakers. "Fall back!"

Union troops in surrounding buildings trickled out of their fighting positions, still maintaining discipline as the good news was repeated over and over down the line.

"We'll be the last off," Araki said.

"Black Knight?" Santos asked. "Isn't that—"

"It is," Cha'ril said. "We need to get to Gideon before he finds Roland."

"But the captain wouldn't—"

"He would. In a heartbeat."

****

Roland snapped his Gustav rifle up and aimed it dead center of Gideon's chest, his former lance commander returned the favor with his gauss cannons. Gideon snapped out his punch spike and readied it at his side.

Gideon side stepped, edging closer toward Roland, who stood his ground, back to the field hospital.

"Using wounded as a shield?" Gideon asked. "How far you've fallen."

Trinia peaked around Roland's side as he and Gideon continued the standoff.

"Tell him what you told me," Trinia said, "before one of you shoots."

"I don't think he wants to hear that just yet," Roland said.

"That's why?" Gideon bellowed from across the damaged square. "That's why you're here, isn't it? You've come for the Aeon. You Templar pretend you're for all of humanity, but the second your matriarch demands you—"

"The Ibarra Nation's here for all of you," Roland said, his rifle still pointed at Gideon. "Drop ships are coming in, enough to get every Union soldier off this hell hole and back home. Check your comms. Your soldiers will confirm it. So do you want to get off this shit hole or do you want round two right here right now?"

Roland and Gideon kept their weapons trained on each other. Gideon said nothing, and Roland hoped that meant the other Armor was scanning comm freqs and verifying Roland's claims that Ibarra Nation drop ships were evacuating Terran Union soldiers

Gideon bent his cannon arm slightly, shifting the aim off Roland. Roland lowered his Gustav.

Cha'ril and another Armor with the fleur-d-lys of the Iron Dragoons showed up behind Gideon and Roland pinged Nicodemus for reinforcements.

"And what about Trinia?" Gideon asked.

"I need her," Roland said.

"Sir, it's that vision," the new Iron Dragoon said. "It was the Aeon and you and—"

"That's enough, Santos." Gideon stomped forward and Roland put slight pressure on his trigger.

If this Santos saw the vision, then Stacey must have reached out to every Armor in the galaxy when she sent her message. She must have been under too much stress to limit the call to just the

Armor loyal to her, Roland thought.

"Your stupid visions don't matter if the Ibarrans jettison us into the void the first chance they get," Cha'ril said. "Of all the Ibarrans they could have sent…"

"No," Roland said, shaking his helm. "We won't do that. You have my word."

"Your word?" Rage seeped through Gideon's speakers. "You think for a second I'll believe—"

Roland raised his rifle.

Trinia stepped around Roland and put her hand on his muzzle. She tried to push it down, but Roland held firm, so she moved directly between his and Gideon's line of fire. Roland canted his Gustav to one side.

"Gideon will remain my guard," she said.

"Then come over here," the captain said, tilting his helm to one side.

"And I will leave this place as soon as the Ibarrans bring down a ship," she said. "I'm leaving with my ward—with all the wounded. Gideon, are you going to come with me or not? What's more important—the warriors following you or your vendetta?"

Gideon seemed to relax ever slightly.

"He can't stay with you," Roland said. "You're needed to—"

Trinia spun around and leveled a finger at his

chest. "Your damn 'visions' gave me up to the Toth." She poked him in the breastplate and winced with pain. "You have no idea what they've done to me. Now your 'visions' bring you back here. Gideon stays with me. He will behave. He owes me."

"How long have you known him?" Roland asked.

"Do you want my help or not?" she asked as her green face darkened several shades. Roland opted not to test her further.

"Then…he stays with you," Roland said.

The sound of heavy footfalls came from behind.

"Roland!" Nicodemus shouted. "Landing zone is secure and—"

The other Templar skidded to a stop next to Roland. His rotary cannon snapped toward Gideon then locked back into its holster mounted on his upper back.

"And you found Gideon," Nicodemus said.

Gideon twisted his gauss cannon arm from side to side.

"Sir, do you not like that Ibarran either?" Santos asked.

"That's enough out of you," Gideon said. "Dragoons, form a cordon around the Aeon and get her to the extraction point." An antenna went up from his helm. "I'll make sure the rest of our soldiers get off this hell hole.

Trinia, go with Roland. I'll catch up."

"Why isn't he going with us?" Trinia asked as Roland guided her to a crumbling stadium.

"He's going to be the last one off," Roland said.

"He didn't say that," Trinia said, glancing over her shoulder several times as she broke into a run. Cha'ril and Santos caught up quickly and formed a flank to her left.

"Doesn't have to," Roland said. "I know him too well."

****

Roland stood beside the ramp of an Ibarran Destrier as Union wounded were carried into the ship. A gaggle of a half dozen children—all wearing oversized breather masks, their eyes scrunched against the blazing sunlight—were led by a team of Strike Marines.

Two of the Strike Marines caught his attention. One carried a little girl in his arms, and was too large for a standard human, with scaly skin and four fingers on one hand. The second Strike Marine was short, but with a larger helmet to accommodate his quills—a Dotari.

A girl squealed and slipped the grip of a Marine as she saw Trinia. She bounded up the ramp and into the Aeon's arms.

More Strike Marines carried a gurney up to the ramp. The man strapped to it had no lower arms or legs and wore a makeshift mask over the gaping hole that was his jaw.

Roland wanted to reach out and call to Aignar, but given the way the two had parted, he decided this wasn't the time.

"Last of the aid station," said a Strike Marine lieutenant as he peeled off from the litter team. "This bird a priority evac?" He looked back at the dusty stadium pitch. "Still got a few more trickling in."

"All birds go wheels up at the same time," Roland said. "Keeps the Kesaht from identifying high-value targets."

The roar of Shrike fighters continued overhead.

"Sounds about right." The lieutenant did a double take at Roland. "You're one of…them."

"Roland."

"Hoffman. We're not surrendering to you. We're catching a ride."

"That's not why we're here," Roland said. "You'll be sent back to Earth. Eventually."

"How 'eventually'?" Hoffman asked, shifting uneasily.

"You're riding space available. Soon as space is

available to get you home, you'll get home…Is that a Karigole in there? And a Dotari Marine?"

"I don't know how it is with the Ibarrans," Hoffman said as he started up the ramp, "but the Strike Marines only take the best of the best!"

"Group Dynamo, this is Shrike leader," came over Roland's IR, weak and broken. *"Got a cleared vector back to the fleet. Break for orbit in two minutes. No second chance. You miss the pickup, you miss the pickup."*

Roland backed up toward the cargo bay. The Destrier's engines revved up and the deck shifted slightly against his sabatons as the anti-grav generators kicked on.

"Gideon…" Cha'ril said, coming down to the ramp's edge and joining Roland.

"Do you have him on IR?" Roland asked.

Cha'ril tapped the side of her helm hard. "Damn thing's been malfunctioning since we set down. I…there!" She pointed to the ruins where Gideon had emerged at a run, carrying someone beneath one arm.

The ship wobbled and lifted a few feet off the ground.

"Pilot!" Roland shouted both through his speakers and over wideband IR. He flagged down a crewman at the other end of the cargo bay. "Pilot, wait! We've got one more!"

The crewman touched his ear then waved his fingertips across his neck several times.

"Got bogies incoming," the pilot sent over IR. *"No close air support. Got to outrun them."*

Roland looked at Trinia, huddled in a far corner with the girl on her lap, then back to Gideon, who was closing the distance rapidly.

"Tell him to hurry," Roland said.

"I will shoot the pilot in the head if he doesn't stop," Cha'ril said, snapping her rotary gun up as the barrels spun to life.

Roland chopped a hand against the rotary gun's base, and it popped off her shoulder, rounds spraying from the ammo belt.

"You bastard!" the Dotari armor cursed as she loaded gauss bullets into her forearm cannon.

"Cha'ril!" Gideon shouted.

The ship lurched forward and into a turn. It rose ten feet off the ground and flew back toward Gideon, giving him a berth of a few dozen yards.

Gideon adjusted his course and hefted the man in his arms up in one hand like a rag doll. The ship rumbled past him and he threw the man…with too much force. The limp figure sailed over Roland's head…and into Cha'ril's arms.

Roland fell onto his belly, the sudden impact of his many tons sending the ship bobbing like a dolphin. He unlocked his sword from his hip and unsnapped the blade. Grasping it near the tip, Roland thrust the hilt out toward Gideon as the Union armor broke into a dead sprint to catch up.

The ship lifted up.

Gideon leaped and got one hand on the hilt. His momentum carried him forward, sending stress warnings from Roland's shoulder actuators across his HUD in giant red symbols.

Roland braced a knee to the ramp and heaved back. Gideon flew up just enough to get a grip on the edge of the ramp then pulled himself up, the sword still in his hand. He looked down at the Ibarran blade, the same one that had so badly damaged his armor when he and Roland last saw each other.

He dropped the blade and went into the cargo bay, not bothering to give Roland a glance.

Roland scooped up his sword and got to the deck as the ramp closed with a bang. A crewman jabbered at him, clearly upset at the stress his ship had gone through. Roland turned his optics to the crewman's face, then snapped his blade back into the hilt.

The crewman went red, then mumbled and turned

away.

Roland stood and looked over the wounded, the children, Trinia…and the Iron Dragoons.

"Nicodemus…you read me?" he asked through their quantum-dot communicators.

"I have you. All birds are skyborne…but don't celebrate yet," Nicodemus said.

"We've done our part." He cut the channel. "Hoffman! Put your Marines in the turrets!"

"Fun's not over!" said a Marine with dressings over half his face and a splinted leg as he tried to get up. A gunnery sergeant sat him back down with a single hand and a flurry of expletives.

The deck tilted from side to side and the afterburners kicked on.

"That you, Roland?" a mechanical voice said from next to his feet. Aignar sat up, the stumps of his arms buried in a foil blanket.

"You look like hell," Roland said as he went to one knee next to his old lance mate. Aignar's blue eyes, one badly bloodshot, locked with Roland's optics.

"Worse than the last time you saw me." The cloth over his missing lower jaw flapped in the irregular air currents. "You seem to be doing all right."

"What are you doing?" A Strike Marine medic put

her hand on the small of Aignar's back, then tried to lower him with a push to his shoulder.

"You want me to talk or not, Booker? Damn jarheads and their asshole ways," Aignar said.

"Call me an asshole again and I'll remember that." She wagged a finger at him. "You start choking on your own saliva, I'll still save you—just don't expect my normal smiling bedside manner."

"Roland, tell her how much of a beast I am in my armor," Aignar said. "She's bold because I don't have my hands and feet with me."

"Maybe you *are* fine." Booker shrugged and left.

"I think she likes me," Aignar said.

Santos came over, walking slowly to keep the ship from rocking.

"New guy, Roland. Roland, new guy," Aignar said.

"Wait…*Roland?* Roland?" Santos said. "I thought the captain…acted that way because you were Ibarran. I didn't know you were…you."

"He's better in a fight than you are," Aignar said. "And he's stuck with us through thick and thin."

"Good to meet you," Roland said, ignoring the barb from Aignar.

Santos offered a hand toward Roland, then snapped his hand shut and lowered it quickly. He turned his helm back to Gideon and Cha'ril, both on the other end of the cargo bay with Trinia.

"I should go," Santos said. "You okay, old man?"

"If I had fingers, I'd show you one in particular," Aignar said.

"He's fine," Roland said. Santos turned his back to his captain, mimed a fist to chest salute without striking his armor, and went away.

"Good kid," Aignar said. "Reminds me of someone."

"We didn't part on the best of terms," Roland said, knowing he was sugarcoating their last encounter. Roland had escaped from a Union prison on Mars, but not before Aignar had tried to talk him out of defecting to the Ibarrans. They'd come to blows, and Roland had left his old friend on the floor, his prosthetic arms broken and his metal jaw knocked loose.

Aignar made a grunting noise that Roland assumed was a laugh.

"You did what you had to," Aignar said. "I should've just let you go. You're a man. You're responsible for your own damn self."

"I'm sorry for what I did to you," Roland said. "You…deserved better from me."

"Well, you're getting me home to my son, aren't

you?"

"In a roundabout way," Roland said. "Got to take care of something first. Gideon...how is he?"

"He hates you. More than you can imagine. You're lucky this bird's full of wounded and a child. Otherwise, he'd be going for round two. Don't pick a fight with him. Cha'ril, new guy, and I...we won't be on your side."

"We need each other for a bit longer," Roland said. "Maybe after that—"

"No," Aignar snapped, the speaker in his throat cracking. "You've got a life out there with the Ibarrans. The only thing Gideon has is his duty and this gap where you, Morrigan, and that Nicodemus guy ripped out a piece of his heart. He's my commander. You...were my friend. Don't think he'll ever forgive and forget. You understand?"

"Why the warning?"

"Again, you're getting me back to my son. That's worth something."

"Later...if we ever come across each other on the battlefield in armor...will we come to blows?"

"Get me home and we're square, Ibarran. If there's war after that...then there's war."

"Fair enough," Roland said.

"New guy said he had a vision from Saint Kallen," Aignar said, narrowing his eyes slightly. "Some of the other Armor did too. But not Gideon. Not Cha'ril. Not me. You know anything about that?"

"Did it come after you were cracked out of your pod?"

"How'd you know?"

"Then you might have seen it," Roland said. Concealing the truth from Aignar didn't bother him nearly as much as it did with Makarov. "Saint Kallen does as she will."

"Her shrine's still on Mars," Aignar said. "Sealed. Unguarded. Doesn't feel right to do that…almost disrespectful."

"Get some rest, old man."

Trinia tapped Roland's shoulder. "You have much to tell me," she said.

"Indeed. I need a slate so I can show you video of—"

Trinia held up a Strike Marine gauntlet.

"I need that back!" called out the wounded Marine with the bandages over his face.

A data port popped open on Roland's arm.

Chapter 25

The Vishrakath hive ship was a massive asteroid, engines built into the aft section burned low, keeping the ship between Mars and Earth. Energy cannons flared to life and sent out a rain of pale yellow bolts from one half of the ship. The fire joined with other alien ships, inundating a section of space as a macro cannon shell shot from the red planet, running the gauntlet of fire from the alien fleet.

A bolt clipped the shell and it exploded into fragments, hurtling for eternity through the void.

The energy cannons fell silent, the barrels poking up from ancient craters glowing faintly with heat.

Over Mars, the Crucible gate's basalt thorns shifted against each other and a white disk formed at the center of the ring. Another disk appeared a few hundred yards off the hive ship's port side, opposite the just active energy cannons.

The *Yalta* burst out of the wormhole and opened fire a split second later. Rail cannons blasted hypervelocity shells into the hive ship's rocky exterior, blowing away new craters and exposing the inner hull built into the asteroid. By the time the *Yalta* cleared the aft end of the ship, the rail cannons had reloaded and fired on the alien's engine works. Cowlings the size of apartment buildings were shot off and went spinning into space. An engine core overloaded, blowing out the rear of the ship and sending a loose hunk of rock toward the *Yalta*.

The battleship angled away from the debris, and a cliff face spun past the bridge, missing it by tens of meters.

An Ibarran cruiser following the *Yalta* took the full brunt of the rock and broke apart on impact.

Ibarran rail guns pummeled the exposed inner hull as they came barreling out of the wormhole. The hive ship tried to roll and move the chink in its armor out of the line of fire, but the loss of the engines sapped its maneuverability.

The last ship in the long line of the Ibarran fleet, the *Stolzoff*, fired its rail cannons at once and pierced the inner hull. Explosions burst from the ship's weapon emplacements and smoke and atmosphere bled out through the ruptures.

The *Yalta* canted on its long axis and brought dorsal and ventral guns to bear on a Vishrakath carrier that was little more than a mobile asteroid run through with fighter and bomber bays. The carrier collapsed under sustained rail cannon fire, ripping apart like a dandelion in a gale.

On the bridge, Valdar tapped out priority targets for the fleet.

"Good shooting, guns," Valdar said. "Ignore the support vessels, hit the ships of the line before they have a chance to—"

Light burst through the bridge windows and the ship lurched forward.

"Think they realize we're here," Marc said, still in unmarked legionnaire armor.

"If you don't have anything useful to add, then shut up." Valdar checked a damage report and cursed. "Zahar! Load porcupine rounds and saturate fire around the next Vish carrier. They've likely launched their ready fighters."

He didn't wait for a response as damage reports came in. The Vishrakath had been surprised and had lost their hive ship, but their off-the-cuff response to the sudden attack had scored several hits on his fleet.

"Three destroyers lost...cruiser *Mohsin* lost engines." Valdar rubbed the back of his gloved knuckles against the chin of his helmet. He smiled as his small squadron of artillery ships—each more rail cannon than hull—annihilated distant targets quickly and methodically.

It took another ten minutes before the remaining Vishrakath ships broke and ran.

"Hail from Mars." Marc touched a screen and made a tossing motion toward Valdar.

A harried woman with thick glasses stared wide-eyed at Valdar.

"Ibarrans? Over my planet?" she asked.

"It's Mable, isn't it?" Valdar asked.

"Wait...you? I thought—you know what? I can figure it out later," she said. "Right now, I need your ships to clear out the Vish in geosynch orbit over Mount Olympus."

Valdar reached into the holo tank and pulled Mars closer to him. Red enemy icons around the planet began shifting.

"Negative," he said. "There's a Vish fleet of corvette analogs coming up my wake and—"

"There are ten mass drivers closing on Phoenix," Mable said. "I need the macros on Olympus cleared to fire or those shells will get past the final interception line."

"Once I gain void supremacy—"

"Phoenix, Valdar!" She slapped her camera, jostling her image. "I already had to choose between Baltimore and Oslo today. Lucky shot from a battleship took out the rock, saved the crab cake capital of the world and saved me a lot of grief. But the alien assholes just loosed ten rocks at Phoenix. We can't lose that city."

Valdar ran a time plot to the Vishrakath force holding over Olympus. A force half again as large as the one his fleet had just demolished.

"It'll be bloody," Valdar said.

"I'll help. Just get their cannons oriented off my guns and we'll play the old hammer and anvil game. Wait...where's the *Breitenfeld?*" she asked.

"Long story. I don't know how it ends. We're moving at best speed to engage the force over Olympus. Valdar out." He sent commands to the rest of the fleet and felt the deck rumble beneath his feet as the engines maxed out.

"Admiral." Zahar hurried over to the holo table. "The *Mohsin* can't keep up at this speed. She'll fall behind."

"And the Vish corvettes will overtake her. I know, captain."

"Even if the crew abandons ship, the Vishrakath

fire on escape pods." Zahar bit his bottom lip and looked to Marc, a plea on his face.

"If we hold back for the *Mohsin*, Phoenix and the tens of millions there will be lost," Valdar said. "Do you have a solution?"

"Ibarran lives for Terran…no, no, Admiral, I don't. Forgive me for questioning you." Zahar turned away, his head low.

"You could've jumped in, 'my Lady,'" Valdar said.

"And undercut your command authority?" Marc asked. "Besides, I may not have a heart anymore, but that doesn't mean I can't empathize with him. Union dogs ordered every Ibarran like him killed if captured. Resentment is a bit warranted."

"If the Union keeps that bull up after all this," Valdar said, "I'll defect for real." He rubbed his thumbs against the side of his fists and opened a channel to the *Mohsin*.

"I hate this part," Valdar said just before the captain of the stricken ship came up in the tank.

Chapter 26

The Destrier's cargo bay was empty of the wounded and children, and ten armor faced off against each other: five Ibarran Templars—Roland, Nicodemus, and three Nisei—across from the Iron Dragoons and two others rescued off of Kesaht'ka.

Trinia worked between the two groups, welding together a device from several open crates of parts. She moved uncomfortably in a bespoke vacuum suit made by the *Midway's* foundry.

The ship rumbled through turbulence and the Aeon clicked her tongue in annoyance. Neither side of armor moved.

"This is fun," Roland said to the other Templar through a private channel.

"None of us can blink," said Araki of the Nisei.

"No contact with the ground elements," Nicodemus said. "Best tactical decision is to come in with as much firepower as one ship can carry. The only way Trinia could get Gideon to cooperate was if the security detail was even. I don't like it either."

"If this wasn't for the Lady," Umezu, another Nisei, said, "they could sit and spin back on the *Breitenfeld* with the rest of the Union crunchies. For all I care."

"It is for the Lady," Nicodemus said, "and we are Templar. Honor and duty are our watchwords. We can assume the Union will be professionals."

Roland opened a channel to his lance mate.

"I know what you're going to say," Nicodemus said. "'Assumptions are the mother of all screwups.'"

"It's Gideon I don't trust," Roland said. "If he's waiting for the chance to deal a mortal wound to the Nation, we're giving him the perfect opportunity."

"The *Warsaw* has a hull full of his people. What does *he* think would happen to them if he goes astray?" Nicodemus asked.

"That we'd void them all. Which we wouldn't. Makarov wouldn't."

"But that's not what he thinks," Nicodemus said.

"We can't let Lady Ibarra's safety hinge on what

we think Gideon is thinking. I want to beat myself up just for saying that." Roland cringed within his pod.

"Is Gideon an honorable man?"

"That…there's no doubt there. Stabbing people in the back isn't his style."

"Then we must believe he is true," Nicodemus said. "But don't take your eyes off him. Ever."

"Agreed."

****

Gideon seethed as he looked from Roland to Nicodemus. The two bore the Templar cross so prominently on their armor, bragging about their treason, practically rubbing his nose in their new loyalty.

He pulled his arms and legs close to his body within his womb, wishing for a chance to lash out. To hurt something.

"Sir?" Cha'ril asked over the Union Armor's channel. "We've crossed into the planet's atmosphere. Nekara, they call it. I'm not picking up any IR traffic, but they haven't let us into their wider net."

"I can try to splice in," Santos said. "Our sensors can pick up atmo scatter from even short-range IR. Our tech is almost the same and—"

"Don't," Gideon said, forcing his muscles to relax. "Don't assume they're amateurs or fools. You stick your hand in the cookie jar, they'll cut it off."

A panel opened up on Cha'ril's shoulder. A data flex-line snaked out and reached to the matching port on Gideon's pauldron. Gideon accepted the suit-to-suit hardline connection.

"They can see us," Gideon said.

"Let them," the Dotari said. "They won't give us complete transparency, we'll return the favor. What's our plan, sir? What are we doing?"

"I'm getting us all home. The survivors are all aboard the *Breitenfeld* and other Ibarran ships. We're not going back to Earth just yet. I still don't exactly understand what they need Trinia for."

"Sir…it's me. I don't trust the Ibarrams. They almost killed my joined when Roland escaped. I was pregnant. The thought that I'd lost him was…But they betrayed the Union. The Union that saved my people from Takeni, that gave us a home on Earth and then returned us all to Dotari. Then the *Breitenfeld* found a cure to the phage killing my people, and the Ibarrans stole that ship from you. And from us. We are a spacefaring culture. To steal a ship with such a history…disgraceful. And if *I* don't trust the Ibarrans. I know that *you* don't trust the Ibarrans."

Blood rushed to his cheeks and adrenaline dumped into his system as he thought of fighting with Cha'ril against the traitors. He worked his jaw from side to side, frustrated as he worked out the second- and third-order effects of her attacking the Ibarrans.

She was Dotari, and the traitors could assign blame to her entire race if she joined him in an assault. Some of assault force had survived the operation on Kesaht'ka, but Earth's combined fleet was spent. There weren't enough ships to defend the colonies…or the Dotari, who numbered barely over a million. Earth couldn't protect itself and its main ally if the Ibarrans came looking for retribution.

No…no, Cha'ril couldn't join him. The act of a lone soldier was just that. A hint of coordination or conspiracy would be enough reason to strike back at the weakened Earth and her allies.

"We keep the Aeon safe," Gideon said to Cha'ril. "Bring her back to Earth and keep her out of the Ibarrans' hands. You saw what the Toth made her do. If the traitors can exploit that knowledge, then—"

"Abominations," Cha'ril said. "Such things should never be."

"And that's why she must come back with us,"

Gideon said. "Earth abandoned the procedurals. We'll never go back to it."

"And if the Ibarrans demand the Aeon?"

Gideon's Armor clenched its fists. "We'll cross that bridge when we come to it."

Cha'ril was quiet for a moment. "As you say, sir. Say the word and it shall be done."

"You're a good soldier, Cha'ril. The legacy of Caas and An'ri live on with you."

Her helm nodded ever so slightly.

There was a whine of servos as the Templars loaded gauss shells into their forearm cannons and ammo belts connected to their rotary guns.

"What're they doing?" Santos put a hand to the hilt of his METL.

"*—say again. Landing zone is hot,*" said the pilot, cutting into the Union's network. *"Unknown hostiles in contact with ground forces. Prep for a combat drop."*

"Pilot, we have a crunchy—I mean, an untrained VIP with us," Gideon said.

"Roger. Better get her schooled up pretty quick."

"Goddamn it." Gideon waved Trinia over as he loaded his weapons. The Aeon toddled over, uncomfortable in her new armor.

"This is not good news, is it?" Trinia asked.

"Button up and just hang on," Gideon said.

Trinia almost put her helmet on backward, then flipped it around and fit it over her head. Loose strands of hair wafted out from under the seal.

"Ow…ow," she said, wiggling her helmet.

Gideon grabbed her by the waist and hefted her off the deck.

"What is this?" She pushed against his forearms and her legs kicked back and forth.

Gideon transformed his legs into treads and pivoted toward the ramp as it cracked open. Wind whistled through the opening. Trinia's feet planted onto the plate over the treads and she clutched to one arm.

"Hang on," Gideon said.

"I am not going to like this. No. I already don't like this. I have bones that can break and nice soft skin that doesn't do well when dropped out of speeding planes like—oh!"

The ramp slammed down and Gideon lurched forward. Trinia broke into a high-pitched scream as Gideon dove off the end and went into a free fall for a full two seconds. He landed hard against the dirt and slid across the ground, kicking up a dark cloud around him as his treads spun to find purchase and keep him from flipping over. He finally slid to a halt, one side lifting a yard off the ground before it thumped back to the surface.

Trinia was still screaming, both arms wrapped around his helm.

"We're here," Gideon said.

Trinia inhaled deeply and let out a cry for a split second.

"Aaah—oh…that wasn't so bad. It was kind of fun," she said, her arms trembling.

"I can't see." Gideon nudged her with an elbow and she hopped off him.

The sound of gauss fire carried through the cloud of thick dust hanging in the air. A metallic rattle rose from the dust and Gideon paused, unsure if some new Ibarran weapon was making the noise.

A shadow coalesced in the tan fog, loping toward them like an animal. Gideon flung Trinia to the ground behind him and swung a punch as a saber leapt through the air. His fist connected with the Geist beast's chin and deflected it to one side. Claws raked across his breastplate as it passed. The saber dug in its front claws and whipped its hindquarters around to bring it face-to-face with Gideon.

Gideon fired his gauss cannons, blowing out a crater on the shoulder and blossoming cubes into the air. The saber lurched back, the threat rattle growing faster.

The armor reloaded and fired again, but both shells deflected off an energy screen, catching Gideon flat-footed. The saber pounced, one claw reaching to rake down the front of his helm, though the dark-green nails missed Gideon by a foot. The saber landed on the ground and jerked backward.

Cha'ril, one hand on the saber's tail, chopped the axe head of her METL into the saber's flank. She wrenched the blade out, chiseling out a good hunk of the beast's side, and pulled back on its tail, moving it even farther away from Gideon.

She swung the axe down like an executioner and severed the saber's head. The Geist collapsed, its body dissolving into tiny cubes and black smoke.

"How'd you know that would work?" he asked.

"Didn't. Seemed like the right thing to do. Shooting them until they stop moving wasn't as effective," she said.

"Trinia?" Gideon spun around and found the Aeon in the dirt, her arms covering her head. She looked up then wiped her visor clean.

"I don't like this place. At all. Ouranos had *voynir* rats, but they just eat your vegetables and let off a scent when threatened."

Gideon grabbed her by the belt and hauled her up

to her feet.

"Sir!" Santos's voice carried through the haze. It had settled to the point where Gideon could make out the Ark. The junior Armor, his suit caked in dust, arrived and pointed to the Ark.

"Sir, the Ibarrans have an entrance secured and—"

"Let's go," Gideon said and gave Trinia a gentle push toward the Ark as the three Iron Dragoons formed a loose perimeter around her.

Trinia tried to run, making a few awkward strides.

"The gravity is too light," she said. "Hard to—"

"Keep. Moving." Gideon made out the heavy crack of armor gauss cannons as they got closer to the Ark.

"New guy, did you foul your landing?" Cha'ril asked.

"Any landing you can walk away from, right?" Santos asked as he swept his cannons toward the temples behind them.

"He broke track." Cha'ril shook her head.

"I did break track," Santos said, raising his forearm cannons and firing once. "That wasn't one of those panther-looking things. What have the Ibarrans gotten us into?"

"The sooner we get out of it, the better," Gideon said, stepping into a thin sheen of cubes mixed into the dirt. The cubes became a blanket as they reached the perimeter wall manned by Ibarran legionnaires.

Gideon noted the claw marks on the wall and human blood staining the ramparts. A gate rolled open and the Dragoons made it inside.

"They didn't panic and shoot us," Santos said. "Maybe they aren't so bad."

Gideon and Cha'ril looked at him.

"For traitors. Maybe they aren't so bad for traitors. They're still traitors, I mean," Santos said.

"And he can hear you," Marshal Davoust said as he ran over. He pointed to the Ark's entrance, where Roland and Nicodemus were waiting on the disk just over the threshold. "Two of you and the Aeon. Go!"

"Santos, hang back." Gideon reached for Trinia, who slipped away from his grasp. "What's wrong?"

"The markings…can't you read them?" Trinia's face had gone a pale green. "This is…this ship belongs to the reaver. The harvester of souls. Do you know what that means?"

"No." Gideon paused, unsure what her concerns meant for the mission.

"He's gone," Trinia said, tucking her arms against

her stomach and hunching forward slightly. "He has to be gone. The Qa'resh had him on Bastion. Stacey made the bargain with him. But if he was still here…he would have come for this ship."

"I have no idea what she's talking about," Cha'ril said.

"I'll go." Trinia started forward, though she kept her gaze off the hull. "I'll go for Maggie, and for all the rest of Earth's children."

Gideon and Cha'ril escorted her onto the dish. Trinia stuck to Gideon's side as darkness swallowed them and the dish lifted toward the crystal sphere.

"By the great line of my people," Cha'ril said, "what is this place?"

"Evil." Trinia shuddered. "Pure evil. If Stacey had said this was what she was after…" She shook her head rapidly.

"Malal is gone," Nicodemus said. "The Qa'resh destroyed him. This place is a tool…just that. A tool."

"Wait," Gideon said to Trinia. "Wait…how can the Ibarrans be after this place and not some Qa'resh artifact or database like before?"

"This Ark can move, my golem," Trinia said. "It must still have its jump engines. You see the soul collectors out there? They're fully charged. This ship is…it can be the ultimate weapon."

Rage flashed through Gideon's heart.

"You lied to us," he said, pointing at Roland. "You never said anything about this."

"Our Lady is trapped here," Nicodemus said. "We need her free. Not this ship."

"Maybe she can't…can't control it," Trinia said. "The Qa'resh were far more advanced than we are. Even I struggled to grasp the basics of how their minds worked. You put a child at the conn of a battleship, they won't accomplish much."

"We're here for your metal queen," Gideon said. "Once she's free, we leave."

"We will do what—" Roland took a step toward his old lance commander, but Nicodemus stopped him with a hand to his chest.

"Free her mind," Nicodemus said to the Aeon, then he looked up as the light from the nearing crystal sphere grew stronger. "Brace yourself. This part is…odd."

Chapter 27

Pallax hissed as an optic image from a dead scythe came through the milieu of hovering screens.

"That one is different," he said, scratching at Trinia in the hologram.

"Another of their battle suits," Noyan said. Her tendrils pecked at the holo sphere around her head, directing new attacks on the Ibarran perimeter. "No...her bio readings are so different. The Aeon? Makes little different to me. Their entire fleet has returned and now they have enough air support to devastating any attack I can muster with the dreck around the Ark."

"Thralls are nothing," Pallax said.

"Do you wish to join the battle?" Noyan asked with a sneer.

"We have thralls to spare. Speaking of…Aiza?"

Aiza's chin snapped up from his chest. His head lolled to one side and a sibilant hiss came from his mouth. The theosar had infected most of his face, leaving his lower jaw untouched. His pure white eyes stared into the distance.

"Identify this." Pallax poked a nail into the image of Trinia and flicked his finger at Aiza.

"Not ours…" Aiza's voice was a death rattle. "Void suit is wrong…custom-made. Fresh from the foundry…can see the mold lines. Too tall for human. Too tall to be one of…them."

"The theosar works quite well on your species. This bodes well for your future," Pallax said. "Not everyone goes to Malal's light willingly, but all will join him in perfection."

"I recognize her," Seru said from her makeshift seat. "The new arrival was in the prophet's mind bleed. This…could be a problem."

"Can you break her soul or not?" Pallax demanded. "If it is a matter of time, then we can overrun the defenders, kill them all, and leave the prophet in your grip until she leads us to Malal."

"She is…resilient." Seru squirmed.

"I will awaken the pilgrim ships," Noyan said.

"The galaxy is alive again. We must harvest them all. This is Malal's will."

"And what good are our deeds if we cannot reach the master?" Pallax asked. "Millennia dormant, waiting...we cannot let this chance slip away."

A holo of the command dais appeared between the three Geist. They watched the Armor assemble Trinia's equipment next to the throne.

"Kill them," Noyan said. "Use the threads and kill them!"

"No..." One corner of Seru's lips pulled into a smile. "No, I see their plan. They will bring her defenses down for me. I will strike soon and she will be mine."

"A little more patience," Pallax said. "Just a little more."

Chapter 28

Stacey ducked through a low tunnel leading through a wall. The musty smell brought back memories of her childhood—excited forays after dark, time away from the scrutiny of bodyguards and an overbearing mother. The few moments she ever had to be normal.

A dead city waited for her at the other end. Phoenix had been the economic and technological heart of Earth once Marc Ibarra brought his inventions to the world. His graphenium batteries had revolutionized energy storage and transformed the world within a decade. Advances in robotics, computing, and material science all made the Ibarra Corporation the richest single entity in the history of mankind.

Phoenix had blossomed around Marc Ibarra, with

skyscrapers linked by walkways, elevated mag-lev trains, and Ibarra Corp solar cells and roads built into everything. Twenty-five million people called the city home before a young Stacey Ibarra had reported for duty aboard the *Breitenfeld*.

Now…it was empty.

The once-constant buzz of delivery drones was gone, replaced with the whisper of wind through decaying apartments. Streets that ran with automated electric cars and buses were still as the grave. There were no people on the sidewalks, in the stores, or chatting on restaurant patios. It was all empty, as though the place had been forgotten.

"Mom?" Stacey hurried across a street to a block of homes surrounded by a wrought-iron fence. There was a gap in the metal, like God had taken an eraser to it. She ran through and glanced at a house where one of Marc Ibarra's many secretaries once lived. The front façade was gone, leaving the interior exposed like an open dollhouse.

Her address was next. The paint was faded, its solar shingles cracked and loose.

A thrum grew in the air as she went to the door. Cracking it open with her shoulder, she peeked inside. A broken mirror lay on the floor, coated in dust. The door swung on rusty hinges, and Stacey froze.

A Xaros drone hovered in her living room, fractal shapes pulsating along its oval body. Stalk tips moved up and down a wall, disintegrating it with a wide, red beam. A glowing cube floating over its top grew slightly larger as the stalks continued their work.

"This…this isn't my home anymore." Stacey backed up, but the door had somehow shut behind her. She jiggled the knob, but it wouldn't move.

The drone's body spun in place, then the stalks snapped toward her.

"No. No, this isn't real. I'm not here." Stacey held out a hand, one made from flesh and bone.

The drone moved toward her, the fractals on its surface coalescing into Seru's face.

"I left this place!"

Silver grew from her fingertips and ran up her arm.

The ruby-tipped drone stalks struck at Stacey and as she threw up her arms, her home vanished.

Lowering her forearm, she found herself in a cylindrical room with a low ceiling. A skeleton wearing a decayed suit lay sprawled out next to a small dais. A Qa'resh probe, just a shining tear of light, bobbed slowly in the air over the dais.

"It had to be me," she said as she looked at the

skeleton, the mortal remains of Marc Ibarra. "But he never gave me a choice."

She reached for the probe but stopped short. Thoughts of a beach and Trinia came to her, floating just behind memories of a long, terrible day.

"You want me here," Stacey said. "You want this from me." She dropped her hand and went to the elevator door on the far side of the room.

"But this is still my mind. All mine, you hear me?" Stacey looked up. "All. Mine!"

The doors opened and she got inside. She hit the only button and an old emotion came to her, one she'd tried to banish for years.

"He's not here with me this time." She buried her face in her hands. "Stay away. Please stay away. Stay away, stay away, stay away, stay…"

****

Morrigan stood at the top of the stairs, looking down at Gideon and Cha'ril as they spoke with Martel and Nicodemus, the point of her sword stuck into the thin crystal carpet. She twisted the pommel against her palm, the blade flashing as it reflected the light.

"You just had to bring him, didn't you?" she asked Roland.

From the equipment case, Roland lifted a metal frame run through with fiber-optic cables and set it down next to Trinia. The Aeon worked within a golden lattice, connecting points and muttering to herself.

"We were in a rush," he said. "Needed a working solution right away, not the perfect answer ten minutes too late."

"Has she said anything since she entered the *taaranjin*?" Trinia asked.

Morrigan looked at her.

"The sub-reality simulation based off her quantum pathways." Trinia tried to snap her fingers at Morrigan, but the metal of her gloves fouled the noise. "You don't have an adequate word for it."

"Nothing," Morrigan said.

"Can you free her or not?" Martel asked as he joined them around Stacey.

"I cannot," Trinia said.

"Wait…then we brought you here for nothing?" Roland asked. "Why would—would Saint Kallen have sent us to—"

"*I* cannot," Trinia said. "Stacey's body is of Qa'resh design. It is meant to interface with this abomination of a vessel. We need a bridge, from her mind to this control station."

"Did you...bring one?" Martel asked.

"We already have it," Trinia said, tapping Morrigan on her breastplate.

"What's she talking about?" the Irish Armor asked.

"Our quantum-dot communicators," Roland said and stepped between Morrigan and Trinia. "You can link us to our Lady through them?" Roland flipped the view port on his chest down and brought his eyes up to a window within his womb to lock his gaze with Trinia's.

Catch on, he thought. *You're thousands of years old. Take the hint. Their faith is strong. If the others realize they've been tricked, they might abandon Stacey.*

The Aeon brushed red-gold hair from her face, and her mouth worked from side to side. "Yes...the dots," she said.

"Then what are we waiting for?" Martel asked.

"It's not so simple," Trinia said. "She's trapped within a reality of her own creation. If you go in there...it is difficult to explain. Your mental projection will skew, distort in ways you can't imagine. You run a significant chance of redlining, of wiping out your entire neural system."

"I'll go," Roland said.

"You've just earned your spurs," Martel said. "I've been Armor for decades. I know my limits. This is my duty."

"Sir...wait..." Roland snapped the view port shut and turned to his commander. "Lady Ibarra has these...episodes. Moments where her mind slips. When that happens, she mistakes me for Ken Hale, the Strike Marine from the Ember War that was with her when—"

"I know who Ken Hale is," Martel snapped. "There have been rumors about her, but I never heard anything like this."

"It's true. I swear it." He touched the Templar cross on his shoulder armor.

"It's too risky, boy-o," Morrigan said. "You lose it in there, neither of you may ever come out again. Let the colonel do it."

"I do not know who Ken Hale is," Trinia said, frowning and working her hands through the golden lattice.

"She was in love with him," Roland said. "The feeling...wasn't mutual."

"Then the young one is right," Trinia said. "I need a strong emotional response from Stacey's mind to connect to, and right now, I see her mind degrading.

Something is grinding away at her control. I need to establish the bridge soon before her mind fades away completely."

"I know what it is to lose a loved one," Morrigan said. "I could connect with her that way."

"No," Martel said, putting a hand on Roland's shoulder. "You can do this?"

"I am Armor." Roland glanced down at Gideon, who paced around the lower platform like a caged lion. "I will not fail. Send me."

"Do it," Martel said and backed away.

Trinia removed a segmented metal tube bristling with sensors from the crate and brought it behind Roland.

"No guarantees," she said. "I had to design the Qa'resh-to-armor adapter during the flight down from the *Midway*. But fear not, I've had thousands of years to study the ancients' technology and I invented most of what's connected to your brain stem—plus, I had almost half an hour to troubleshoot this device."

"Are you telling me this to make me more or less confident?" Roland asked.

"Eh," Trinia said, shrugging before she lifted an access port beneath his back armor plates and plugged in the adapter.

"What do I need to do in there?" he asked as a

tingle grew at the back of his mind.

"You'll have a token. When you find her, activate it and a door will appear. She has to go through it of her own free will. If she fights, it will rip her psyche apart," Trinia said. "There's something else in there with Stacey. It's not Qa'resh…shadows come and go. I don't fully understand yet."

"Fair enough. What happens next?"

Trinia went to the lattice and traced an arch in the light.

"Hold on."

Fire shot through Roland's body. He opened his mouth to scream, when his reality exploded into pure-white light.

****

Stacey sat in the corner of the small elevator, her face buried in her hands, a cold dread building in her chest.

"Stacey?" a voice asked, one she knew.

"Stacey, we have to get out of here. Come with me." Ken Hale put a hand, one clad in power armor, on her knee.

She looked up, and he was just as she remembered: armor dirty with blown sand, hair shaved down to a classic Marine high and tight, face wide and eyes kind.

"We've got what your grandfather sent us for. Let's get out of here before the Xaros find us, yeah?" he asked.

"Ken…you're back? But you left me. You went someplace…"

"A mistake," he said as he took her by the hands and helped her to her feet. "I should've stuck with you. I'll stay with you now. I'll be with you forever. It was wrong to leave."

He smiled and her heart skipped a beat.

"Come with me?" His now bare hand touched the side of her face and a tear fell.

"Ken…" She embraced him and felt his warmth.

The elevator doors opened to the Qa'resh station, the final place she'd seen Malal and the last of humanity's first alien ally. She looked to a view port and saw the twin rings of light around a massive black hole, a wall of stars off in the great distance.

"I remember this," Hale said. "I was here with you when…something happened. What was it?"

"They brought us here." Stacey took a step away from Hale, still holding his hand. "The Qa'resh needed Malal here after he'd fed…on the Toth…"

Malal appeared before a large portal. The disk resolved into crystal cities floating in endless clouds. The portal darkened, and a mouth formed to bite at one of the cities.

Stacey yanked her hand away.

"What happened here?" Ken asked. "I've…been gone so long, I can't remember."

"You should know," Stacey said, feeling the walls closing in on her. "You were there. You can't forget—you're not real. You're not Ken."

Hale's face darkened. His eyes went pure black and he advanced on her with a snarl. He grabbed her by the shoulders and shoved her back.

She crashed into the back of the elevator and pain shot through her body. The doors closed behind Hale as he grabbed a fistful of her uniform, picking her up and slamming her against the wall as he brought up his right gauntlet.

A Ka-Bar blade snapped out and he pressed it against her bare neck.

"We are losing patience." Ken's words mingled with another, a female voice. "Your kind believes in a hell, a place of eternal suffering and pain. If you do not give in, we will take you to hell and torture your mind until nothing but clay remains—clay we will mold to our liking!"

The elevator rumbled, and Hale cocked his head to the ceiling, a moment of confusion on his face.

"Malal...Malal was a necessary evil," Stacey said.

Ken looked back at her and morphed. His hair grew into long, oily strands and his face elongated into demonic proportions.

"One we used and threw away!" Stacey's body snapped into silver and she threw a punch into the Malal standing before her. Her fist passed through his body like he was a ghost.

Malal pinned her to the wall and grabbed her by the chin. Light shone from his palm and cold crept through her face.

"Time for the theosar," Malal said. "Time to die."

A giant metal hand punched through the ceiling. Servos squealed as the fingers gripped the edge of the hole and peeled open the roof. A suit of armor towered over the opening, and the sight of the soldier standing there sent a pang of guilt through Stacey's heart.

"Elias?"

"Get away from her!" the armor shouted and punched into the elevator.

Malal vanished and the fist beat a dent into the floor. The massive arm pulled back and the armor tore the elevator in half, leaving Stacey in the middle of a disheveled parking lot just outside a massive tower.

"My Lady, we need—no…" The armor's paint shifted from the old slate-gray, Ember War–era colors to matte-black, Templar crosses on the chest and shoulders.

"Stacey?"

The armor shrank into an older Ken Hale, wearing a decent civilian suit and carrying a slight paunch to his stomach. He looked at the gold wedding band on his left hand, then hid it behind him.

"Stacey…it's me. You remember—"

"No," Stacey said, shaking her head. "No, don't lie to me."

"This is hard for me too. I need you to come with me," Hale said.

+TRAITOR+

The word boomed from all around.

Hale morphed into Roland, wearing only his skin suit. The sky darkened and lightning lashed beneath sudden thunderheads.

"Trinia?" Roland asked the sky. "This is not…this is not working."

"Liar!" a woman shouted behind them. Makarov stalked toward them, hair loose and flowing in the growing breeze. "Betrayer! You protect her when she has done nothing but trick you!"

"She's not here," Stacey said softly. "But are you?"

Makarov evaporated like a wisp of steam.

"Traitor," Gideon said and stepped through a broken door, wearing his full dress uniform, his chest full of medals. He reached to his right shoulder, ripped away the Iron Dragoons patch, and tossed it at Roland's feet.

Roland looked down, and a metal hand grabbed his ankle. Aignar, his prosthetic jaw swinging from one joint, looked up at his old friend.

"You abandoned me," crackled from Aignar's throat speaker.

"No!" Roland shuffled back, growing taller and transforming into his armor. "No! I saved you from the Kesaht. Saved all of you. You…Saint's bones, I hate this place!"

"My Black Knight is here," Stacey said. "You're here to destroy me like I asked?"

"No, my Lady. I'm here to save you. The Nation…" He stopped as a thrum in the air grew louder. Pebbles and bits of glass shuddered against the ground.

A half dozen Xaros drones flew around the tower and collided together, turning into a jumble of stalks and fused bodies. The mass rolled across the ground and formed into something humanoid.

Seru looked up, her statuesque face at odds with

the chaos of the rest of her body.

"You both know this," the Geist said. "You both fear this."

"No," came from Stacey, but in the voice of a different woman. Roland looked down and saw a woman with braided blonde hair in a wheelchair where Stacey should have been. "We fear the lie. The lie we have become."

"Saint Kallen?" Roland dropped his guard for a moment.

Kallen fell out of her chair and her hair shortened and darkened. Stacey looked up at the armor.

"I need you, my Black Knight...I can't do this anymore." Stacey's arms went silver, then began to fade away.

"No! You're mine!" Seru shouted and charged forward, the massive feet of her Xaros construct cracking the pavement.

Roland snapped his hilt off his leg and ducked slightly as he closed on his foe.

Seru lifted an arm to the side and massive claws grew from her hand. She swiped at Roland just as he thrust one knee forward and dodged under the strike.

The metal on his back leg sparked against the ground as he slid, extending the blade from his hilt as he drew it across his body. The blade cut through Seru's chest, sending a spray of tiny cubes into the air. Seru stumbled forward, one arm locked against the deep cut through her chest.

"No," she said. "We can work together. Yes? Share paradise."

Roland marched up to the Geist and flipped the blade point down. He raised the hilt up to his helm.

"You are an abomination!" Roland drove the sword through the base of her neck and impaled her to the ground. Seru slid down the blade, her body disintegrating into cubes that floated into the air and shrank away to nothing.

"My Lady?" Roland went to Stacey, who lay in a pool of blood, both hands over a bullet wound to her chest.

"Stacey, can you hear me?" Roland asked as his armor shrank to normal human size. He touched her shoulder and she looked up at him, blood trickling from her mouth.

"Makarov will do well," Stacey said. "Help her. Help me, Ken…Ken, just come back…"

"No, I'm not going to lose you like this. I—" Roland tucked the chin of his helm to his chest and willed himself back into Ken Hale's form, from the time he met the war hero face-to-face at a restaurant in Phoenix.

"Stay with me," Roland/Hale said and Stacey's eyes went wide.

"I always loved you," she said, "but I know you never did."

"But I—I—" Stacey's face changed to Makarov's and Roland's heart swelled. His body changed back to his own, and Stacey looked away from his face to the scar on his hand, the kiss-shaped scar she'd given him.

Running her fingertips over the abused flesh, she asked, "Roland?"

"My Lady?"

"You came for me?" Her body grew more coherent.

"Of course. You are our Nation. You love us all. We would never abandon you."

"Ken left me...but you came back." Stacey got to her feet and she went silver. "I am needed. Take me home, Roland. I grow tired of this lie."

Roland stood and looked around. "We need Trinia to make a—oh, there's one." He pointed to a simple wooden door in a frame a few feet away. He opened it, and warm light shone through.

She took him by the hand, her normal chill gone.

"Faith," she said. "My faith in you was rewarded.

Saint Kallen is real, no matter what we know between us."

They stepped into the light together.

****

Seru screamed and thrashed against the metal vines holding her up. The seat retracted into the wall and she fell to one side, hands clawing at her face as her wails faded into a weak groan.

"What's happening to her?" Pallax reached for Seru but pulled back when cracks broke out across her naked body.

"I'm losing access to the Ark!" Noyan shouted.

As Seru stretched a hand toward Pallax, her fingers crumbled and fell to the ground like ashes.

"My love," Seru said as half her face shattered and sloughed off. "My love, hellllllll—"

Her head twisted to one side and fell, separating cleanly from her neck. Her body froze into a statue and all color drained away.

"Seru?" Pallax nudged her head with his foot. "You have failed Malal. Such a pity."

"I never liked her," Noyan said. "My connection to the Ark is fading. The prophet is waking up and if we don't—"

"Awaken the pilgrims," Pallax snapped. "All of them. This is a sign from the Perfect One. We must cleanse the galaxy of life, just as he did. Then we will be found worthy. A final test before paradise."

"Shunting power." Noyan's Medusa-like hair went into overdrive, tapping out commands and blurring around her face. "What of the humans?"

"Kill them. Kill them all."

****

Cold, thick fluid enveloped Roland. He was in total darkness and his first reaction was to panic. He opened his mouth to gulp in air, but his mouth and lungs were already full of liquid. He lashed out, bumping hands and feet against the inside of his womb.

"Calm yourself," Trinia said.

Roland stopped, his limbs braced against the inside of his pod.

"Your mind is present again," Trinia said, "though you're dangerously close to redlining. Relax or I will pump you full of tranquilizers."

"Stacey? My Lady?"

"She's free," Trinia said. "Though I'm not sure how much damage was done to her in there. Optics back online."

The command platform snapped up around him, and he looked from side to side. Metal vines lay on the side of the throne, white and steaming. Stacey was there, unmoved from the last time he saw her. Roland tried to move, but his armor wouldn't obey his commands.

A tremor rattled through the bridge and Morrigan unsnapped the blade of her sword, raised her gauss barrels, and looked around.

"What's going on up there?" Gideon shouted from the bottom of the stairs.

The small Qa'resh probe emerged from Stacey's chest, hovered for a moment, then began to move away. Stacey's hand snapped out and closed over the probe, red light pulsing from between her fingers.

"Now where do you think you're going?" Stacey asked.

"Are you here?" Trinia asked her. "Completely here?"

"Trinia?" Stacey leaned back against the throne. "I didn't think you'd be so tall…and so green."

Motes of light flashed within the lattice, sending out ripples like rain across the surface of a pond.

"The quake have anything to do with your interface going malky?" Morrigan asked.

Trinia frowned at the display. "It's coming too fast for me to read," the Aeon said.

"The Geist are draining the Ark." Stacey's eyes shone with light as she spoke. "They…my God, the power they have. I can slow it down, but then…"

"My Lady, if we possess the ability to leave, may I suggest we use it?" Morrigan asked.

Stacey cocked her head to one side. "What have I done?" she asked. "What have I awoken?" The Ark shook and the upper platform dipped up and down.

"My Lady?" Morrigan braced Roland before the disturbance could topple him over.

"It's too late," Stacey said. "Far too late…time to go."

Chapter 29

Santos spun up his rotary gun and sprayed rounds in an arc across the oncoming thralls. Bullets chewed through the Geist foot soldiers, blasting into sand as they died.

He picked up an increase in gauss rifle fire to his left and swung his higher-caliber cannons toward the shooting. A scythe emerged from the dirt as rifle fire chewed up the earth and gouged out hunks of the scythe's body.

Santos put a double shot into the beast's head, and it collapsed back into the hole. A legionnaire tossed a grenade into the hole, blowing apart thralls as they climbed over the scythe's remains.

"You're useful, for a Union dog," Marshal

Davoust said from his spot on the parapet as he slammed home a fresh magazine into his pistol and landed three head shots with as many pulls of the trigger.

"You're not so bad yourself for someone so…bald," Santos said, ejecting his rotary's magazine and commanding his auto-loaders to attach another. An error message flashed across his HUD. "Running out of bullets. Good thing I can swing an axe and never get tired. Your boys can say the same?"

"If my legionnaires draw breath, they can kill," Davoust said, peering over the parapet at a black tide forming in the distance.

Beams of light blasted out of temple domes, forming pylons of white light with crackles of blue lightning between them. Santos followed the beams up and saw them fracture into rays high in the atmosphere.

"Ah!" Davoust ripped his helmet off and leaned against the bulwark, digging a knuckle against his right ear. "My quantum-dot comms just went berserk."

The pylons sputtered out and the domes faded back to normal.

"We going with sky beams bad or sky beams good?" Santos asked. "Because the only thing up there is your fleet, which would make sky beams bad if all those ships just got hit, and those pyramid things…which probably means sky beams bad. Bad. Let's stick with bad."

"Does all Union Armor talk so damn much?" Davoust put the edge of his helmet to his nose then sniffed the inside. He pulled out a small charred box, then tossed both items aside. A legionnaire nudged his shoulder then pointed out over the defenses.

The rumble of thousands and thousands of feet rose in the distance as a dark tide of thralls advanced toward them at a run.

"*Sancti spiritus adsit nobis gratia,*" Davoust said, putting one hand on Santos's armor.

"Not how I planned on dying," Santos said, "but…we'll make these Geist remember us."

The oncoming wave of attackers stopped just beyond the fog. Arms and crude weapons flailed up and down, but they didn't come any closer.

Santos fired a single bullet from his gauss cannon. A ripple of energy burst from in front of the Geist and the shell ricocheted back, striking the Ark a few feet over Santos's shoulder.

Ibarrans cursed in Basque and ducked behind the wall.

"Cease. Fire," Davoust said.

"Hey, now we know there's a force field. Also, my bad," Santos said, watching light glow from beneath the

Ark's hull. "That's new. Not sure if it's a good new or a bad new."

The whole planet moved like a wave beneath their feet, and the Geist beyond the force field fell away. Santos looked up and watched as clouds lowered toward him.

"We're moving?" Davoust stomped on the ground. "But it doesn't feel like it."

Nekara's sky stretched out around them as the Ark ascended higher and higher.

"Brave warriors of the Ibarra Nation," Stacey said through an open IR channel, *"don't panic. I have this under control."*

****

"Admiral!"

Makarov looked away from the *Warsaw*'s holo table to the bridge. Her XO was on his feet, a red light growing from the twin rings of pyramids around Nekara and flooding him and the rest of the crew with firelight. The event ended before Makarov could get to her command seat.

"Get me Davoust," she said. "Try the Lady's Templar guards again. Anything from the surface!"

She went to the sensor officer and put one hand on the back of her seat. "Change detected from the pyramids?" the admiral asked.

"Everything got overloaded in that…whatever it was," the sensor officer said, rebooting systems and tapping against her keyboard as progress bars filled far too slowly.

"Give me a telescope from the prow point defenses," said Makarov as she looked over her shoulder. "XO, ready the Keystone gate. Withdraw all personnel to the construction ships and leave all equipment behind. If we're about to leave, we'll need to do so in a hurry."

"But what about our troops on the ground? Lady Ibarra?" Andere, the executive officer, asked.

"What chance do any of us have if those pyramids just came back online?" She unsnapped a small data slate from her belt and keyed in a code. "Authenticate Fleet Admiral Makarov, Ivana, delta phi 9909. Arm all denethrite charges on the Keystone."

The sensor officer looked up at her, eyes wide.

"You want to see a thousand of those Geist ships over Navarre?" Makarov asked.

"Negative, ma'am." The officer touched a screen and a camera feed came up.

The pyramids glowed from within, slowly rotating

their apexes away from the planet's surface and toward the *Warsaw*.

"Battle stations!" Makarov ran back to the holo table and brought up local space around Nekara. The two rings of Geist ships fluctuated as sensor data trickled in from the rest of the Ibarran fleet. The tiny plots within the holo, each a pyramid several times the size of her *Warsaw*, stretched away from the planet and toward the Keystone.

A red diamond—an unidentified detection—pulsated over the Ark's location.

"XO, order the—"

Red energy beams snapped across the prow of her ship and Makarov braced herself against the holo table.

"Damage report!"

"No hits," the XO called back.

In the holo, error messages appeared over the frigates *Biscay* and *Rutledge*. Neither ship responded to Makarov's hails.

"*Warsaw!*" The captain of the carrier *Victoria* appeared in the holo. "We just lost two of our picket ships. Both destroyed in that volley."

"Then why are any of us alive?" Makarov looked at the last-known location of the ships and found her answer.

"Fleet, this is Makarov," she said on a wide

channel. "The enemy is after the Keystone. Close on the jump gate at best speed. Put your hulls between the gate and the Geist. I believe they won't fire if there's a risk of hitting the Keystone."

She touched another of her ships in the holo.

"*Breitenfeld*, how long until we can get the hell out of here?"

A timer appeared over the Keystone.

0:21:17

"Too long," Makarov hissed and ran a time plot from the leading edge of the Geist ships to the Keystone. They had half that time before the enemy reached them.

"Shall we open fire?" her gunnery officer asked.

"Like trying to stop a wave with a lit match," Makarov said. "Keep all power to the engines." She set the small slate on the table edge and stared at a pulsing red button. One press and the Keystone—and all hope of ever leaving this system—would be blown to dust.

Mother didn't waver, she thought. *Her fleet couldn't stop the Xaros, but she fought on. Bought Earth time to get ready for the invasion. If I'm to die for the same purpose…at least I can face her with honor in heaven.*

"XO, send the destroyer *Kalaris* to the gate. They're to return to Navarre and warn the Nation of what happened here," she said. "Guns, bring the rest of the fleet about. We'll do our best to buy the *Kalaris* time."

"Aye aye," Adere said, a knot in his throat.

"Makarov…" Her name came through her helmet speaker, high-pitched and tinny, but there was no new channel open. "Makarov, you must hold true."

"Who is this?"

"Destroy the Keystone. I will bring us all home."

Makarov tapped the side of her helmet, unsure if stress was inducing audio hallucinations.

The Geist ships shifted toward each other, like a hand grasping at something.

Makarov zoomed in and found the Ark, trailing jagged rock beneath it like it had been ripped out of the planet. The Qa'resh ship rolled over, and the tips of the shell-like protrusions wavered.

A curtain of pure energy blasted away from the Ark and the holo field scrambled. Makarov spun toward the bridge and her jaw dropped. The attack from the Ark had expanded into a fan thousands of miles across. It angled down, sweeping over half the Geist ships and over the outer edge of Nekara's surface.

The blast snapped off and Geist ships shone like embers against the night. On Nekara, a slice of the planet was gone, leaving magma exposed, pulsating like a wound.

Makarov crossed herself.

"Destroy the Keystone," the voice said again. "Now, Makarov! You were not born to follow every single one of your mother's footsteps."

"The Geist wouldn't tell me to destroy the gate," Makarov said, taking a deep breath before she hit the trigger.

The Keystone exploded outward, sending millions of fragments scattering across the system.

"The *Kalaris* didn't make it through the wormhole," her XO said.

"Just wait." Makarov went to her command chair and clasped her hands behind her back. She made out the pearl-colored hull of the Ark as it approached. "Our faith in Lady Ibarra is well-placed."

A white field formed behind the Ark, expanding dozens of miles as they kept pace with the Qa'resh ship. Makarov said a silent prayer as the new jump gate passed over her ship.

Chapter 30

Valdar shook his head, wishing he could wipe the sweat from off his brow.

"Order our Eagles—I mean Shrike—fighters off that Vish rock and back to the *Guzman*," he said. "She's been vulnerable for too long, whatever small craft the ants still have will think she's an easy target."

"Aye aye." Zahar nodded and worked a screen in the holo tank only he could see. The captain's eyes narrowed as the plots within the holo began changing. "Admiral…the Vishrakath are moving off. They're breaking orbit from Mars. Course plots for deep space."

"They're running?" Valdar frowned. "That flotilla coming around from Deimos was about to—"

The holo tank went wild with static and Valdar

took a step back.

"By the Saint!" a bridge officer shouted.

Valdar turned around and his jaw dropped. The Ark was there, gleaming in pearl and ivory, contrasting with the ruddy red of Mars. A lance of light shot out from the shell tips of the Qa'resh vessels and broke into smaller rays. Each annihilated a Vishrakath vessel. Sparks seemed to fly off the tip of each lance and ray as the aliens were picked off with terrifying speed. After a minute, the Ark went silent.

"Scope's....clear," the gunnery officer said. "No active threat ships detected."

"Oh," Marc said. "Oh no."

"You know what that is?" Valdar asked.

"You are in so much trouble." Marc took off his helmet and tossed it onto the holo table.

Zahar put one hand to the commo suite in his helmet and stared daggers at Valdar.

"Whelp, the jig is up." Marc looked down and his shell returned to his true self, growing slightly and ripping out of the legionnaire armor. He shrugged off what remained and backed against a bulkhead.

Lift doors opened and armsmen swarmed onto the bridge, their gauss carbines trained on Valdar and Marc.

"Admiral," Zahar sneered, "you are relieved. Guards, secure them both."

Armsmen grabbed Valdar and flung him to the deck. He didn't resist as they cuffed him.

****

Gideon watched the holo over the Ark's throne as the Ibarran fleet finished off the Vishrakath. In his many years of war, he'd never seen a battle ended so quickly…or persecuted more ruthlessly. The Vishrakath must have lost hundreds of ships; their wreckage would form a small asteroid field near where Ceres had once orbited the sun.

Santos stepped off the disk.

"All troops are inside the Ark," he said. "Internal air is almost to Earth standard."

Gideon switched to short-range IR for just the three Iron Dragoons.

"You get vid of the internal layout?" Gideon asked.

"Mission accomplished," Santos said, tapping a thumb against his forefinger. "Lot of the energy cells went dark. Guess this thing will need a recharge soon."

"You saw what this thing did—to the Geist, the

Vishrakath," Cha'ril said. "Nothing can stop the Ibarrans now."

"At least they're on our side, right?" Santos asked.

Gideon shifted his gaze to the four Templar surrounding Stacey Ibarra and the Aeon on the upper deck.

"What makes you think that?" Gideon asked.

"They just...wiped the Vish and Kesaht fleets attacking Earth. They didn't have to. The war should be over." Santos's suit shifted from foot to foot.

"Did Earth win? Surviving on our knees isn't what I'd call a victory," Gideon said.

"The only one controlling this ship is the silver Ibarran," Cha'ril said.

"I see that too," Gideon said and clenched his fists within his womb.

"What? What—I'm confused," Santos said.

"Head down, mouth shut, Santos." Gideon flexed his hands and a plan formed. "The Ibarrans still have our Strike Marines and all our wounded from the attack on Kesaht'ka. We need to free them. Get them home. We need to behave."

For now, he thought.

Stacey stood up and the light around the throne dimmed slightly. She made her way down the steps, her

Templar in a cordon around her, Trinia following a few steps behind her. The Ibarran leader stopped next to Gideon.

"We meet again," she said.

"Ibarra."

"You're the Union commander, yes? You and your Armor will board the *Breitenfeld*. I have some business to attend to, then you'll be taken back to Earth. Agreed?" she asked.

"That ship is Union. It was always Union. We—"

"Are testing my patience," Stacey said. "Trinia vouches for your conduct. Because of this, I am extending a courtesy. Don't push it."

"She will stay with me," Gideon said. "This is her wish."

Stacey looked over one shoulder at the Aeon, and the tall alien nodded slowly.

"She and I have some business that we must conclude together. After that, I'll bring her to you on the *Breitenfeld*." Stacey motioned toward the disk. "Go. There's a shuttle waiting for you all."

Gideon hesitated. With all four Templars around her…

"You will deliver Trinia to me personally," Gideon said. "On your honor."

"You'd accept my word?" Stacey's shell rippled with light.

"A lot of trust has been offered lately," Gideon said, and a snarl broke out across his face. He betrayed his emotion within his womb, not through his words.

"Agreed. I'll bring her to you," Stacey said and dismissed him with a flick of her hand.

"Dragoons," Gideon said. Turning his back on them, he went to the disk.

"What are you doing?" Cha'ril hissed at him over a suit-to-suit link. "This is our last chance to—"

"Let it go," Gideon said. "This is not your concern, Dotari."

Ibarra's flush with victory. Power. Gideon thought. *She's overconfident now…and that will make her sloppy. Just have to wait a little bit longer.*

Gideon turned his helm to Roland as the disk pulled away and light enveloped them.

Chapter 31

Drool glistened from Charadon's teeth. The old Toth clicked claw tips together as a timer on the data globe neared zero.

"We'll clear the horizon soon, master," he said to Bale. "Full bombardment of…Seoul? That is the first population center in range."

"How many there?" Screens came up on the inside of Bale's tank. "Only a few hundred thousand. Shall we demand surrender until we have a better target…Adelaide, perhaps?"

The data globe shimmered and Charadon hacked out a curse. The globe morphed into a giant conch shell, the bottom encrusted with rock.

"What is that?" Bale asked. "Some sort of message

from the humans?"

"It's there." Charadon pointed a long finger out the forward window. The Ark was squarely between the *Last Light* and Earth.

Thin rays of light snapped out from the Ark's shell tips and crisscrossed over the Toth dreadnought. Charadon slunk back, hands covering his face.

"Our ships," he said. "All our Kesaht escorts are gone."

"Prepare my escape pod!" Bale practically leaped off the throne and made for a door. "Do…do what the humans did! Set a collision course. Charadon, this is your ship. You should go down with it."

New rays leapt away from the Ark and the *Last Light* rumbled with impacts.

The throne exploded with sparks as a nearby energy cannon on the hull overloaded. Charadon found himself in a puddle of yellow Toth blood and saw Bale exit the bridge. He tried to crawl out from under what was left of the throne, but both his hands were gone, replaced by blackened, smoking stumps. He hissed a menial to help, but the smaller Toth flicked its tail and bolted off the bridge, following Bale.

Charadon felt the spine of the *Last Light* crack under the Ark's assault, and realized he would follow

Bale's final order. Like it or not.

****

A half-wrecked Toth escape pod lay canted on the *Warsaw*'s flight deck. Armed and ready legionnaires formed an outer ring around the craft, while Ibarran Armor made up an inner ring. Trinia peeked over Roland's shoulder as Nicodemus wrenched open a ramp and tossed the garage-door-sized piece of hull to one side.

A Toth menial jumped out of the hole, small claws brandished and tail whipping around furiously. Nicodemus caught it by the neck and broke its spine with a twist of his wrist, then tossed the still-twitching body aside.

"I'm prepared to negotiate!" came from within the escape pod.

Nicodemus raised his gauss blaster and stepped back. Bale emerged slowly, three of the four mechanical legs of his tank functioning normally, the fourth catching and sputtering as he crawled out of the pod.

The Toth overlord straightened his legs against the deck, trying to bring his disembodied brain level with Nicodemus's helm. When he came up almost a yard short,

Bale crouched back down, one leg prodding the dead menial.

"I don't remember that one's name…" Bale said. "But let's make a deal, yes? An armistice, perhaps? Yes, yes…a cessation of all hostilities. I'll need transportation back to Kesaht Prime to make sure everything comes to a complete end. Ending a holy war is just as easy as starting one, in my experience."

"You are a monster," Trinia said as she stepped out from behind Roland. "They know what you've done!"

"I got carried away," Bale said, his tendrils writhing within his tank. "After you humans wiped out my race, I thought a little 'eye for an eye' was in order. Can you blame me? And look where we ended up! Earth needs a little repair work and the Kesaht can—I can turn their passions elsewhere. Let's just wipe the slate clean and I'll—"

A legionnaire stepped forward and removed her helmet. Silver skin and hair shone beneath the deck's lighting.

"We are at the end," Stacey Ibarra announced. "Millions are dead because of you, Bale. The Kesaht were no threat to the galaxy until you turned them loose. Trinia told us of the abomination you forced her to create. We know your plan for all of humanity."

"It wouldn't have been that bad," Bale said, backing away as Stacey walked toward him. Nicodemus gripped the upper edge of his tank and stopped him cold. "Remember Nibiru? What old Mentiq had in place? Happy humans! Living and working and—"

"Cattle," Stacey said. "You would have turned us into cattle to be bred and slaughtered."

"When you put it that way…but let's deal with reality. The Kesaht still have their holy war against you. You want to kill me now? The Kesaht won't stop just because I'm gone. Make me a martyr, you've got a long-term problem—one I won't be able to rein in. Yes? Yes. So send me back and I'll—"

"Nicodemus."

The armor put one foot against a leg joint on Bale's tank and pried the limb away, tipping Bale over. Nicodemus ripped the other legs off and tossed them over his shoulder, then put a sabaton on the tank to keep it from rolling away.

"The Kesaht are tearing themselves apart right now," Stacey said. "Their fleets have pulled out of Union space. Every ship that makes it back to their home system joins in the new civil war…and the side that sees you as a savior is losing. Badly."

"This is madness!" Bale shrieked. "I am the last of

the Toth! I'm an endangered species. Think of what the rest of the galaxy will do when they hear of this murder. This xenocide. Don't you have regrets for what you did to my planet? I'm a second chance! Turn over a new leaf, Ibarra."

"The only thing I regret is not wiping every last one of you out the first time," Stacey said, removing her legionnaire gauntlets and dropping them to the deck. She flexed her silver fingers against each other.

"You had a chance, Bale," she said. "You know why I chose to sacrifice your people to win the war against the Xaros. The Toth were a scourge on the galaxy. Slavers. Murderers. Your entire species was dedicated to feeding overlords like you…getting your fix through new and different minds to consume. And when you had the chance to turn away from all that…you proved irredeemable."

"A trial! I deserve a trial. Humans love justice, don't they? I'll need a barrister and we need a neutral race to serve as a judge—"

"You're the last of the Toth." Stacey looked back to the Aeon. "Others in your place chose to do good works with the time left to them. Trinia?"

"Do it," Trinia said.

"Do what?" Bale's brain swam from side to side in

the tank. "This is insane! You can't do this to me!"

Stacey bent over, her face even with Bale's eye stalks. "The Toth believe hell is a cold...cold place," she said. "If only my body could spit."

She slapped her bare hands against Bale's tank and frost crept across the surface.

"There's no need for this," Bale said as his neural system moved to the bottom of the tank. A tendril poked at the ice crystals forming in the surrounding fluid. "You can't kill me! I'm the last of the Toth. Don't let me—it's getting cold in here...Okay, you've made your point! Let me repent! I'll be your slave, do whatever you want if you—"

"I'm giving you a chance to die with dignity," she said. "Though this is what I expected."

"You do this, you'll be worse than I am! Humans would have lived..." Bale's words came slower. Tendrils pushed his brain off the tank wall and danced around as ice nipped at the ends. "Pleassssss..."

"I've learned to accept a number of things about myself," Stacey said, peering closer into the tank as the fluid grew opaque with ice.

The Toth's brain bumped against the glass next to her face and stopped moving. Ice squealed as it solidified the neural tissue.

Stacey pulled her hands away with a snap.

"Nicodemus? Would you mind?" She took a step back.

The armor lifted his sword high over his head and swung it down like an axe chopping into a felled tree. The tank shattered, spilling chunks of ice and Bale's frozen remnants across the deck and around Stacey's feet.

"Satisfied?" she asked Trinia.

The Aeon gagged for a second then nodded furiously.

Stacey picked up a broken piece of Bale's ornate goldwork that had broken off the tank and tossed it to a bodyguard.

"There is a Karigole aboard the *Breitenfeld*. See that he gets this with my compliments. Now, to Earth. Time to set things right with the Terran Union."

Chapter 32

President Garret hurried down the cramped hallway. His dress shirt was nearly soaked through with sweat and he badly needed one of the pills rattling around in a coat pocket. He stopped at a vault door guarded by a pair of Rangers.

"Everything okay, Mr. President?" a Ranger asked.

"I'll tell you after this," Garret said, smoothing his hair and doing his best to straighten out his suit. "Open it up."

There was a clang and the door rolled to one side. In the vault was a small box with a lit projection lens on a wooden stool. Stacey Ibarra stood in front of the lens, her shadow on the wall. Garret stepped inside and closed the vault.

"Lady Ibarra," Garret said, flopping his hands against his legs, "I suppose thanks are in order."

"You 'suppose.'"

Garret sighed. His breath fogged and he noticed a distinct chill in the air. "Your fleet arrived in time to keep Mars from falling," he said. "Then your new…ship? Is that what it is? Your new ship put an end to the siege, so I—"

"Now my Ark is over Earth and you're worried I'm going to turn this planet into a cinder," she said as light from the lens played across her chrome surface.

"There's no reason for that! There are a billion people here who—"

"You're right." Stacey held up a finger. "There's no reason for me to punish Earth for what you've done."

"What *I've* done? I don't know what you're talking about. Relations between the Ibarra Nation and the Union were strained, surely, but—"

"Do you know what I did to the last worm that sniveled and squirmed at my feet?" Stacey took a step toward Garret and the chill grew stronger.

Garret did a double take at the box then looked to Stacey as she stepped out of the light and grabbed him by the wrist. He yelped as his flesh began to freeze. Stacey put a finger to his chest and pushed him back into the wall.

Garret reached for the panic button on his belt.

"Don't," she said, wagging the finger at him. "Let's not ruin your sterling reputation for grace under fire. We need to get some issues worked out between us. Do you want to talk or do you want to piss your pants?"

"Talk," Garret said, his voice going an octave too high, and he cleared his throat. "Talking is always good."

"Something has…awoken," Stacey said. "Something ancient and terrible. They're called the Geist, and I don't know when they'll get here, but they're coming. For you. For me. For every soul in this galaxy. You must reopen the procedural farms. You must rebuild your fleet. Your armies. All of it must be stronger than ever."

"We can't just…do that," Garret said. "The Hale Treaty—"

Stacey grabbed the projection box and hurled it at Garret. It exploded against the wall behind him.

"Fool! You kept to that damn treaty and the Vishrakath took advantage of your stupidity and weakness. You will not survive the Geist unless you restart the tubes. I slowed them down, but I don't know for how long."

"Bastion!" Garret said, brushing bits of plastic off his shoulders. "Bastion will never go along with that. You think they'll believe some Ibarran boogeyman is the reason we just abandoned a treaty that we spent so much political capital to keep in place? Maybe you can convince them."

"I won't have to," Stacey said. "My next stop is Bastion and I'm bringing a very large, very fast comet with me. I'll aim it at that pathetic city and give them hours to get off world. They will see me in my Ark, a horrible and awful god, and I will tell them that human space—all human space, Ibarran and Union—is off-limits. Any incursion by any race, any attack, and that race will face my Ark—my Ark that doesn't need the Crucible gates. I am out of mercy."

"If there's some new threat coming, won't we need the other—"

"No!" Stacey backhanded the quantum projector and smashed it into fragments. "Bastion is corrupt. The rest of the galaxy thinks we are the enemy. We must divorce ourselves from them, let them fight amongst themselves and learn that we are not the threat. By the time the Geist reach them…they will be ready to fight beside us."

"The Senate will never go along with this," Garret said. "We have a long-standing relationship with—"

"I'm not asking," Stacey said, cutting him off. "I need a strong Union as my ally against the Geist. I will accept a conquered Earth fighting under my orders."

"You wouldn't," Garret sneered. "Your soldiers

are still human. They won't do it."

"They are mine, you weakling. They are all mine. Do you want to test my resolve? Do you want to see the full power of the Ark?"

Garret wiped cold sweat from his face. "You're insane. We're not your slaves. No matter what doomsday weapon you've found."

"I only ask you to act in your own self-interest. In your Union's interest. I will ensure the Ibarra Nation will endure the coming darkness. It is better if the Union is an ally in that fight and not fodder for the Geist. Reopen your procedural crèches. Rebuild your defenses. If you do not act quickly…I will."

Garret's shoulders slumped. "I'll do what I can."

"You don't want to see me again, Garret. You won't like how that ends. Now…we have some business to take care of."

"More?" Garret chuckled. "You want the Union to break off from the galaxy and prepare for a war against some phantom mena—"

"Saint Kallen," Stacey said, interrupting him again and putting a hand to her hip. "I'm taking her bones to Navarre. Her legacy belongs to the Ibarra Nation. Your armor lost the mantle when they turned on the Templar."

"Agreed…if you return the *Breitenfeld* and all

Union prisoners. Especially Admiral Valdar." Garret licked his lips.

"I will return the *Breitenfeld*'s crew. Masha. I need her back."

"Valdar. His ship. That strike carrier has significant historical and cultural significance to the Union. You can't have Kallen *and* the ship that won the Ember War," Garret said, leveling a finger at her chest.

Stacey snatched the finger and Garret gasped in pain. He went to his knees, whining as her freezing touch burned down his hand.

"Valdar killed my sailors. Tricked them into a fight that wasn't theirs. He will answer for those deaths. I just might destroy the *Breitenfeld* while he watches. Let him feel that loss. You will return Masha to me…and you will send one more person along with her." Stacey flung Garret's hand to one side and he fell on top of it, clutching the frostbitten flesh to his chest.

Garret heard his pill bottle rattle within his coat. His hand was numb, but the tingle of nerves promised a world of pain in the near future.

"This was never a negotiation," Stacey said. "Take your 'meds,' and get ready for more instructions."

****

Valdar was on his knees, a hood over his head, hands bound behind his back. He could tell from ambient noise that he was in the *Yalta*'s main hangar bay. He'd been kept blind for hours and felt a Crucible gate jump just before he was dragged from the brig to the bay.

The hood came off and he blinked against bright light. Through the open bay doors, he saw Ceres and Earth through the force field holding in the bay's atmosphere.

Marc was on the deck next to him, an Armor's foot pinning him down.

"Valdar, we are not in a good situation here," Marc said. "Let *me* do the talking."

Valdar's breath fogged as a chill washed over his face.

Stacey, the real one, and Captain Zahar stopped in front of Valdar. Her doll-like face was inscrutable, but Valdar could feel the anger inside of her. Zahar looked cowed, ashamed.

"Granddaughter!" Marc called out. "So I take it things went great on Nekara."

Stacey held up a finger and the Armor pressed its sabaton against Marc's chest. Deck plating groaned under the pressure.

"Shutting up! Shutting up!" Marc shouted.

The foot eased against him.

"Captain Zahar tells me you tricked him into leaving Navarre and helping Earth," Stacey said. "Is that accurate?"

"Zahar believed he was following your orders," Valdar said. "No Ibarran but that one," he cocked his head toward Marc, "knew any wiser."

"Why did you do it, Valdar? Why go along with this charlatan? This…lying piece of garbage."

"For Earth." Valdar got to his feet and looked Stacey in the eye. "For the Union. You knew we were losing. Knew how many were about to die. Why did you ignore us?"

"I came around eventually," she said. "Once I realized just how badly I'd need Earth in the near future."

"Before that? You could've sent the Fifth." Valdar motioned to Zahar.

"And more Ibarran lives would've been lost," she said. "I destroyed every Kesaht and Vishrakath ship with the Ark. No human casualties. Ibarran or Union. Though I wish I could have arrived sooner."

"And Phoenix would be destroyed if I'd arrived any later. Can that Ark of yours bring people back to life? Rebuild a capital?"

"No…it can't. But Zahar is blameless for what you did?" she asked.

"He fought well. Fine commander. You can't hold him responsible for what I did," Valdar said.

"Captain," Stacey held up a hand, "you are dismissed. Return to your duties."

"My Lady." Zahar bowed slightly and hurried away.

"As for you…" Stacey grabbed Valdar by the collar and the cold of her touch numbed one side of his neck. She ripped the rank insignia off his uniform and tossed it to one side. She tore away the Ibarra Navy patch on one shoulder and plucked the ship commander insignia off his breast, leaving his void suit in tatters.

"You don't deserve those honors," she said.

"No apologies from me," Valdar said.

"Ibarrans are dead because of you."

"And more live for it." He looked up at the Armor still holding Marc down. "Tell everyone in Phoenix they would be dead if you'd had it your way. Which lives are more valuable to you?"

"Things…are different now, Valdar. But you…are right. I acted too late," she said.

"Sorry, what?" Marc raised his head off the deck. "Valdar mentioned that this was all my idea, right? Sure, he commanded the ship and blew up the Vish part, but everything else was all me."

"Nicodemus." Stacey looked away from Valdar and the Armor lifted his foot off of Marc.

"There." Marc brushed off his chrome chest as he got to his feet. "See, a little humility can go a long way. Just let Valdar and me go back to Earth and the healing process can—"

"Marc Ibarra!" The name echoed off the bay walls as Stacey's voice went so loud, it stung Valdar's ears. "I have had enough of you. By my right as leader of the Ibarra Nation, you are hereby exiled for time and all eternity. Nicodemus."

"Now you wait one second." Marc held out a hand.

The kick from the Armor sent a rush of air past Valdar. There was a clang of metal on metal and the last Valdar saw of Marc was his silver body tumbling end over end through space as he hurtled toward Ceres.

"Am I leaving the same way?" Valdar asked.

"You have blood on your hands, Valdar," she said. "Our blood. You think I can just forgive that? You're going to internment with the rest of the *Breitenfeld*'s crew. I'll decide what to do with you later."

Valdar got one last look at Earth, his home,

before the hood went over his eyes.

****

Masha came down a Mule ramp with a bounce in her step, her hands cuffed behind her back, Major Kutcher leading her by the elbow. Legionnaires waited for them on the flight deck of the *Warsaw*.

"So good to be home." Masha smiled. "And a warm welcome from such big, strong men."

She stepped off the ramp and shimmied her hands up and down, rattling the chain between the cuffs.

Kutcher, avoiding all eye contact with the Ibarran troops, put a fob to the cuffs and they unsnapped.

Masha slipped out of the restraints and dangled them in front of Kutcher. "You can keep these. I'm not into that sort of thing, my dear."

Kutcher turned away and started up the ramp, but a hand grabbed him by the collar and yanked him back. He landed hard and slid until a legionnaire boot pinned him to the deck. One of Stacey's honor guards bent over and looked him in the eyes, then grabbed him by his thinning hair and whacked the back of Kutcher's head against the metal.

"I'm just delivering the prisoner! Let me go!" His

breath fogged and he went white with fear. The intelligence officer squirmed, but the Ibarrans kept him in place.

"I'll let you go," Stacey said, kneeling next to him. "But you and I...there's blood between us."

Kutcher tried to pull away from her, but the honor guard slapped an unkind hand against his chin and kept his face toward Stacey.

"You killed him," she said. "His name was Tyrel. Remember? You pulled him from an escape pod over Nunavik and you shot him in the head for being a procedural. You executed him for the simple crime of existing without your permission."

"It was the Hale Treaty. The Omega Provision!" Kutcher beat at the foot pinning him to the ground. "I—I had to. Bastion had witnesses there. Witnesses! If we'd let him live, Earth would have gone to war with *all* the members—not just the Vish, not just the Naroosha. It...I was just following orders!"

"There it is." Stacey shook her head. "You had integrity until just a moment ago. I know what it is to make hard decisions, little man. I could almost forgive you for what you did..."

"I'm sorry! So sorry! I didn't want to kill him, but I had no choice."

Stacey looked over her shoulder to Masha. "No choice? Masha is just as illegal as Tyrel...yet you didn't shoot her in the back of the head."

Kutcher sputtered.

"You did just what our alien enemies wanted you to do. You shed your brother's blood on their order. On their terms. You vile...little worm. You coward," she said as she removed a glove from one hand.

"I was just following orders!"

"I know. Oh, how I know that. That's why I won't kill you. Your commanders need a reminder that Ibarran blood is Union blood. We can't fight each other anymore...but actions must have consequences. I'll give you more of a chance than you gave Tyrel. Keep your brand—your mark as a murderer—and you will keep your life."

"Mark? Brand?" Kutcher's eyes darted from side to side.

Stacey put her bare hand on Kutcher's face, spreading her fingers across his brow but leaving a gap so she could look into his eyes.

Kutcher stifled a scream for a moment then howled in agony as her freezing touch bit into his skin. Stacey pulled her hand back, leaving an ugly print of blackened flesh across Kutcher's face.

"Keep the brand. Keep your life," Stacey said, flicking her fingers up. The boot moved off Kutcher's chest.

The intelligence officer scrambled back into the Mule, steam trailing from his face.

Stacey folded her hands over her knees and asked, "Masha, you were well treated?"

"They learned nothing from me, my Lady," the spy said as she rubbed her wrists. "Forgive me for failing you. For being captured."

"I have need of your talents," Stacey said as she rocked back onto the balls of her feet and stood. "Escort Admiral Valdar to internment on Zelara. See if you can sway him to our cause."

"He's not to be punished for stealing our fleet?"

"I have a knife in the Union's gut," Stacey said. "I wish to twist it—Valdar and the *Breitenfeld*, both in the Nation's service. Get it done."

"Yes, my Lady," Masha said.

"Medvedev will join you on Zelara," Stacey said and left, followed by her honor guard.

Masha grit her teeth and mumbled under her breath.

****

Pathfinder Tomas bounded over a small crater edge on Ceres. The low gravity made for easy travel across Earth's second moon, but hopping across the dusty landscape was still a tax on his muscles, even with the slight assist of his lighter power armor.

"This is nuts," his partner, Pathfinder Gerns, said through her suit link. "No way anyone survived without a suit. We'd pick up their emergency beacon."

"Today's had all sorts of crazy." Tomas looked up at the Ark, stationary in space near the Crucible. "Pilot saw a Dutchman. We go find a Dutchman. That's what Pathfinders do, remember?"

"Yeah, I remember that part of training," she said. "This Dutch better be alive to appreciate that we're on pod duty. I'm tired of busting my ass just to pick up remains."

"Bad attitude." Tomas vaulted over a crater lip and slid across the basin. A sprawl of dust and rocks spread from an impact point a few yards away. "There?"

"No weather on this rock." Gerns took a scanner off her belt. "Could be a meteor hit from eight million years ago. Nothing on the scope. I'll get the body bag out."

Tomas shuffled toward the impact and made out a humanoid shape just beneath the dust. He went to the neck and brushed the dark brown dirt away. Silver flashed in the sunlight.

"The hell?" Tomas reached for the chest, when a hand snapped out of the ground and gripped him by the wrist. He shrieked in a manner not befitting a Pathfinder as a dirt-encrusted hand clamped down on his visor.

"Settle down." The words came through without tone or inflection, vibrating through the fingers and against the glass of his visor.

"Holy—"

Tomas heard his partner panting as she fumbled for a gauss carbine locked to her back.

"Hold on!" Tomas raised a hand.

The figure sat up and dirt fell away from his silver face.

"Pathfinders. Good. I need you to contact anyone with stars for rank in Camelback Mountain," came through the touch on Tomas's visor. "Tell them Marc Ibarra needs a favor. We don't have much time to rescue Admiral Valdar."

Chapter 33

Santos scrubbed a towel against his scalp. His face tingled, a sensation normal after being so long in the pod. He wiped amniosis off his brow and looked up at his dirty, battered, and damaged Armor within a coffin-shaped maintenance bay. He leaned against the catwalk running chest height across all the bays.

"The *Breitenfeld* cemetery." He whistled and looked around. Cha'ril, one bay over and wearing a skin suit, stepped into an unmarked jumpsuit. "Maybe the Ibarrans will give us the ship back."

Aignar banged his cane against the bars of the catwalk.

"Stop gold-bricking," Aignar said. "Captain wants us on the flight deck. Not sightseeing."

Cha'ril zipped up her jumpsuit and joined her lance mates. She cast a quick glance at Ibarran legionnaires guarding the doorway.

"Why did the captain order us to dismount?" she asked. "If there's an issue, then—"

"I don't think we're prisoners," Aignar said. "But we're not their guests either. The captain worked out a deal. We're in orbit over Earth. They should let us go soon."

"Aignar, did you see that giant shell-looking thing?" Santos asked. "You see what it did? That Stacey lady could crown herself the Queen of Earth right now if she wanted. What the hell are we going to do about it?"

"The Ibarrans just pulled our asses out of the fire," Aignar said. "Broke the siege on Earth. I don't like them," he nudged his prosthetic jaw, "but let's accept the obvious: they're on our side...at least now they are."

"And Captain Gideon's been so...reasonable," Cha'ril said.

"Not like him with the Ibarrans." Aignar shook his head. "Now that we're all safe back in Union space, we...wait, where's the captain? His Armor's not here."

"Flight deck. Trinia's coming back from whatever she was doing with their Lady," Santos said.

Cha'ril's quills flared and she looked at Aignar.

"He wouldn't," Aignar said.

"This would be his last chance." She looked back at her suit and trilled with frustration.

"What're you two going on about?" Santos put on a pair of fresh boots.

"We need to get to the flight deck." Aignar hobbled away. "We need to get there now."

Chapter 34

Roland stood guard on one side of the Ark's command throne, Morrigan on the other. Stacey was in the seat, palms turned up, fingers twitching. The Qa'resh probe floated a foot in front of her chest, its light white and faint.

Earth hung in the portal above their heads.

"Never thought I'd see it again," Morrigan said through their suit link. "So many new cities…you can see their lights on the night side."

"I…have some concerns," Roland said.

"About Earth? The Vishrakath fleet is destroyed. Kesaht too. No more mass drivers coming to pummel the planet. All the out-system macro cannons are silent for once. What's there to worry about?" she asked.

"Our Lady dealt with Bale. Now she comes for the Union," he said.

"Ach, Bale was a war criminal. A monster. President Garret isn't in the same league."

"He signed the Omega Provision. Ibarrans are dead because of him," Roland said.

"She's...she wouldn't," Morrigan said, looking at him. "You still doubt her?"

"Toth are not humans. Templar don't take oaths to defend them."

"She's not going to fry our home world, Roland. Do you need some time out of your suit?"

"My synch rating is amber. Pulling Stacey out of that...purgatory...left me a bit fuzzy," he said. "I could use a checkup."

Stacey's head snapped back and the reflection off her face rippled.

"Trinia?" The word was high-pitched, the syllables almost a song. "Oh, Trinia...you won't believe what I've found!"

The Aeon came up the steps but stopped well short of the upper level.

"This place is tainted, Stacey," Trinia said. "Destroy it for good before Malal's legacy can bring more suffering to the stars."

"The Qa'resh had toys!" Stacey lifted a hand next to her face. "Toys and gizmos and gadgets we never imagined. It begs the question why they never shared any of it with us on Bastion. It could have made the fight against the Xaros so much easier. Look…"

She swiped through the air and a lattice appeared before Trinia. The Aeon looked it over, her face impassive.

"I see why," she said. "Look at the power source for all of them. They all draw from the reservoirs. They're all powered by soul energy. Death fueled them. The death of sentients. That's why the Qa'resh hid it from us, because we would have had to sacrifice ourselves to use them."

"The Ark still has some power left in it," Stacey said, "enough to set things right."

"You can't use it," Trinia said. "Malal drained the life from entire worlds to—"

"The dead are still dead!" Stacey rose from the throne. "I cannot siphon the power back into corpses. The reservoirs and this ship are simply tools to my will, and tools are neither good nor evil."

"I do not fear power," Trinia said. "I fear those who wield it."

"And I am to be…no…" Stacey looked down at her hand. Her wrist quivered and the motion traveled through her fingers. She clutched the palsied limb to her chest. "You were promised Earth—your freedom—if you helped me. But...could you stay with me just a little bit longer? This probe was corrupted, but with a little work, it could—"

"No." Trinia shook her head. "No. I've done enough. I helped you save the galaxy against the Xaros. I will not be part of what you do next."

"I...I understand," Stacey said as she put a hand on the throne and crouched slightly.

"My Lady?" Morrigan moved toward her.

"Fine! I'm fine!" Stacey straightened up. "I have a fair amount of control over one of the new toys. Let me flip a mental coin...Roland wins."

"My Lady," Morrigan said, putting a hand to Roland's shoulder. "He needs a bit of time to—"

Stacey snapped her fingers.

Colors melted together then reformed into a different place. An Ibarran transport was beside Roland, the ramp open, and Terran Union soldiers were staring at him, their jaws slack. He looked over a flight deck devoid of any other fighters or utility ships. A group of three Union Armor and a handful of Strike Marines were on the far side of the flight deck.

He was on the *Breitenfeld*.

Stacey looked at the fingers she snapped, then flexed her hand open. "Now there's a trick," she said.

Stacey's honor guard swarmed out of the shuttle and formed a circle around her and a bewildered Trinia.

"My Lady," one of the guards said, "you're on time…we thought you'd be late as—"

"—as I hadn't left the Ark." Stacey put two fingers to a temple. "Indeed. I can get back the same way…in a few minutes. Tell the Union to send Gideon over. We'll meet him halfway."

Roland tried to take a step forward, but his armor wouldn't respond.

Stacey got a few steps ahead of him, then paused. "Is there a problem?" she asked.

"My plugs are…a moment, my Lady," he said.

"Let me." Trinia went to his back and attached a data wire from an oversized, bespoke gauntlet on her left arm.

Gideon, on the other side of the flight deck, went to one knee and looked to a Strike Marine as he touched his arm, a normal devotion done to honor Saint Kallen.

"He's picked up religion?" Roland asked.

"Your neural stasis is fluctuating," Trinia said. "Stay back and do a full reboot cycle. Then unplug soon as you can. Make a note of how…teleporting affects neural systems. I'm a bit foggy myself. Your Lady doesn't have this problem—no flesh to bother."

Gideon stood and his ammo canisters fell from his armor to the deck. He flicked off the ammo belt connected to the gauss cannons mounted to his forearm.

"No time," Roland said, ejecting his own ammunition and taking a wobbly step forward.

"Trinia," Stacey said, "a moment. *Ysir meg nass'harr.*"

The Aeon responded with words and sounds he didn't think human vocal cords could reproduce just as a message request came up on his HUD. A short text message read "1836."

The year the Dragoon regiment was first constituted on Earth, Roland thought. He opened the channel, already knowing who was on the other side.

"Roland," Gideon said over the tight-beam IR, "you know what that Ark can do."

Stacey and Trinia started forward, still speaking in Aeon. Roland followed, though his armor's legs felt like rubber through his plugs.

"And?" Roland asked. His left hand flexed and the empty gauss cannon barrels felt heavy on his arm. Leaving his bullets suddenly felt foolish, but he wasn't unarmed.

"And only Ibarra can use it. It's too dangerous,

Roland. We've heard she's borderline insane. Is it true?"

Roland almost reached out to pull Stacey back but hesitated. Gideon had seen reason before. He'd fought beside the Ibarra Nation when the need arose. If he could sway Gideon to peace…

"She…she's got us this far. Ended the war with the Kesaht. Saved Earth. She's no threat to those who will leave us alone," Roland said.

"*She* is Saint Kallen, you fool," Gideon said. "It's all a fraud. There's a component in your Armor—"

"I know."

"You what?" Gideon stopped dead in his tracks. Then moved forward again before Stacey and Trinia could react.

"I know what she's done. Ibarra has iron in her soul, Gideon. I've seen it. She only wants what's best for all of us. I could have taken Trinia by force, left you all back on—"

"You expect me to believe that?" Gideon rumbled. "I know you. I don't believe you'd let a psychopath control a doomsday weapon. The Ibarrans have corrupted you with their damn cult of Kallen. You know the truth but refuse to see how blind you really are."

But he just let a Strike Marine use him as an icon…why would he talk of Kallen like that if he knows what Stacey's done?

He looked at Gideon's gauss cannons and a realization hit him. "Gideon. Don't. We want peace with Earth. Our Lady is—"

"I'm not one of yours." A whine went up as Gideon powered up the magnetic accelerators in his forearm cannons. Gideon's speakers clicked on.

"And I do this for *me*, traitor!"

Roland dove in front of Stacey as Gideon cocked his cannons and fired both barrels.

One shell hammered into his breastplate, cracking the armor and punching a dent into his womb. The other ricocheted off his shoulder, wrecking the servos within. Roland's mind went white-hot as pain lanced through his spike and his body felt the damage his suit had just taken.

Shouting a war cry, Gideon charged forward, pulling a METL hilt off his back and snapping the blade out in the shape of a gladius.

Stacey grabbed Trinia by the belt and yanked her back. The Aeon went sliding across the deck and away from the oncoming armor. Stacey raised her chin slightly and opened her hands to her side, offering a clean target.

"All your fault!" Gideon pulled the gladius up to his shoulder and leapt at the Ibarran leader.

Stacey didn't move.

Roland shoulder-tackled Gideon, turning his body

sideways. The two armor crashed into Stacey and sent her careening into the bulkhead.

Gideon got off Roland and swiped his gladius at his optics. Roland flinched and the blade sliced off his antenna. Roland unsnapped his hilt and drove the extending blade at Gideon's chest. The gladius parried the strike on one side and Gideon reversed his momentum to send the tip of his weapon skidding up Roland's arm and off a shoulder plate.

Ducking before the gladius could chop off his helm, Roland swung his longsword up and felt it connect against Gideon's thigh. The sword chopped into armor plate, and Roland twisted, cutting deeper as he drew the blade across the damage. There was a squeal of failing hydraulics and Gideon stumbled away.

Roland looked to Stacey, who was on all fours against the wall. The deck and bulkhead were coated in frost as her body worked to repair the damage. He got to his feet and backed toward her, his HUD alive with warnings, his left arm twitching against his side as his suit struggled to regain control of the damaged shoulder joint.

Gideon twisted his METL's hilt and the gladius snapped into a spear longer than Roland's sword. He stabbed at the damaged area of Roland's suit, where his gauss shell had found its mark, and the tip ripped across the shell of Roland's womb, spilling amniosis fluid out like a bleeding wound.

Roland got his left arm up and grabbed the spear haft. Gideon put his suit's strength into the weapon, and it pierced deeper into Roland's womb.

Roland swung his sword up to strike the haft, but it went wide, snapping back into the METL's hilt. He bounced against the wall, shielding Stacey with his body.

Gideon shifted his weapon into an axe and chopped off Roland's sword hand. Roland's HUD fizzled and his vision went red. He collapsed to one knee and raised his arms just in time to deflect another blow from the axe. Gideon punched Roland in the helm, badly denting the face and crushing half his optics.

The Union Armor transformed his weapon into a long spike and stabbed—not at Roland, but at Stacey braced against the wall just behind him.

With his remaining hand, Roland deflected the strike up and the spike punched through the bulkhead. He grabbed Gideon by the arm and pulled his other arm out to one side.

His punch spike emerged from the hole where his hand should have been, and he rammed the diamond-tipped point into Gideon's chest. The spike pierced the outer layer of armor, but not the inner womb.

Gideon tried to pull back his arm holding his weapon, but Roland's grip was too strong. The two suits struggled against each other, servos grinding.

"You hate me," Stacey said. "And you're right to hate me."

"You betrayed us all!" Gideon struggled and Roland pressed the punch spike closer against the womb. Gideon stopped, realizing his former lance mate could kill him in a split second.

"I am horrible," Stacey said. "I am everything you think I am…but I don't hate you, Gideon. I want to live. The battle that's coming is far worse than you can imagine. I want you to live because Earth will need you. Don't choose to die now. Please."

"Gideon," Roland managed through damaged speakers, "I…I'm redlining. Stop this."

Gideon looked at Roland, then to Stacey. He pulled his weapon free from Roland's grasp but kept it poised high and ready to strike.

"Never!"

Gideon drove the tip at Stacey's heart.

Roland twisted and punched his spike through Gideon's chest. He felt the inner wall give and the weapon strike home against the back of the other man's pod. Gideon's armor locked up and fell to its side, Roland's punch spike still embedded inside. Blood dribbled out of the womb and down Gideon's breastplate.

"Gideon?" Roland asked as his vision swam. He yanked his spike out and amniosis—thick with blood—poured down Gideon's Armor. Roland collapsed to his knees as he lost feeling throughout his body. Through one eye, he could see light shining off the blood covering his weapon and a pool spreading across the deck.

"Didn't…didn't want this, sir. If we could still be Iron Dragoons together…forgive…me."

His vision went red and his mind cut out.

Chapter 35

Santos pushed through a group of Strike Marines.

"Move. Move!" He shouldered Lieutenant Hoffman aside and looked across the *Breitenfeld*'s flight deck. An Ibarran shuttle took off and passed through the force field.

There, halfway across the deck, a pair of Armor lay entwined.

Santos and Cha'ril ran to Gideon, their feet splashing through a puddle of amniosis run through with blood.

Roland's black armor was cracked open, the womb gone. The Black Knight's fist spike still punctured Gideon's chest.

"No no no!" Santos tugged at the spike arm then

put his hands against the spike to stop the dribble of fluid.

"Stop…Santos." Cha'ril put her hands atop Gideon's arm. "It's no use. One of them was always going to die."

"We should've been here." Santos sank to his knees. "We could've stopped him or—"

"You know why," Aignar said as he limped over, Hoffman at one elbow keeping him upright. "You know why we weren't here. Don't you?"

"To protect us," Cha'ril said. "He went after…he tried to kill Ibarra, and we would've helped him. No question."

"And if he succeeded with us at his side, then the Ibarrans would've blamed all of Earth." Aignar raised the tip of his cane to the Ark in orbit over Ceres. "Alone…it was just him. Ah, Gideon. You stubborn…stubborn…"

Aignar's metal hand creaked open and he touched Gideon's helm.

"You didn't have to do it. Now look at you."

There was a whack of metal against the deck.

Santos looked over his shoulder at one of Stacey's honor guards, halberd in hand.

"Transports are coming," he said. "The Lady, in her grace, wants you to give honors to your dead. Take him with you."

"You son of a bitch!" Santos made for the guard, but an iron grip took him by the elbow. Aignar kept a painful hold on the younger Armor.

"Think, kid," he said. "Think about every Union soldier on this ship."

Santos shrugged his arm free, scowling at the guard.

"We've got Strike Marines," he said. "You know this ship, don't you, Hoffman?"

"Try it." The guard's leather gloves creaked as he gripped his weapon. "Please."

"*Breitenfeld* means a lot to people," Hoffman said. "But it's a hull. A thing. Can't replace people. Once they're gone…gone for good."

"I'm going to remember this." Santos pointed at the guard's face.

"And you best hope the Lady…doesn't." He backed up, not turning his back until he'd put distance between him and Santos.

Santos took an involuntary deep breath and spun back to Gideon. He wiped a sleeve across his eyes, chest heaving as he fought back tears.

"It's okay, kid." Aignar bumped his arm against Santos's, attempting real contact, not the cold touch of his prosthetics. "Let it out."

Santos went to his knees and bent his head against Gideon's foot. He covered his head with his arms and wept.

Chapter 36

There was pain—pain and a world of white light, like he was trapped in a Crucible portal and every nerve ending tingled with agony. Roland felt the sensation at a base level as a dark, massive shape loomed over him. A childhood memory of suffering through a fever subsumed him...and he questioned if he was even alive as he made out long strands of hair around a face.

"Mom?" he asked, his voice little more than a rasp.

"That is unlikely."

Roland bent his fingers, but his joints felt rubbery. "I hurt too much to be dead...but I redlined." He scrunched his face, but broken glass beneath his skin made him want to go back into the white light.

"You redlined. Hard," the voice said. A hypo spray touched his neck and a cool wave passed through his body, taking the edge off the pain.

Roland blinked hard and realized he was talking to the giant Aeon, Trinia.

"Your mother had green skin?" Trinia asked.

"Not…in the mood," he said as he shifted against his hospital bed and pain shot down his legs.

"Locomotion is not recommended," she said. "There is very little clinical data regarding the aftereffects of a neural overload. Take your hand out of the fire, yes? It won't hurt so much."

"I redlined." Roland smacked dry lips. "How am I here? No one comes back from that."

"Incorrect. You are the second. An armor by the name of Elias achieved partial recovery following the Tagomi procedure. Your Saint Kallen was involved in that event."

"It wasn't Saint Kallen that brought me out…was it?" The nozzle of a water bottle worked between his lips and he took a long sip.

"No. It was me," Trinia said. "I designed your neural bridge. I was on hand to stop the complete degradation that normally follows a redline. Remember?"

"You were there," Roland said, turning his head

away from the nozzle. "You…the Lady?"

"Safe. We're back on Navarre."

Roland felt a weight grow in his chest. "Gideon?"

"Dead…and we are less without him." Trinia frowned.

"I didn't want—"

"I understand humans will not speak ill of the dead, but I am Aeon." She stood, dwarfing his hospital bed, and went to a holo bank of diagnostic machines to swipe through overlays showing Roland's biometrics. "Gideon attacked during my handover—a time of truce, one you honored…until he didn't. Our cultures may have dissimilarities…but our concept of honor overlaps in a number of places. What Gideon did was wrong. I misjudged him. Misjudged Stacey. I'm old, yet I've failed to achieve perfect wisdom."

"You're on Navarre…not Earth."

"Correct. You required my close and personal administration to recover. Now that you're awake and alive…I've decided to remain with the Nation," she said. "You're not the only miracle I'm working. Plus, the Ibarrans are more…open to some projects I have in mind. I have a purpose here. On Earth, I would be put in a gilded cell to be gawked at."

"Welcome," Roland said, lifting a hand and

dropping it when shivering set in.

A text message flashed within the holo screens.

"Speaking of miracles…I must go," Trinia said. "Just relax. You have a visitor coming." She came and leaned over him, looking like a mother worried for a sick toddler. She put a palm to his forehead then gave his cheek a quick pat.

"Don't think I'm going anywhere," Roland groaned. He looked to one side where IV lines connected to several ports on his left arm. He sank against his cushions and marveled at the tiny stabs of pain working up and down his body.

He didn't hear Trinia leave. He zoned out until a new shadow appeared.

"Roland?" Makarov pushed strands of her black hair behind an ear.

"Oh, hi," he managed. "I'm a little…fuzzy."

Placing her hands on either side of his face, she gave him a lingering kiss on the lips. He mumbled non-words and tried to raise a hand.

"Don't try and be clever." She pushed his hand down and held on to it. "You'll just wreck the moment."

"That works," he said, taking a deep breath as strength returned to his limbs. "So…what happened? How long have I been out?"

"Eight days," she said. "Lady Ibarra destroyed New Bastion—though she let the diplomats escape—and all our ships are back home. We have a nonaggression pact with Earth. The rest of the galaxy knows well enough to leave us alone. No sign of the Kesaht. The war is over."

"Huh…we won. The Ark?"

"In orbit over Navarre," Makarov said, her face darkening. "It's…unsettling. We're still coming to terms with just what it can do."

"Lady Ibarra's safe. I'm kind of glad you're not in charge. Would be awkward for just some armor soldier to be around…the Lady," he said.

"Don't jinx it." She put a finger to his lips. "And you'll never be—wait. You're not just any soldier, Roland. You're the Black Knight. *My* knight. You saved her. You went past the redline to do it. The Nation knows you're a hero, no matter what happens next."

Roland squinted at her. "There's…what aren't you telling me?"

Makarov put a hand over her mouth and a tear fell.

Roland shifted up on his elbows, confusion writ across his face. "What? Is Lady Ibarra okay? Are you—what's wrong?"

Makarov hugged him and moved a hand over the

back of his head. Her touch was almost electrifying, but he winced as her fingers passed over raw flesh. Which was wrong.

He touched the base of his skull.

His plugs were gone.

"No…no, no, no!" Roland felt around, searching for the neural link that made him Armor. "What happened? This can't be right. Bring Trinia back here. Now!"

"You redlined," Makarov said, gripping him by the shoulders. "The damage was too much. The Aeon could bring you back, repair what she could, but if you ever donned your armor again…you'd be dead. No way for you to survive."

"But…but Elias! Saint Kallen brought him back and he—"

"Was trapped in his armor for the rest of his life," Makarov said slowly. "The Aeon…is no Saint Kallen. Trinia did the best she could."

Roland leaned forward, face buried in his arms. "I am Armor. I must *be* Armor…no…now I'm nothing." He recoiled when Makarov tried to take his hand.

"Your plugs did not make you who you are," she said. "Roland Shaw is not his suit."

"How would you know?" He pressed his

fingertips into the scar tissue where his plugs had been.

"Because I don't care if you walk in metal…I only care that you can be with me," Makarov said, wrapping her arms around his shoulders. "Where's your iron, Roland?"

Roland fought back a sob as his anger grew, replacing the fear and shock from the loss of his plugs. Of his identity. He fought the urge to lash out and tightened his arms around his head.

Then a still, small voice whispered to his mind.

Fight.

Roland lifted his face up to Makarov's. He wiped the back of a hand across his eyes and nodded.

"There's no…nothing left of the plugs in me?" he asked.

"All gone. I'm sorry, Roland."

"Huh…then where did that…ugh, what the hell do I do now?" he asked.

"You've got a stint of physical therapy ahead of you. After that, Marshal Davoust has already promised to take you under his wing. You'll make a fine commander, or that bald bastard will break you in the process."

"Not the Navy?"

"I love you, Roland, but you don't have the talent to drive a ship."

"Wait. You what?"

Makarov pursed her lips. "Oops."

Roland managed a smile. "When I was in the Geist cage, that menagerie, trying to pull our Lady out, I had the chance to lie to her…pretend I was Hale, her long-lost…all I had to do was lie and say that I loved her, but I couldn't do it. When I tried, she became…you. It was weird in there."

"Is this your way of saying—"

"I love you too. I'm just not the man I was…sorry." He touched the scars on the back of his head.

"I never loved the armor. I love the man inside," she said and gave him a better kiss on the lips.

"It's going to take me awhile to catch up to your rank," he said, sinking back against his pillows.

"Worry about getting back on your feet." She gave his hand a squeeze. "As much as I want to stay and feed you Jell-O, I'm still a fleet admiral. I've been off the grid for almost half an hour. I wouldn't be surprised if everything's on fire."

"I get it," he said as a brush of vertigo hit him. "See you soon."

"Tomorrow. That's when the procedure will be ready."

"Procedure?"

"Lady Ibarra is taking a risk—one I've tried to talk her out of. Get some rest, my Black Knight. She wants you there when it happens." Makarov raised his hand and kissed his knuckle, then left.

Roland stared up at the ceiling. He lifted a hand, remembering the feeling of his suit obeying his mind, a sensation he'd never feel again. His hand fell against his chest and tapped his dog tags.

He fished out the metal-beaded necklace and ran his thumb and forefinger over two of the oval tags, both stamped with his parents' names and serial numbers.

"I'm not done…not done making you proud of me."

Chapter 37

Roland tugged at the collar of his dress uniform. The Ibarran Armor Corps of a white tunic with the Templar cross and black tunic, pants and boots always made him feel like he was meant to dress up as a medieval knight outside of his armor. The connection wasn't lost on him, though he would never don his suit again, and wearing the uniform grated at his mind, calling him out as a fraud.

He touched the raw flesh at the base of his skull and felt small, useless.

His elevator slowed to a stop and his knees buckled. Roland braced himself against the walls as the nerves down his arms and legs tingled.

"Maybe I should've asked to stay in my Armor,"

he said to no one. "Least then I could manage something like gentle deceleration."

The doors opened to a pair of Lady Ibarra's Honor Guard. The two hulking soldiers in ornate armor beat a fist to their hearts in salute when Roland looked up.

Roland returned the courtesy as best he could, although his hand felt like rubber when it brushed against his tabard.

"They're about to begin," a guard said as he swung to one side and opened a path for Roland.

Roland nodded quickly and hurried past them. He felt a burning where his plugs used to be, and wondered if the guards were staring at him like he was some sort of a cripple.

Walking into a high-domed laboratory, he saw the ever-present Navarre rain lashing at the glass ceiling. Senior Ibarran military formed an outer circle around a workstation Roland couldn't entirely make out. Trinia, the exceedingly tall Aeon, busied herself in the middle of the room, not paying any attention to the surrounding Ibarrans.

Roland picked out Davoust's bald head and the back of Makarov's void-black hair to the right. A swath of white tunics were to his left. He hesitated for a moment, not sure which side he belonged to. His only communication with Marshal Davoust was a reading list from the older man, a long reading list of military history classics.

Roland bit his lip and went to the group of Templars.

General Hurson, the Corps commander, was the first to greet him at the back of the circle, clasping forearms with Roland and giving his shoulder a gentle shake.

"Good to see you up and about, son," Hurson said. "Trinia likes to claim all the credit for bringing you back from the redline, but we know the truth." The general brushed the back of his fingers against the Templar cross emblazoned on his tunic.

"Saint Kallen is ever with us," Roland said as a knot formed in his throat.

"More than ever," Martel said from over Hurson's shoulder. "We received her reliquary before we left Earth. A proper tomb is being built now. You should be well enough to participate in the consecration ceremony by then, yes?"

Roland looked to one side as Nicodemus passed, and a touch of envy shot through his heart as he saw the man's skull plugs.

"I imagine it will be an…Armor ceremony,"

Roland said.

"Martel's face darkened. "It...will be. Yes."

"You're a test case, Roland," Hurson said. "Once we earn our spurs, the only way anyone's ever left of the Corps is feet first. You are Armor. Let no one ever doubt that."

"But I'll never fight with my lance again." Roland gripped an imaginary stylus and mimed writing. "Pencils to push. Beans to count."

"The marshal promised me you will rise to the limits of your capability and talent," Martel said. "You won't disappoint us."

"By my...Armor and my honor." Roland felt an invisible weight press against his shoulders and his legs went rubbery. "Excuse me, sir."

He took an uneasy step, when someone grabbed him by the elbow and helped prop him up.

"If I didn't know better," Morrigan said in his ear, "I'd say you'd had one nip too many."

"Trinia has me on so many pills, I'm surprised I didn't float in here." Roland smirked.

"Fair is fair. I was sent for you. They've got a spot up front for you," she said.

"Who sent?"

"Who do you think, boy-o? You made this all

possible." Morrigan flapped the back of her hand against the arm of an admiral and a gap opened for the two of them.

In the middle of the laboratory was a glass cylinder holding a frozen young and bloody woman. She was in her mid-twenties, face locked in pain and despair as she reached for someone to help her. Her other hand clutched a red wound over her heart.

Nearby, the Qa'resh probe recovered from the Ark floated in the middle of a glowing sensor suite.

"She…looks familiar," Roland said as Morrigan led him to a single seat on the inner edge of the crowd.

"You don't recognize Lady Ibarra?" Morrigan raised an eyebrow at him.

Roland stopped behind the chair and put one hand on the back to steady himself. He'd heard how Stacey Ibarra had been badly injured, and her mind transferred to the silver body he was familiar with, but he never imagined that her flesh and blood had been preserved in such a state.

"Huh," he managed.

"Bullet tore the outer wall of her aorta," Morrigan said. "She was seconds away from passing out from blood loss when they got her into the stasis tube. There was no way to get her mind back into her body after all the

Qa'resh probes destroyed themselves after the Ember War. And even if she could transfer…"

"But now we have a probe and Trinia," Roland said.

"There you have it. Sit down before you fall down," Morrigan said.

"I'll stand." Roland fought a wave of dizziness but held on to the seat back.

"Maybe a cane." Morrigan sniffed. "Like old Colonel Carius used to carry."

"Did our Lady summon us here to watch her…final moments? Seems only one piece of the problem's solved by the probe," Roland said.

Ibarran military within earshot cleared their throats then went quiet.

"Don't be macabre. Trinia has a solution. Surgical medi-bots with their own null fields. They should be able to heal our Lady before she's…lost to us. The Aeon's been such a boon to us since she arrived. Makes me ashamed that we failed to bring her back the first time we were sent for her. What the Toth made her do…"

"She doesn't have a problem working with us?"

"Night and day. Martel's been telling me about her plans for the next generation of Armor. We'll need every advantage when the Geist come for us. Trinia saw what they are, knows we need her help against those soul thieves."

"Lady Ibarra used Malal to win the Ember War," Roland said. "And that led to the fight against Bale and the Kesaht. We found the Ark to save humanity from the Kesaht and awoke the Geist in the process. It won't ever end, will it?"

"Only the dead have seen the end of war, boy-o. You're still Templar, suit or no. You ever think you'd beat your Armor into a plowshare?" she asked.

"No…"

"At least we fight on the side of the light. And we did just win against the Kesaht. Hell of a lot better than losing, eh?" She gave him a nudge with her elbow.

"I'm a little—" He touched his temple. "Sorry to be so dark."

"You're a strong man, Roland. I can see what you're going through, but I can't feel it. For what it's worth…Gideon deserved to die. He had more hatred than honor in his heart. I'm shite at touchy-feely. Maybe some time with a chaplain? Time in prayer?"

"I'll settle for not throwing up or falling over for right now," Roland said.

He looked over to Makarov, who seemed stiff and pensive, despite a world-class poker face and her hands clasped behind her back. She gave him a slight nod and some of his strength returned.

Lady Ibarra walked through a door in the back of the lab, and the room snapped to attention. She went to Makarov and put a gloved hand to her arm.

"I have need of your champion one last time," Stacey said.

"Of course. He will never fail you," Makarov said.

Stacey looked to Roland then crooked an arm.

Roland swallowed hard and took a tentative step away from the chair. He felt the room staring at the back of his skull as he crossed over and put his arm in Stacey's. She motioned toward Trinia and propped him up slightly as they went.

"If there's a fight to be had, you should've picked someone else," Roland said.

"If you can keep going…so can I," she said quietly. "This procedure is risky. Several miracles have to happen in sequence. Medi-bots that can install an artificial heart without blowing the entire stasis field. A lobotomized probe that's been hacked to make the transfer. My mind that's…less than stable. The Geist did some damage that…my periods of lucidity are growing shorter. I have to do this now before there's nothing left to put back in my old home. No matter what happens, I have one last wish for you."

She stopped them next to the stasis tube. Roland's own heart ached to see Stacey's true body locked in a moment of anguish.

"I told myself that this shell is better," she said. "That my mind trapped in metal is better than pain. Better than death. But immortality has its own price. One that's proving too high for me to pay. I stay like this and I *will* come undone."

"Your wish, my Lady?"

"Yes…let them keep their faith, Roland. They are stronger with it, and the Nation will need that strength, no matter how this day ends."

Roland looked over one shoulder to the Templar, then back to Stacey.

"There's more to Saint Kallen than miracles," he said. "The Templar…have their hand on a rod of iron, guiding us…us away from hell. From the fate the Xaros and the Kesaht meant for us all. That faith will endure. Even after Saint Kallen stops appearing to the Armor."

Roland removed his arm from hers and faced her directly.

Stacey tilted her head to one side slightly and Roland could sense the emotions behind her doll-like face.

"With the war against the Kesaht over and Saint

Kallen interred on Navarre…her spirit can rest now."

Roland worked his jaw from side to side and nodded.

"What do you need from me?" he asked.

She touched gloved fingertips to his cheek and Roland twitched at the chill.

"Your face is…comforting. I want it to be the first thing I see when I live again, or the last before I die. Will you do this for me?"

"Yes, my Lady."

"I see why she cares for you so much. Take care of her." Stacey withdrew her hand. "Excuse me."

She left Roland behind and went to the Qa'resh probe. Trinia spoke to her in Aeon, and Stacey reached out and grasped the crystal tear.

Lights dimmed, then snapped back up.

In the stasis tank, chrome wires wiggled out of the top and connected to Stacey's chest and back. The space around the wires wavered then glowed with a dim blue light.

"The medi-bots are functioning…poorly," Trinia said from her workstation as she tapped hard against several different panels. "The stasis field is fluctuating more than I anticipated. The bots aren't adapting as designed."

"Then end this!" Makarov shouted. "Don't throw our Lady's life away!"

"She made me swear to see this through." Trinia swiped up a screen and a golden lattice appeared in front of her face. "No matter the outcome."

A red tube sank through the tank and a needle tip punctured the side of Stacey's neck.

Light grew from within Stacey's metal fist.

"Consciousness transfer initiated," Trinia said.

Roland put a palm to the tank and looked into Stacey's pain-filled eyes.

"Come on," he whispered. "Come back to us. Fight. Fight, my Lady."

A ragged breath came from Stacey's true body and her eyes focused on Roland. Her bloody hand hit the glass, leaving a red streak.

"Trinia? What's happening to her?" Roland asked.

"I don't know! The probe took over the transfer and—"

The tube twisted open and Stacey fell into Roland's arms. Hot blood soaked through Roland's tunic and spread against his chest as he lowered them to their knees.

"My Lady?" Roland moved her hair out of her face, and he smelled her copper-laden breath as she exhaled with a weak rattle. He put a hand to the back of her head and lowered her to the floor, her blood smeared across his uniform.

Stacey's bare skin was cool to the touch, and she grew pale.

"Stacey?" Roland cupped her face and looked into her unfocused eyes. "Come back to me. You're too strong to leave. We need you. Do you hear me? The Nation needs you!"

Roland looked up as a medical team came through the crowd.

A blood-slick hand grabbed him by the collar.

Stacey coughed and took a shallow breath.

"Stay back!" Trinia shouted.

Stacey got an arm around Roland's neck and clung to him as she fought to breathe. Roland held her gently, the smell of blood nearly overpowering.

"You…" Stacey said, and Roland jolted with surprise. "You were never Ken Hale. Never."

"I'm sorry for that, my Lady."

"Never him." Stacey looked up and Roland smiled.

"You're…okay?"

She pushed him away weakly then prodded the bullet hole in her shirt.

"I'm a real girl now." She smiled and swiped bloody fingertips against the corner of her lips. "I feel again…air and—" she…" She smacked her lips. "Thirsty."

Trinia knelt beside them, her height dwarfing them like they were children. The Aeon ran a sensor up and down Stacey's back.

"I'm thirsty, Roland." Tears ran down her face. "And…I feel awful. It's wonderful."

"The medi-bots worked as intended," Trinia said. "Your artificial heart is functioning well. I'll need to monitor you. That is a one-of-a-kind piece of equipment in your chest."

"*Ferrum corde*," Roland said. "You have an iron heart."

"Help me up." She lifted her arms and blood dripped to the floor. Roland obliged as best he could, struggling to keep his feet planted in the red slick.

"*Ferrum corde!*" Makarov shouted.

The Templar went to one knee and began praying in unison.

"*Ferrum corde!*" Davoust beat a fist to his chest.

The room broke out in a chant.

Ferrum corde. Ferrum corde. Ferrum corde.

"See what you've done?" Stacey asked.

"I didn't mean to." Roland shrugged.

Stacey hobbled to her silver body, determination on her face.

"I hate this thing. A prison for my own mind for so long. Every waking moment a reminder that I was going to suffer forever. Now...now I want to destroy it. Live life...no chance to escape time and death. But I can't do that, can I, Trinia?"

"The consciousness transfer can be done again," the Aeon said.

"Why would you go back to that?" Roland asked. "You're free."

"Because I can't control the Ark in this bloody bag of flesh and bones," Stacey said. "The Geist are coming...the Ark will be the difference. I just don't know if it'll be enough. I spent most of the power when I destroyed part of their armada. I won't...won't sacrifice any souls to charge it back up. Still, the jump engines will be useful, and the Ark still has teeth."

Stacey hissed and leaned against Roland.

"Something hurts," she said through grit teeth.

"Your adrenaline is wearing off," Trinia said. "Your doctors can take over from here."

Roland waved the medical team over.

"I'm so hungry." Stacey smiled as medics helped her onto a gurney. "I've been waiting so long to eat a proper sandwich. Roland…thank you." She kissed the back of his hand where she'd left her brand on him.

Stacey waved to the officers as she was wheeled out of the room to their thunderous applause.

Roland stayed with Stacey's metal body for a moment. It was a statue now…and he could feel that Stacey's soul was gone from it.

"Well done," Makarov whispered in his ear and took him by the elbow.

Roland's knees buckled for a split second. He looked down at his bloodstained tabard. The Templar cross gleamed red.

"The fight goes on, doesn't it?" Roland asked.

"It does. And you and I will be there to win it." She tilted her head and pressed her forehead to his. "Now…how about you get some rest."

"There's an idea. Maybe pizza?" Roland turned around and paused as he realized the assembled senior officers and all the Templar were looking at him and Makarov.

"Uh oh. I think they know," Roland said.

"They don't matter to me," she said. "Only you do."

Davoust stepped forward and looked Roland square in the eye. The marshal beat a fist to his chest in salute and stepped back and to one side. The crowd saluted Roland and cleared a path to the elevator.

Roland set his face firm and tried to straighten up as he walked out on unsteady legs. Makarov stayed arm in arm with him until they made it to the elevator.

The doors shut and Roland slumped against the corner.

"How do you feel?" Makarov asked.

"Worthy...for once."

Chapter 38

Wind swayed trees around the cemetery. The rustle of branches and shifting bushes carried over an open grave, where the Iron Dragoons gathered around a tombstone. Aignar and Santos stood to one side, Cha'ril opposite the hole. A dull gray casket sat at the bottom of the grave, a broken Armor helmet set at the head.

Cha'ril, in a Dotari dress uniform modeled after a void suit but done in fine fabric, shifted her feet in the loose dirt along the edge. Aignar and Santos, both their Class A's with medals and ribbons, stood silent as they stared down at Gideon's final resting place.

"Forgive me," Cha'ril said. "The custom is to spread soil over his…box?" She angled a foot, as though to kick.

"Like this." Santos picked up a fistful of dirt and held it over the grave. Dust blew out with a gust and his hand trembled. "Not just yet. Not yet."

Cha'ril scooped dirt into her hands and stood, holding it against her stomach.

"I don't understand," she said.

"You bury him when you place it on his casket. It's how you let go," Aignar said.

"The Dotari…we speak truthfully of the dead before they're interned. It lets their spirit grow unburdened," she said. "Even if that truth is…ill. As you say."

"I don't think he'd be offended by Dotari custom," Aignar said.

"He was wrong," Cha'ril clicked her beak and looked away from the grave. "He should not have attacked the Ibarran. Even if he'd succeeded…it was still wrong. They saved us on Kesaht'ka. Saved Earth. Despite it all, the scales balanced in the Ibarrans' favor."

"Gideon could never see that," Aignar said. "He was dishonored when his old lance defected without him…and he never got past it."

"I can envy a life without compromise," Santos said. "The captain was true in his beliefs. Never wavered. Never faltered. We would have broken on Kesaht'ka without him."

"And you see where he ended," Cha'ril said. "He could still be with us, still in his Armor. The Corps is in shambles. We are less without him because of his…fury."

"Strange to hear this from you, Cha'ril," Aignar said. "I thought you hated the Ibarrans just as much as Gideon."

"What if it was me there?" She motioned to the casket. "What if I'd died in his place? For what? Vengeance? My hatchling would have grown up without a mother. What would Man'fred Vo carve on my grave to remember me to our child? 'She died for her hate.' That is no lesson for a little one."

"You think his life was wasted?" Santos asked, his face flush with anger.

"Gideon was more than how he died," Aignar said. "He fought through the Ember War. Fought for years in Armor, and like it or not…he saved that Aeon. And she brought an end to the Kesaht and the Vishrakath. Even if those bastards died under Ibarra guns, the war is over. Gideon helped win the peace—if that's what we have now."

"I will miss him," Cha'ril said and opened her hands over the grave, sprinkling dirt across the coffin. "I will speak of him with honor to my hatchling, and to the

Dotari. And I will miss you both."

Aignar looked at her and raised an eyebrow.

"My egg is nearly ready." She wiped a dirty hand across one side of her beak. "It is time for me to go home and…roost, you can say. Man'fred Vo wishes to move from being joined to a proper marriage. I accepted. I will not return to Earth. He and I will raise our child on Dotari Prime."

"But you're an Iron Dragoon," Santos said. "I think…aren't you the lance commander now?"

"It isn't about the lance," she said her quills bristling slightly. "My home world has had a number of…difficulties lately. Our population surged with the reintegration of those rescued from the Golden Fleet. The war against the Kesaht has made my people wary of the galaxy. There is a movement to withdraw from our Alliance with Earth. I—and other veterans—need to be home and fight against such cowardice. The Dotari owe a debt of honor to you. To Earth."

"Don't." Aignar shook his head. "Don't try and hide why you're going home. You have a child to raise. You can't do that from Mars. I failed to be a father to my son. Be a mother. There is more honor in that than sticking around the Terran Union as we rebuild."

"Old guy's right." Santos shrugged. "Fighting's

over. Bastion's gone. Ibarra put the fear of God into the rest of the galaxy with that Ark of hers. And I know what it's like to have only one parent around. Kids deserve better."

"Would Gideon be so accepting?" Cha'ril asked.

"Huh." Aignar's eyes narrowed. "He never talked family. Lost his like everyone else during the Ember War. All he had was his Armor. The Corps."

"Farewell, captain," Cha'ril touched the plugs at the back of her head. "I leave…but I remain Armor." She took a small nut the size of a golf ball from a pocket and held it out over the grave to Aignar. "For a *garuuda* tree. Dotari plant one with the deceased's loved ones carved into the shell. This way, our spirits are always entwined. May I?"

Aignar nodded and Cha'ril dropped the nut into the grave.

"The deeper we plant, the stronger the bond," she said.

"I am Armor." Santos spread soil over the coffin.

"I am fury." Aignar gripped a clump of dirt in his metal hands and tossed it into the grave.

"We will never fail," Cha'ril said. "The Iron Dragoons live on in you two." She looked down at the coffin and said, "It was my honor to fight at your side."

Aignar's hand snapped straight and saluted, holding it long enough for Santos to match him. They lowered their hands slowly. As one.

Chapter 39

A Geist pyramid orbited far over Nekara. The base oriented to the planet, each corner lit with soul fire and trailing a faint wisp of energy. The planet's atmosphere was alive with storms;, and smoke and ash hung over the continent-sized pieces sliced off by the Ark like scabs.

Pallax stood in a grand bay, silent as he regarded the broken planet. The concave wall lined with blisters the size of city blocks, the nascent shape of Geist war creatures writhing within. He wore a robe made of obsidian flakes, each glinting with internal life.

Noyan wore platinum armor, the tendrils of her hair squirming against her head and shoulders. Slack-jawed and dead-eyed thralls huddled behind her.

"It's coming," Pallax said.

"You're a fool." Noyan's hair twisted into braids. "We let the Ark slip through our fingers. This is not how we pledged to serve Malal."

"No, no, my dear, this was Malal's will. The prophet showed us where to find Malal. A gate at the center of the galaxy. He laid out the path...now we have one final test to prove we're worthy to exist for all eternity at his side."

"It will take centuries at sub-light speeds to find planets full of the unenlightened ready for Malal's word," Noyan hissed. "The prophet decimated our pilgrim fleet. Our offering to Malal is a shadow of what it once was. There is a path...but a difficult one."

"Malal demands every soul." Pallax raised a finger. "And every soul will be his. The pilgrims ships can be replaced, our ranks of thralls replenished with the unworthy."

"We have to find them first," Noyan said. "They're not coming here."

Pallax reached to the void and something flashed against the endless black, like a new star.

"Faith is not its own reward." Pallax's mouth pulled back to smile. "You must trust Malal, my dear...he may try us, but he also grants us the occasional boon."

A dark basalt hunk tumbled through the bay's force field and smacked into his palm.

"Now...what have we here?" He peered closer at

the material and snarled with pain. The basalt stuck to his palm like it was glued as he tried to shake it off. He dug claw tips into the basalt and ripped it out of his other hand, taking off several of his fingers.

Pallax hurled the material into the chest of a thrall. The thrall's jaw worked as the dull gray of his body morphed into basalt, lit from within by gold sparks. Pallax raised a hand and the thrall's feet lifted off the deck before the transformation could spread to the ship.

The thrall broke apart, reknitting into a crown of thorns.

"This…is helpful," Noyan said. "Their star gate—their Crucible—it can be rebuilt."

"And then we will take Malal's glory across the galaxy." Pallax twisted his hand around and the small Crucible rotated slowly. "We will bring his word to every planet with intelligent life. Those that refuse the word will have their souls offered to Malal in tribute. We will stand in glory beside him. No one will stop us. Not the prophet. Not her Armor. No one."

Chapter 40

Sunlight burned through the last of the morning fog. Distant towers resolved from the waning gloom and Roland felt a moment of awe as he realized just how many arcology towers made up Navarre's capital.

He stood on the Roost, the highest balcony on Tower 1 from where the Lady led her Star Nation. Those gathered stood in ranks, the crowd almost identical to Stacey's transfer back into her flesh and blood body. Roland was in the front rank, Makarov and senior Navy officers to his left, Davoust and Legion to his right. The Templar had their own small formation, just apart from the rest.

Roland still felt out of place, though he wore a Legion uniform. His white tabard was gone, and a red Templar cross medal at his neck was his only token of his former battle brothers. He rolled his shoulders against his new uniform. The black fabric had taken on some of the humidity. He tugged at his high collar and got a quick and disapproving glance from Marshal Davoust.

A V-formation of Shrike fighters soared overhead, the rumble of engines drowning out all other sound. Roland looked up and caught his breath when he realized the Ark was in low orbit, gleaming in the sunlight. The rock that once encrusted the bottom of the Qa'resh massive ship was gone, and the unsymmetrical structure struck Roland with a certain beauty.

The double bang of spiked halberd pommels against the floor announced Lady Ibarra's arrival. Roland straightened his back and raised his chin slightly as he locked his ankles and legs together, hands pressed firm to his sides in the position of attention.

There was no chill as Stacey passed through the ranks to the front. She wore a simple uniform with only the Ibarra Nation crest pinned to her upper chest. Seeing her as a young woman still unnerved Roland, as the soul within was a good deal older and more tested than her appearance let on.

She went to the edge of the Roost and set her palms against a bronze handrail. A cheer rose from below.

"Front rank," Stacey dropped a hand below the bar and motioned forward, "join me."

Roland went forward in step with Davoust and the cheer grew louder as he walked straight ahead and ended up to Stacey's right, Makarov to her left. Small video drones buzzed around them, and multi-story screens on each side of the arcology towers broadcast a live feed.

Brigades of legionnaires filled a massive parade ground several stories below the Roost. Armor, to one knee and with swords drawn and points down in prayer, formed a line between the Legion and the Roost, echoing the Martyr's Square on Earth that memorialized the final sacrifice of the Iron Hearts, Templar, and Hussars at the end of the Ember War.

Roland's heart ached to see Armor, their rain-slick metal glinting in the sunlight.

"You're still the Black Knight," Stacey said to him. "You're still our champion."

"I can't fight for you with sword and plate, my Lady. But my iron is within," Roland said.

"And you'll temper that iron into something greater than your Armor," Stacey said. "And soon. This Nation will need you."

"By my honor and my ar…"

Stacey smiled at him, an expression he still wasn't used to seeing from her. "We're both getting used to a simpler existence," she said. "But we are our decisions and our actions. Not our shells. Let's begin."

Stacey raised her arms up and the cheers from the

Legions changed to a chant.

Ferrum corde...ferrum corde...

She lowered her hands to the rail and the chant faded away. A drone the size of a sparrow flit near her and hovered just ahead of her chest.

"My Nation." The words echoed from the towers and across Navarre. "My Nation, we are victorious. The Kesaht have crumbled, and the final Toth with them. Bastion, which called for our destruction...is no more. The Terran Union remains, and through your sacrifice, this Nation earned their respect and honor. This Nation stands secure. Our fleets will colonize new worlds, and any who threaten our worlds or our way of life will feel the fury of our retribution."

She looked up to the Ark as the crowd broke out in thunderous applause.

"First, humanity defeated the Xaros. Now we stand dominant over the galaxy...but not for long. There is a darkness rising. The Xaros and the Kesaht wanted our lives, wanted to spill our blood for the crime of existing...but this new threat will come for our very souls."

Roland felt a tinge of fear as memories of Nekara came back to him.

"The Geist are coming," Stacey said. "They are

coming for all of us. And we are not ready."

The crowd went silent.

"Nearly a century ago, an Ibarra was warned of a coming threat to all of humanity. It was enough. Now I warn the Ibarra Nation of the Geist, of soul thieves dedicated to worshiping Malal, the greatest monster this galaxy has ever seen. I don't know how much time we have, but with us is the last Aeon, the Ark, and the iron heart of this great Nation."

Ferrum corde! shot from the crowd.

"There is no rest in victory," she said, "for another war is coming, and that war will see us victorious or our Nation utterly destroyed. There can be no peace with the Geist. No coexistence. We will fall or we will triumph."

Stacey put a hand on Roland's shoulder and his face appeared on every tower.

"Saint Kallen is with us," she said. "God is with us. Legends fight beside us. It is up to every soul in this Nation to prepare, to build fleets and train warriors for the coming war. When we go before judgment in the next world, let none be found wanting…myself most of all."

Stacey gripped the handrail and Roland realized what an awesome mantle she'd taken upon herself. After all she'd been through and suffered, she still fought not for herself, but for humanity. The pity he'd felt for the loss of his plugs melted away. She was right; his strength and iron were within. They did not come from his shell.

He said a silent prayer for Saint Kallen, the crippled soldier whose inner strength had inspired so many to fight on.

"A great work lies ahead of us," Stacey said. "A…crusade across the stars that will ensure humanity endures. Let all who carry the Templar cross be united in faith and purpose. Today, our crusade begins. And we will cleanse this galaxy of the Geist and any who would join them."

Stacey put a fist to her heart then thrust it overhead.

"*Ferrum corde!*" she shouted.

Roland beat a fist to his chest and raised it high.

"*Ferrum corde!*"

THE END

The Ember War Saga continues with the

THE IBARRA CRUSADE! Coming 2020.

FROM THE AUTHOR

Richard Fox is the author of The Ember War Saga, and several other military history, thriller and space opera novels.

He lives in fabulous Las Vegas with his incredible wife and two boys, amazing children bent on anarchy.

He graduated from the United States Military Academy (West Point) much to his surprise and spent ten years on active duty in the United States Army. He deployed on two combat tours to Iraq and received the Combat Action Badge, Bronze Star and Presidential Unit Citation.

Sign up for his mailing list over at www.richardfoxauthor.com to stay up to date on new releases and get exclusive Ember War short stories. You can contact him at Richard@richardfoxauthor.com

The Ember War Saga:

1.) The Ember War
2.) The Ruins of Anthalas
3.) Blood of Heroes
4.) Earth Defiant
5.) The Gardens of Nibiru
6.) Battle of the Void
7.) The Siege of Earth
8.) The Crucible
9.) The Xaros Reckoning

Printed in Great Britain
by Amazon